STAGE ROAD TO DENVER

Denver, 1876 — the burgeoning capital of a rough new state. When Terry Woodford rides in with his partner Slim, he dreams of showing Colorado how to save starving cattle by herding them to lush grazing grounds in the mountains over the winter. What he doesn't expect is trouble with Milo Patterson, kingpin of the city. By incident and design, Terry learns how Patterson cheated a dying miner, Frank Barber, and his family out of seven quarts of gold stashed on the roof of his cabin. And now Patterson is wooing Frank's beautiful niece, Faith, while running a crooked gambling joint. Terry vows to find the gold and get it back to its rightful owners — and to put a stop to Patterson's shady dealings once and for all. It's time for a showdown, and a thousand eyes will be watching . . .

SPECIAL MESSAGE TO READERS

STAGE ROAD TO DENVER

ALLAN VAUGHAN ELSTON

SAGEBRUSH
Large Print Westerns

First published in Great Britain by Ward Lock
First published in the United States by Lippincott

First Isis Edition
published 2020
by arrangement with
Golden West Literary Agency

The moral right of the author has been asserted

A catalogue record for this book is available
from the British Library.

ISBN 978–1–78541–860–0

Published by
Ulverscroft Limited
Anstey, Leicestershire

Set by Words & Graphics Ltd.
Anstey, Leicestershire
Printed and bound in Great Britain by
T. J. International Ltd., Padstow, Cornwall

This book is printed on acid-free paper

To Steven Payne and Forbes Parkhill, tellers of tall tales, and a journey they made long ago to the author's mountain camp, up the old stage road from Denver.

CHAPTER
ONE

Dust swathed Denver, rising in tawny clouds wherever wheel or hoof churned it. Churning it just now, up Wazee Street, came a trail-weary freight outfit, five small mules abreast and four yokes deep. Lesser outfits came and went, all giving off the odors of flesh and sweat and dust. Farmers, freighters, merchants, miners, some heading in, some heading out. Most of the ranch folk had a discouraged look; for this, the summer of 1876, made the second straight year of grasshopper plague. Grass and crops, everywhere east of the front range, had been devoured to the roots. Only in the upcountry, the high mountain parks, could stock hope to find forage.

In conspicuous contrast were the freighters and merchants. Eager, confident of quick high profits, these were. And why, not? Wasn't hay a hundred dollars a ton, once you got it to Leadville, and flour a hundred dollars a sack there? Didn't word of new and fabulous strikes blow in on every canyon breeze? Why worry about grasshoppers when a man could get rich in a single season?

In the wire room of the Denver Pacific depot, a message clicked from a telegraph sounder. A

1

triumphant message of two words. The operator shouted it to the dispatcher. The dispatcher rushed it to the superintendent. A clerk opened a window and yelled it to the street.

Off it went, from lip to lip, through the heat waves of Denver. Like fire on a prairie up Wazee and down Blake, up both sides of Cherry Creek and down the long row of saloons and bawdy houses fronting Holladay. "We're in!" men yelled. And this time they didn't mean gold or silver. In a very few minutes nearly all of Denver's eighteen thousand citizens knew it. "We're in!" Whistles blew. Bells rang. Cowboys fired into the air. And at the American House bar, for the next hilarious hour, drinks were on the house.

Terry Woodford and Slim Baker drew rein there. Having just lost their jobs, they were in a mood to drown sorrows. A teamster came out of the bar. "Go in and hoist a few, gents," he counseled. "Won't cost you a cent."

Terry dismounted, letting the reins drop. He was ten years younger than Slim, an inch taller, broader of face and shoulder, copper-hued under the line of his wide, heavy hat. Slim's step-down from the saddle had the same unconscious grace. Both men wore tight-fitting denims. Each had a cartridge belt which sagged from the weight of a holstered forty-five.

Slim was in the lead as they pushed the twin lattices back and entered the American House bar. Customers were two deep there, noisily convivial. Tables and booths were full. Slim pushed back his hat and grimaced. "Looks like we're outa luck, kid."

2

Then a Chinese boy in full native costume bore down on them. On his tray were assorted libations. "You likee, please?" the boy chanted. The newcomers helped themselves. "What's all the excitement?" Terry queried.

Response came from a thin-chested young man who'd been scribbling in a notebook. "Statehood," he explained.

Slim Baker downed his drink. "So Colorady's a state now, is she? Allasame like Ioway and Illinoy!"

"Allasame," amended the thin-chested young man with a grin, "like Pennsylvania where the Centennial Fair's whooping it up right now. So with the compliments of the Liberty Bell there they're nicknaming us the Centennial State." He pocketed his notes and picked up a jigger of rye.

"Helluva lota good it'll do us!" This from a jaded rancher who sat hunched over a beer. "Grasshoppers done et everything out my way. So what the heck difference does it make if we're a state?"

A burst of song drowned him out. The prevailing mood was for celebration and never mind the grasshoppers. Glasses clicked, were quickly emptied and refilled. The Chinese boy kept circulating and none said him nay. Out on the street a band of cheering riders galloped by, their guns belching skyward. Here some of the, crowd surged to a piano, cheering for Colorado, cheering for President Grant, cheering for the bartender. It made room for Terry and Slim at the bar where the thin young reporter wedged in between them.

3

"I'm Tony Raegan," he told them, "of the *Rocky Mountain News*."

An hour later the two cowboys, feeling even gayer than their usual gay selves, went out to their horses. Terry wore a high flush and his sky blue eyes had a moist brightness. Slim's booted foot missed its first punch at the stirrup. He'd had at least two more than Terry. In this country one never insulted a bartender by refusing his treat.

They rode south along Sixteenth at a sedate gait. Not because they needed to go that way but because they didn't want to miss anything. Sixteenth was abuzz with commerce. Here and there a new brick-front was springing up. Slim, to prove he was sober, sat straight as a cavalryman in the saddle.

They crossed the horse-car track on Larimer. Three blocks further the brick-fronts petered out and they turned east on Curtis. Here, by comparison, the vista was almost pastoral with cottonwoods lining the gravel walks and an irrigation streamlet gurgling down the south gutter.

Presently Terry reined to a halt, sniffing. "Somethin' smells awful good around here, Slim."

Slim looked to the right, to the left and behind, sniffing in each direction. "Must be that there bake-shop," he concluded. "They're bakin' up a batch o' bread in there."

"It sure smells awful good, Slim. Why don't we go in and buy a chunk of it?"

4

Slim pondered it gravely. "We'll have to wait," he decided, "till they take it out of the oven." He leaned forward with both hands on the pummel, in a pose of patient waiting. Terry Woodford did the same.

"What's that there game them kids are playin'?" Slim wondered. In a vacant lot adjoining the bakery two ten-year-olds, a boy and a girl, were using mallets to knock wooden balls through wire wickets.

"They call it croquet," Terry said.

Slim cocked an eye. "Looks like the little gal's awinnin'." He splashed his horse through the irrigation ditch and across the gravel sidewalk for a better look. Terry followed him. Keeping in their saddles, they observed the next several shots in absorption. Warmly partisan to the little girl, they cheered every time she made a wicket.

Her ball bumped the goal post and the game was won. Preferring then to rest on her laurels, she declined when the boy wanted another game.

Slim turned sportively to Terry. "Le's you an' me play."

"You wouldn't stand a chance, Slim."

"The heck I wouldn't!" Slim was grievously insulted. "I'll show you, cowboy. Dibs on the first shot."

He spurred his horse a little to the left. There, still mounted, he took squint-eyed aim with his Colt's six-gun. A ball chanced to lie about two feet in front of a wicket. Slim squeezed his trigger and the gun roared. His bullet hit the ball and drove it accurately through the wicket.

5

A chortle of glee from Slim. A grimace from Terry Woodford. A half-muffled shriek from the little girl as she scampered around a corner of the bakery. But the small boy stood his ground and looked up with undisguised hero worship at Slim. "You did it!" he crowed. "So you get another shot."

Slim maneuvered his mount to a favorable position. Again he took aim and fired. This time the ball bounced forward about a foot and fell apart in equal pieces. The heavy slug had split the grain.

"My turn now!" Terry exclaimed. He chose a ball which wasn't too far from a wicket. Standing in his stirrups he took solemn aim. The gun boomed and the ball jumped forward. It stopped short of the wicket with a chunk the size of an apple blasted off of it. The bullet went in a whining ricochet across the street and knocked a picket off a lawn fence.

"Stop that! Stop it at once!" The command came furiously from behind Terry. He twisted in the saddle to look into a beautifully indignant face. A young woman had dashed from the bakery. Her dark eyes snapped and her tongue lashed. "You drunken rowdies! Why don't you stay in the saloons where you belong?" She burst into Terry's blurred vision like an avenging angel, too lovely to be real, yet scourging him none the less mercilessly. He gaped at her, fascinated, forgetting the smoking gun in his hand. "Even our children aren't safe! Now get out! If you aren't off this lot by the time I count ten I'll call the police."

Mentally she began counting.

"We better skin outa here, kid," Slim whispered sheepishly. "She ain't foolin'." He spurred his sorrel and was off in a streak of dust up the street.

Terry followed only as far as the ditch. There he dismounted and stood humbly, hat in hand. "Sorry, ma'am." His penitence was abject. "We didn't go to make any trouble." All at once he was completely sober and ashamed. "We just didn't think . . ."

"Of course you didn't!" she agreed scathingly. "A drunken cowboy never thinks. All he can do is go shoot up the town."

"It won't happen again." Terry made the promise fervently. At the same time an impression struck him that he'd seen this girl before. Only before her glossy black hair had been coiled on her head in thick braids. Now it was parted and brushed back over her ears. And now she wore a white apron with a bib and her sleeves were rolled to the elbows. A smudge of flour on her nose meant that she'd been mixing dough.

"I should hope not!" She turned her back severely and re-entered the bake-shop. As she let the screen door slam a bell tinkled.

It tinkled again as Terry, hat still in hand, Went in after her. "I'd like to buy a loaf of bread," he said desperately. Any excuse would do if it kept her in his life even half a minute longer.

"My aunt will wait on you." Her face still stonily uncompromising, she started for the kitchen.

"I remember now," Terry blurted. "I saw you up on Elk Creek, one time."

She stopped, whirling toward him. "You *did not!* I was never there."

"It was your picture I saw. In a frame on the wall of Frank Barber's cabin."

Her eyes narrowed incredulously. Clearly he was just trying to make up to her. Whoever heard of a cowboy wanting to buy a loaf of bread? And now he was pretending to know Uncle Frank! Almost anyone would know that Frank Barber had for years kept a cabin in Elk Valley.

"You're even prettier'n your picture," Terry said.

This, for a fleeting moment, chased the severity from her face. Then she remembered the croquet game and was stern again.

A plump, white-haired woman came in from the kitchen. She had a tray of oven-hot loaves. Her face, broad and calm and spectacled, bore a distinct family resemblance to Frank Barber's.

"Here's a customer, Aunt Emily," the girl said. "He's ridden all the way in from his ranch to buy a loaf of bread. Are you sure, sir, that *one* loaf will be enough?" Her tone mocked him. Everyone knew that ranch cooks made their own bread. A cowboy might be sent in for a barrel of flour, but never for a loaf of bread.

"One'll be enough," Terry said. "Happens my boss laid everybody off yesterday, includin' me. Grasshoppers kinda cleaned him out."

The older woman looked at him with a gentle sympathy. "Oh, what a shame!" She wrapped the loaf and Terry paid for it.

"You're Mrs. Frank Barber, are you?"

"No. I'm Emily Barnes, Frank's sister. You know Frank?"

"Stopped overnight with him once, that's all."

She took off her spectacles, wiping them, and Terry saw a worry in her eyes. "I fret a lot about Frank," she said. "More than ten years he's been at it and it's wearing him out. He's getting old and thin. I tell him he ought to quit grubbing for gold and settle down right here in town."

"He seemed right snug up there," Terry said. He turned to say goodbye to the girl. But she'd disappeared into the kitchen.

With a wrapped loaf under his arm he went dismally out to his horse. Riding down Seventeenth he turned left on Larimer Street. He stopped at a store and bought a brightly painted croquet set. "Deliver it," Terry instructed, "to the Home Bake-Shop on Curtis."

A short jog took him to the Bull's-Head Corrals on Wazee. There he unsaddled and penned his bay. In the same pen he saw Slim's sorrel. He found his friend perched on a fence facing the corral office. Terry climbed to a seat beside him. "I tried to square us, Slim, but I didn't have much luck."

No answer from Slim. Gazing fixedly at the office door, over which was mounted a shaggy bull's head, Slim seemed profoundly preoccupied.

"She thinks," Terry mourned, "we're just a coupla no-good hell-raisers."

Still no response from Slim.

Terry unwrapped his loaf, which was still warmish from the oven. He held it under Slim's nose. "Take a whiff, cowboy. Smells like home in Indiana."

When his friend again failed to respond Terry broke off a chunk and began chewing on it. "Tastes good too, Slim. Have some? Maybe it'll settle your stomach." But when he broke off another chunk the older cowboy brushed it away.

"I ever tell you about Rex Kelly?" Slim's query came with seeming irrelevance.

Terry gave a quizzical stare. "Not that I recollect. What about him?"

"He was tried for a killing in Taos, coupla years ago. I was the state's witness. An eyewitness. I told about it in court."

"Did they hang him?"

"They should've. But he was acquitted. His lawyer rigged up an alibi."

"So what?"

"So as we left the courtroom, Kelly sidled up close and called me a snitcher. Said next time we met he'd fill me fulla lead."

"Ever see him again?"

"Not until about fifteen minutes ago." Slim pointed to two saddled horses tied at a rack just outside the corral office. One was a blue roan and the other a buckskin. "See them two broncs over there?" Terry hadn't noticed them till now.

"Two guys rid up on 'em," Slim said. "They went into the office and they ain't come out yet. One of 'em's Rex Kelly."

Terry didn't like it. No matter who got the best of it, a gun-fight with a Taos bad man wouldn't do Slim any good. The sensible thing was to be somewhere else when Kelly came out of the office.

"Let's blow, Slim. You're in no shape for a gunplay. Not after tossin' down eight or nine fast ones at that bar. You might miss . . ."

"I didn't miss that croquet ball, did I?"

"Sure you didn't. But the croquet ball wasn't shootin' back at you. So let's be on our way, Slim."

"Drunk or sober," Slim scoffed, "nobody's ever yet run me off a corral fence. I was settin' here when them guys rid up. So I'll be settin' here when they come out." His jaws clamped stubbornly.

Terry knew him too well to argue.

"Okay, Slim. Just promise you won't start anything."

"There they come now," Slim warned. The office screen slammed as two men came out.

Terry whispered, "Which one's Kelly?"

"The tall guy. The one with the flashy vest. Used to deal faro in Santa Fe."

The tall man also wore a cream-colored sombrero with four neat dents. In looks, in spite of a narrow face and a too deeply cleft chin, he was considerably more personable than his short-coupled companion. Each man wore a belt gun.

They went directly to two ponies barely ten yards from Slim's perch on the fence. "Where do we go from here?" the short man growled. Trail dust encrusted him and he needed a shave.

"To a hotel," Kelly told him, "and wait for Milo Patterson. We're some early. He's not due to meet us for coupla days yet."

The man still hadn't noticed Slim Baker on the fence. He stood beyond his roan horse, tightening the cinch.

The shorter man mounted. "What's Milo got on the fire?"

Kelly didn't respond. At that moment he spotted Slim. A quick recognition flickered in his eyes. Small, cold, dangerous eyes, Terry thought. The man stood frozen, and yet poised. Being hidden from the shoulders down by his horse gave him a slight advantage.

For Slim couldn't see his hands. Neither could Terry. It meant Kelly could draw unseen. And Terry had to keep an eye on the short, hairy man, in case of a four-man fight.

"Hello, Baker," Kelly's voice came in a monotone. Only his eyes held a threat.

"Hi, Kelly." Slim's hands rested loosely on his thighs.

Kelly looked right, then left. A dozen teamsters were within sight. "Kinda crowded around here," Rex Kelly observed.

"I've seen lonesomer places," Slim admitted.

Kelly stared for a moment longer. Again he looked right, then left. "See you again some time, Baker," he decided, "when we ain't so crowded."

"Any time, any place," Slim said.

Kelly stepped into his saddle and spurred away. The short man rode at his stirrup and neither of them looked back.

Slim relaxed and broke off a chunk from the loaf which Terry, all this while, had held in his left hand. Biting into it he smacked his lips. "You're dead right, kid. It smells good and it tastes good. Just like home in Indiany."

"They said they're here to meet somebody," Terry brooded. "Milo Somebody."

Slim nodded. "Patterson, sounded like. Milo Patterson."

CHAPTER
TWO

High in the South Platte Mountains, two riders dipped downward through a wilderness of lodgepole pine. One rode a bony mule and the other a powerful, iron-gray gelding. They had nothing in common, these two, except that each was heading for Denver. They'd stopped overnight at Jefferson, at the crossing of Tarryall Creek, where the Denver-to-Leadville stages always changed horses. One timid, the other bold, the timid traveler had asked permission to ride on in company with the bold. Holdups and killings were not uncommon on this trail.

And Milo Patterson had condescendingly consented. Glancing sidewise now at his companion's threadbare coat and flat-crowned hat, he smiled with a sardonic tolerance. It rather amused him to jog along with a circuit-riding preacher like Jethro Bell. Often the wilderness made strange bedfellows.

Arriving at Bailey, where the road crossed North Fork, they found today's Leadville-bound stage changing horses.

A stage passenger hailed Patterson. "Didja hear the latest?"

The man on the iron-gray shook his head. "Another strike up in Gilpin?" he hazarded.

"Nope. Statehood. The word hit Denver just as we were pulling out."

Patterson and the shabby little preacher rode on. The steep grade up Crow Hill slowed them to a walk. On this second day of August the hillsides were in gay dress, columbine and lupine in riotous blues and purples against curtains of aspen and pine. The air was balmy at this high altitude, moist from the almost daily showers, and grass grew rank in every meadow. "A beautiful land" murmured the little preacher.

Patterson, deeply preoccupied, made no response.

"But alas," sighed Jethro Bell, "it has many wicked men."

Again no response from Milo Patterson. He rode straight, yet loose, in the saddle, and a stranger might mistake him for a stockman. No man in all of Colorado wore finer boots, or rode a better saddle, than Milo Patterson. Yet his black, crinkly hair gave him an urban look. Women, both kinds, looked twice whenever he passed by. A career gambler, he'd learned to mask his emotions and nothing of his inner self showed on his face. Not even now, high in this wilderness, did his clear brown eyes mirror any of his roughshod ambitions.

These ambitions absorbed him and made him completely ignore Jethro Bell. Some day Milo Patterson meant to be the biggest man, the richest man, and politically the most powerful, in all the Rocky Mountain region. But thus far he'd gone at it wrong.

He'd been playing from the wrong side of the table. From the sucker's side. He'd been riding from camp to camp bucking the house games, rolling dice and riffling cards. And due to uncanny skill, winning much oftener than he lost.

Yet recently he'd realized how stupid it was. Solid, permanent fortune didn't come that way. In the long run percentage was always with the house. So instead of bucking the house he must be the house himself. He must establish and operate the biggest gambling place in Colorado.

Where? Leadville, claiming to be the biggest city in the state, and certainly the wildest, gayest and most spendthrift, had naturally tempted him. Yet Central City, whose diggings were known far and wide as the richest square mile on earth, could house him in a much finer hotel. Hadn't the Teller House there laid a pavement of silver bricks from cab to lobby, on the occasion of President Grant's recent visit? At both Leadville and Central City, hard cash flowed like water.

Yet a place called Denver, Patterson had finally concluded, in the end would outgrow both of those Eldorados. True it had no mines either of silver or gold. By comparison it was drab and farmerish, at times dust-choked and at the mercy of insect plagues. A treeless prairie. And just now not a blade of grass within miles of it.

But some inner hunch whispered to Patterson that Denver would never be a ghost town. Alma might; or Fairplay; or even Leadville. But never Denver. For the very good reason that people had to pass through

16

Denver to get anywhere else. Railroads of standard gauge track could get that far and no farther. And now this news of statehood would some day mean a great Capitol and all the trappings of state government.

So he'd decided on Denver. He was on his way there to get the project started. He'd even sent word to certain old associates of Taos and Santa Fe, asking them to meet him in Denver. He'd use them as dealers in a money trap he planned to call Patterson's' Palace.

A doe with fawn by her side leaped across the trail, crashing out of sight into juniper brush. Further on grouse whirred from the trailside, sailing gracefully over the brow of Crow Hill. From the summit the trail dropped gently toward Elk Creek Valley. Patterson spurred to a trot and Jethro Bell, bouncing on his mule, had a hard time keeping up. This he was determined to do because Shawn's Crossing, the next stage station, had been called a rendezvous for robbers and killers.

"Damn!" muttered Patterson as he recalled something unpleasant.

"What did you say?" asked Jethro Bell from a length behind.

Patterson ignored him. The unpleasant memory concerned a poker game at Fairplay night before last where the cards had been maddeningly perverse. In fact the evening of bad luck had cost Patterson more than half the stake with which he'd planned to make his start in Denver.

Elk Creek Valley, cloud-shadowed, spread out below them now. The slopes dipping down to it were pine clad, but the valley floor itself was mainly an open meadow. Here and there an island of aspen dotted it. Elk Creek hugged the far edge of it, this trail fording it at Shawn's Crossing. Dimly Patterson caught a brief sight of the buildings there; then, as he descended the last half mile of slope, timber closed in on him and again shut off all distant view.

They came to the floor of a tributary ravine from which a creeklet riffled into the main valley. Here, for a few hundred yards, the forest was dense. Jethro Bell's mule shied or perhaps they wouldn't have seen a man sprawled on the grass a little way off in the pines. He lay face down, his arms outflung. Beyond him, Patterson glimpsed the outline of a cabin.

Jethro Bell slid from his mule and ran to the man on the ground. He kneeled for a quick look, then called to Patterson. "He has been shot! We must help him."

Patterson joined him there. The victim had long white hair and there was blood on his shirt. Jethro Bell opened the shirt and exposed a bullet wound in the chest. The man looked like a miner. Hard work, a full life of it, was printed on his gaunt face and horny hands.

"He is alive," murmured Bell. "We must fetch help to him without delay."

It wasn't likely there'd be a doctor nearer than Denver. The settlement of Morrison was fifteen miles nearer than that. Shawn's, at the far side of this valley, was only a stage stop with a saloon and corrals.

Patterson stooped for a closer look. Presently he identified the man. "Name's Barber," he announced. "An old mountain rat prospector they call Frank

Barber. Ran on to him at Alma one time. I remember they said he kept a cabin in Elk Valley."

The cabin was of logs with a sod roof. Preacher Bell scurried to it and came back with a canvas cot. They put Frank Barber on it and used it as a stretcher. After carrying him to the cabin they put him on the bunk there.

Jethro Bell removed the shirt and heated water. Carefully he cleansed the wound. The man was conscious by then, although his eyes had death in them. "Who did it?" Patterson asked him.

"Tom Redding." The answer came faintly but both Patterson and Bell caught it. Patterson gave a slow nod. Everyone in the hills knew about Tom Redding. Early in the season he'd held up the bank at Golden, killing the cashier. Since then he'd been hiding in the mountains, presumably feeding himself by raiding an occasional cabin.

Frank Barber had no strength or voice for any detailed account of the raid. But when Patterson suggested that the outlaw had been prowling for food during Barber's absence, and that Barber's return home had surprised the man, a nod from the victim confirmed it. Patterson turned to Preacher Bell. "One of us will have to stay with him while the other rides for help. Take your choice."

He was sure the little circuit rider would prefer to stay while Patterson rode on. But Bell surprised him with the opposite choice. His personal timidity evaporated in the face of another man's desperate need. Also he was scheduled to perform a marriage ceremony

19

tonight at Morrison. At best it would take him till dark to get there. The people at Morrison. could send on to Denver for a doctor.

The choice annoyed Patterson. It didn't suit him to be held up. But it need only be for an hour or two. "Stop at Shawn's," he directed, "and tell them to send someone here. A boy or a squaw will do. Anybody who can sit by this bunk till a doctor comes."

Jethro Bell promised. Presently he was on his way. Patterson stoked the cabin's stove and put coffee on. Waiting for it to boil he went out and unsaddled his horse. Then he twisted a cigaret and relaxed. When relief came from the Crossing he'd push on. Meantime an hour's rest at midday wasn't too unwelcome.

The coffee boiled and he poured a steaming cup. Frank Barber's haggard eyes were on him. "How 'bout some yourself?" Patterson suggested.

"Not coffee. Whisky," the man murmured, his gaze shifting to a cabinet. Patterson found the whisky there. He held it to the dying man's lips.

The stimulant revived him a little. "I'm a goner, ain't I?" he whispered.

"We sent for a doctor," Patterson evaded. He took his coffee and sat by the bunk.

"You got any folks?" Patterson asked.

"A sister and a niece," the man murmured.

Patterson found paper and pencil. "Names? And where?"

"In Denver. My sister's Emily Barnes. She has a bakery on Curtis."

20

"I'll notify her," Patterson promised. He wrote the name down.

"I want to tell her goodbye," the dying man pleaded. "Write her, I mean. Her and my niece."

"Okay, mister." Patterson put pillows under the man's shoulders and head, propped a breadboard in front of him, gave him paper, pencil and envelope. "Don't strain yourself."

Painfully Frank Barber began writing. Patterson finished his coffee, then went out to watch the trail for passersby. Maybe he could flag down some traveler and get him to take over here.

Just now the trail was deserted.

This stage road to Denver, Patterson knew, was the only one left. For during the last few years rail tracks had supplanted all the others. A standard gauge track from the east, and another from the north, were now feeding Denver. And from it narrow gauge lines ran south to Pueblo and west to the Clear Creek diggings around Central City. Three years ago men had even promoted a narrow gauge line to Fairplay and Leadville, up this very trail, but the panic of 1873 had nipped it in the bud. The Denver and South Park Line, they'd planned to call it, and rumor said the project would be revived next season.

Presently Patterson went back into the cabin, expecting to find that the exertion of writing had exhausted the man there. Instead he found that the old prospector had turned the sheet over and was writing on its other side. Then he saw Frank Barber cup a hand over the writing. As though to hide it from prying eyes.

Patterson picked up the liquor bottle, took a pull from it. Again he went outside and watched the trail.

When next he went into the cabin Frank Barber had sealed and addressed his letter.

"Will you mail it, please?" The request was urgent, though barely audible. It was the last effort Frank Barber ever made. Writing the letter had sapped his final reserve of strength. He closed his eyes. And Patterson, watching him, knew he'd never open them again.

In only a little while he stopped breathing.

Patterson covered him with a blanket. He lighted a cigaret and cocked an eye at the sealed letter. A sister and a niece in Denver! Probably the old sourdough's only surviving relatives. Had he left them anything?

Patterson glanced around the room and saw nothing to indicate that Frank Barber had been more than, an impoverished failure. The place had a dirt floor. Plank shelves had the usual camp supplies. Coffee, sugar, flour, salt. A dozen quart cans were labeled "PENDLETON'S PEARS." The coffee was packaged in heavy manila paper, a bright yellow with borders and cross bars of red. Patterson idly observed this because putting out coffee in pound packages was a new wrinkle. "ARBUCKLE'S," he noted, was the name on the package, and underneath this was the figure of a flying angel with long flowing skirts. Other food supplies were under paper, canvas or glass. Only the fruit was packaged in sealed cans.

On the walls Patterson saw two decorations: one a calendar advertising the Jay Joslin store in Denver; the other a framed photograph of a pretty girl. So pretty that Patterson crossed the room for a closer look.

And although he found her on the wall of a rude mountain cabin, Patterson sensed at once that she belonged to a world that he himself had been shut off from. Here was the opposite of the coarseness he'd met so often in the gold camps.

This girl, Patterson guessed, would be the niece Frank Barber had mentioned. Shrugging her from his thoughts he turned to the blanket-shrouded figure on the bunk. This sealed letter! Something highly confidential was in it, he sensed, else the dying man wouldn't have cupped a hand over it. A secret? Patterson could imagine only one one kind of a secret for a gold-hunter like Barber.

Scruples never bothered Patterson. A coffee pot was still on the stove, steaming. It took only a minute to steam the envelope open. The message inside, penciled in a shaky hand, said:

Dear Emily:

I wanted to surprise you with it. So many winters I've gone down to you empty-handed. This time it's different. Found a rich placer pocket. It played out on me but while it lasted it panned big. Enough dust and nuggets to fill seven quart cans. Was aiming to pack them down to you and Faith. Now I can't. But it's awful good to know you won't have to sweat over that bake oven any more. Goodbye and God bless you both.

FRANK

P.S. The seven cans are on the cabin roof under the sod there.

Patterson stepped warily outside and looked at the cabin's flat roof. Spruce poles had been laid across the top logs; on these a layer of clay, the clay itself covered with squares of tough sod.

A perfect cache! What vandal would look for gold on a roof?

Seven quarts of gold! How much would it come to? Patterson's mind flashed into swift calculations. A quart of water weighed two pounds. Seven quarts of water would weigh fourteen pounds. And the specific gravity of gold being nineteen point three, seven quarts of gold would weigh about two hundred and seventy pounds.

Gold being worth twenty dollars per ounce, Patterson could make an accurate evaluation. If completely full the seven cans would be exchangeable for eighty-six thousand dollars. And no questions asked. In fact gold dust, in this region, was accepted in lieu of cash over nearly every bar or counter.

Yet seizing the cans now, Patterson reasoned, would be risky and stupid. A relief from Shawn's Crossing might arrive at any minute. Or a freighter might pass along the trail and see him grubbing on the roof. Moreover, packing two hundred or more pounds on his saddle would be awkward. The job called for a pack-mule and should be done by night.

Best to leave the treasure where it lay. He'd flag the first Denver-bound freight outfit and load Barber's body on a wagon. He himself would ride along with it as far as Morrison. Later, after all questions had been asked and answered, he could return and camp overnight in this conveniently empty cabin.

Patterson smiled. The wheel of fortune had spun many times for him, but never to a pay-off like this one. Eighty thousand dollars dropped in his lap! Enough to launch, and handsomely, his Palace of Chance in Denver.

Hoofs coming up the trail clashed on gravel; and through the pines he saw an Indian woman on a burrow. Shawn's Crossing was sending her to watch till a doctor came. She wouldn't be needed now. Patterson struck a match and held it to Frank Barber's letter, watched it burn to an ash.

CHAPTER
THREE

They met the doctor only a few miles above Morrison.
"You don't need to go any further," Patterson said. He
thumbed toward a canvas-covered wagon. There were
many wagons in the train, all loaded with loose wheat
from the San Luis Valley for Denver.

"I half expected it," the doctor said, "from what
Preacher Bell told me." He reversed his direction and
they all trailed down into Morrison. At the log store
there Jethro Bell had made a concise report and to it
Patterson added a few details. Preacher Bell, he
learned, had performed his ceremony last night and
could be found at Trimble's Boarding House, on
Lawrence Street in Denver.

After complying with every proper formality,
Patterson rode on swiftly and alone. He was out of the
hills now, on the broad flat plain which stretched
interminably eastward. A bleak land, grassless, ravaged
for two straight seasons by grasshoppers. As Patterson
followed down Bear Creek he saw that even the leaves
had been stripped from creek willows. What few cattle
he sighted were gaunt and generally bawling in distress.

Diverging from Bear Creek he struck the South
Platte just below the mouth of Cherry Creek, which

26

came in from the other side. A bridge here had light metal trusses and a plank roadway. Cantering across it Patterson hit the foot of Fifteenth Street at the D & RG tracks. A tiny engine was bunting cattle cars down a narrow gauge siding.

There the rider turned left down Wazee into a traffic of hacks and wagons. It was a shabby, track-front street lined mainly with framed false fronts.

But after Patterson had turned south on Sixteenth the vista improved rapidly. Here was an occasional three-story brick. Here, instead of trail wagons, were buckboards and carriages. Here was a strictly urban commerce and the change since his last visit impressed Patterson. He'd left it a rude frontier supply town, a mere jumping off place for the gold hills, and what he returned to was a city in violent birth pains.

One block above Wazee brought him to the American House, a three-floor brick with projecting iron balconies. Not as palatial as the Teller House up in Gregory Gulch. But fine enough to be called Denver's best, definitely grander than a competitor, the Interocean, across the street.

Old associates from Santa Fe were to meet him at the American House. But for the moment Milo Patterson didn't stop. He continued up Sixteenth, crossing Holladay Street, known as Red Light Row, and on to Larimer. The Larimer corner had a bank, a hotel and two stores. A tram track centered Larimer, another one branching off up Sixteenth. But even here there was no pavement; sidewalks were board, frayed at the edges where hitched horses had pawed the wood.

Crowding them was a mixture of traders, builders, women shoppers, cowboys, cooly-coated Chinese, bell-hatted Mexicans and lank Yankees, even a few Ute Indians with strings of wampum, fringed leggings and straw hats.

As Patterson stopped to let a horse tram pass, a man he knew came out of the bank and climbed into a buckboard. An English aristocrat who ran a big ranch up Golden-way. By his glum look perhaps the bank had just handed him some bad news. Ranch after ranch was going bankrupt this season.

Patterson turned east on Lawrence and soon he was again riding past shabby frames. The shabbiest of all was Trimble's Boarding House and there, fanning himself on the porch, sal Preacher Jethro Bell.

"Our man died," Patterson announced. "They're teaming the body in right now."

Jethro Bell sighed. "It was to be expected, of course. Does he have people here?"

"A sister and a niece. They run a bakery on Curtis. The Home Bake-Shop. That's why I looked you up, Preacher. I want you to break the news to 'em."

Bell made no effort to evade the errand. Consoling the bereaved, after all, was much nearer his province than Patterson's. "I will attend to it at once," he promised. He put on his low-crowned black hat and went trudging off, up Eighteenth toward Curtis.

Milo Patterson rode in the opposite direction, toward the river. At Seventeenth and Larimer he noticed two cowboys in front of the Grand Central Hotel bar. A row of saddled horses stood at a hitchrack there. One of the cowboys picked up the left hind foot of a blue roan. He examined the hoof critically and Patterson heard him say, "It ain't this one, Terry."

Mildly puzzled, Patterson continued on. He turned north on Sixteenth and at Blake dismounted in front of the American House. He tied the gray and went in. The high-ceilinged lobby had ornate chandeliers. There was an oil mural of a buffalo hunt. Men of affairs stood in groups or overflowed the leather-padded divans. Cigar smoke choked the room.

Patterson was bearing toward the registry desk when, on a hunch, he turned aside into a dimly lighted ladies' parlor jutting from the lobby. A woman, her back to him, sat at a writing desk. Patterson smiled. He knew that chic, straight back and graceful neck. And the way she was dressed, no one would ever guess that Serena had been down on her luck this past year.

Tiptoeing to her, Milo Patterson put his hands over her eyes. "Guess who."

A gasp of shocked delight came from her. She sat quite still as though it were a moment she wanted to prolong.

Then she murmured: "Long, slender, sensitive — thrilling — those fingers over my eyes! Sensitive from dealing cards; and thrilling because I love you, Milo Patterson."

She stood up, twisting around to face him with her cheeks glowing. Her coiled hair, to Patterson, seemed even a richer gold than ever. And always it amazed him that she could keep so young. Barely twenty, she seemed, although he knew she was past thirty. It was an art she'd learned in Santa Fe where, as a gambling club hostess, she'd first come into Patterson's life.

"What happened to your earrings, Serena?"

"I had to hock them, my dear. Which doesn't matter now, because you will redeem them for me." She looked quickly about the room. "But you're forgetting something, aren't you?"

He knew what she meant, and kissed her. And oddly the thought came to him that he didn't really want to; that he hadn't really missed Serena, this past year.

She made him sit by her on the sofa and took his arm coaxingly. "Tell me about our plans, man of mine."

He rolled a cigaret and she lighted it for him, puffing it herself before putting it between his lips. "Just as I wrote you, Serena. I'll open up the swellest joint between Chicago and Frisco. Which naturally calls for the most beautiful hostess. So I sent for you — and for Rex and Cimarron to be dealers. Those fellows showed up yet?"

She nodded. "They have a room here. But this morning they took a ride down the river. I don't know where or why. Maybe they're back by now. If so you'd probably find them across the street, at the Interocean bar."

When Patterson looked askance she added: "Drinks are a dime cheaper over there. And you know Rex Kelly. He's still got the first penny he ever lifted off a blind man's eye."

Patterson smiled. "Don't be too hard on Rex. After all he's the best faro man west of Kansas." He stood up and looked at his travel-stained hands. "Time I'm washing up. Be here at seven and I'll take you to supper."

The desk clerk, whirling the book and offering a quill pen, remembered him. "Nice to have you with us again, Mr. Patterson."

"I left a bag in storage, last time I was here. Please send it up. That big iron-gray at the rack is mine."

"We'll see that it's stabled, Mr. Patterson." The clerk tapped a bell and a boy came. "Show Mr. Patterson to room 210 and then get his bag out of storage."

The boy led the way up thickly carpeted stairs. Room 210 had French windows with dark red drapes. "Bathroom at the end of the hall," the boy said. He scampered off to fetch the stored bag.

Patterson peeled off coat and shirt, filled a water bowl, lathered his neck and hands. He dried himself on a towel with "American House" embroidered on it in pink. After which, since he couldn't change till his bag came, he opened a window and stood looking out at the street. Obliquely across it he saw the Interocean, slightly less select than the American. Saddle horses were switching flies at a hitchrack in front.

Two cowboys rode up and dismounted over there. Milo Patterson, watching idly from his upper window, remembered seeing them in front of the Grand Central on Larimer. There they'd showed interest in the left hind hoof of a blue roan. And now again he saw one of them go to a roan pony and examine a left hind hoof. Patterson wondered why.

They were gunslung range hands and looked more than commonly competent. The one at the roan's hoof

31

glanced up with a nod. Some interchange passed between them. Then the two men crossed the wide board walk to the Interocean's barroom entrance.

However they didn't enter. They merely peered over the latticed screen and then drew back on the walk. Patterson, mildly curious, saw them hold a whispered colloquy.

"No use tyin' into 'em, Slim," Terry Woodford warned. "The barkeep'd stop us before we got started."

Slim Baker agreed. "Reckon you're right, kid." The Interocean bartender would be like any other. Chances were he kept a sawed-off shotgun at hand to enforce order.

An idea sparked from Slim's narrow slate eyes. "They said they was waitin' for somebody, didn't they? A guy named Patterson."

"That was the name. Milo Patterson."

Slim took off his high-crowned sombrero and looked grimly at jagged holes. A bullet had passed through the crown. "Somepin's gotta be done about it, Terry. And fast. I'm gonna sign up for a room here. After I go up, you tag along a minute later."

He led Terry into the hotel's lobby entrance. There Terry idled on a divan while Slim went to the desk and registered. The name he signed was Milo Patterson. "Seein' as my baggage hasn't showed up yet," he offered, "I'll pay in advance."

"Very well, Mr. Patterson." The clerk accepted two dollars and assigned him a second-floor room. A boy took him to it.

"Here you are, buddy." Slim flipped a fifty cent tip. "And say. Friend o' mine named Rex Kelly's down in the bar. Page him there, will yuh? Tell him Milo Patterson just blew in and wants to see him."

"Sure will, Mr. Patterson. And thanks." The boy went out and scampered downstairs.

On the landing he passed another cowboy coming up. Slim was watching from the open door of his room. "This way, compañero." He beckoned Terry inside.

Slim's grimness had disappeared and he was in high spirits again. "Chances are they'll both come," he chuckled.

"First thing we better do is grab their guns."

They took ambush to the left of the door. Anticipation of Kelly's surprise brought a grin to Terry's face. It was a broad, bronzed face with white high on the forehead as he tipped his hatbrim back. Less reckless perhaps than Slim Baker's, yet vivid and gay and resolute to meet fun or trouble head-on. "Other feller calls himself Dodds. Cimarron George Dodds. Listen. Here they come now."

Spurs were clinking on the stairs. Then boots thumped along the hall. Being to the left of the door, Slim and Terry wouldn't immediately be seen when it opened.

A knock. Then Kelly's voice. "Milo? You in there?"

"Come in, Rex." Slim gave the invitation throatily.

The door opened and two gun-belted men came in. A tall man with a narrow face and cleft chin, wearing a plaid vest. A blocky, bull-shouldered man who needed a

33

shave. Terry punched a forty-five into the ribs of one; Slim gave similar welcome to the other.

"What the hell!" gasped Cimarron George.

Kelly froze. His small black eyes fixed shiftily on a bullet hole through Slim Baker's hat. Terry kicked the door shut and stood with his back to it.

Slim, using his left hand, stripped the gun belt from Kelly and tossed it on the bed. Terry disarmed Dodds.

"I'm liable to ketch cold, wearin' a lid like this," Slim complained amiably. "Kinda makes a draft on me, whistlin' through them holes. So I figger maybe I'd better get me a new hat." He turned to Terry. "How much does a new hat cost, compañero?"

"Seventeen-fifty," Terry said. "I just priced one at Joslin's."

"Okay." Slim held an open hand toward Kelly. "Seventeen-fifty, please."

A bellow of protest burst from Rex Kelly. "I won't . . . I didn't . . . what is this, a holdup?"

Slim drew his own gun and tossed it on the bed. Terry did the same and all four men stood unarmed. "Makes us equal." Slim grinned.

The fact brought color back to Kelly's face and Terry saw his knees bend a little. He was tensing for a spring. Terry put a hand against the barrel chest of George Dodds and gave a shove. It sent the man reeling to a corner. "We're staying out of it," Terry warned. "All I'm here for's to see it's an honest deal."

"What's it about?" Kelly demanded.

"You don't know?" Slim baited. He stood bare-handed, inches shorter than Kelly, twenty pounds

34

lighter. "You mean you didn't follow us this morning as we rode downriver? You didn't cross the river and hide in the willows to drygulch me as I rode back?"

Slim took off his hat and looked sadly at the holes there. "Reckon you must've heard me ask the corral man where I could get a cow job. And heard him advise me to try the Circle K downriver. You was smart, Kelly, pickin' a spot where the river can't be forded easy. So by the time I got across to them willows you was a long way from there. All I could see was your bronc tracks. Three cleated horseshoes and a flat one. The flatty was on the left hind hoof. After a play like that, we figgered the first thing you'd need was a drink. A blue roan, we remembered. So we sashayed around to all the bar hitchracks lookin' for a blue roan with a flatty on the left hind hoof."

"It's not so," Kelly rasped. "I was right here in town all day. Wasn't I, Cimarron?"

"Sure he was," Dodds confirmed.

Slim looked surprised. "You mean you ain't gonna buy me a new hat?"

Kelly's lips took a twist. "Try and make me." His confidence was mending. These cowhands had been stupid enough to toss their guns on the bed.

"Maybe I can't make yuh," Baker admitted sadly. "But I can sure try. How's this for a starter?" His open-hand slap flashed to Kelly's mouth and rocked the man's head back. It left blood trickling down the chin.

Kelly lunged, punching. But Baker wasn't there. He was lean and quick and sure-footed. His sidestep was

35

like a puma's and again he slapped Kelly's mouth. They circled the room, Kelly beet-red and missing swing after swing as Slim countered with flat-palmed slaps.

Each slap had two stings, one physical, the other mental and unbearably humiliating. The blood trickle widened on Kelly's chin. The path of combat brought Slim near to Cimarron George, who, backed in a corner where Terry had shoved him, put out a sly foot to trip. Slim almost went down. He recovered his balance and again slapped Kelly across the lips.

Terry stepped up to Cimarron. "I told you to stay out of this." His punch to the jaw dropped the man. Cimarron crumpled with barely a sigh. Terry, his grin irrepressibly boyish, went to the bed and sat down. He brought out makings and rolled a cigaret. "Roll one for me too, kid," Slim said. "I'll be done in a minute." Again he slapped, this time across the eyes.

Kelly, with a swelling eye and bleeding mouth, kept missing his swings. Fury choked him; the fury of ignominy; this slim cowboy wouldn't even accord him the respect of a clenched fist.

The slaps kept slashing, to lips, to eyes, to ears; in the end Kelly doubled to his knees. "Any time you feel licked," Slim invited, "you can slip me the price of a hat."

Kelly kept on his knees, maudlin, eyes bloodshot, hands hiding his cut and livid face. In a profane hysteria he brought out a wallet and extracted a twenty dollar bill. "Take it, damn you!"

Baker accepted it cheerfully. "Here's your change." He dropped two silver dollars and a fifty cent piece into

36

Kelly's vest pocket. "I won't need this old one any more." He took off his bullet-punctured hat and put it on Kelly's head. Being a size too large. Slim was able to push it down over the man's ears so that it almost covered his eyes. It gave him a grotesquely comical look, like a vaudeville comedian.

Cimarron still sprawled in a corner. "We better make sure they don't foller us too quick," Slim said.

"We can take off their pants," Terry suggested. He promptly removed Cimarron's while Slim performed the same operation on Kelly.

Terry wrapped Cimarron's gun in one pair of pants; Slim wrapped Kelly's in the other. After recovering their own hardware, they retreated from the room.

Rear steps led to an alley.

Half a block up the alley was a trash can. Into it went two pair of trousers, each wrapped around a forty-five gun.

Terry and Slim circled to the street and reclaimed their horses. At Jay Joslin's Slim paid exactly seventeen dollars and a half for a cream-colored, high-crowned range hat. Proudly he wore it as, with Terry siding him, they jogged down Sixteenth to the Bull's-Head Corrals.

CHAPTER
FOUR

Milo Patterson, on the day following the funeral of Frank Barber, read an account of it in the *Rocky Mountain News*. The same issue reviewed the well-established facts about Barber's death. Law officers were combing the hills for the killer, Tom Redding. The account mentioned Patterson's name, and favorably. Both he and Jethro Bell had been interviewed by a *News* reporter named Tony Raegan.

Such interviews were inevitable, so Patterson had taken pains to make himself available. For that reason he hadn't gone back to pick up the seven quart cans of gold. Yet nerveless gambler though he was, it wasn't easy to let a jackpot like that remain unclaimed. Naturally he'd confided in no one. To Serena he'd merely explained that a bit of unfinished business would soon take him out of town for a few days. After which he'd be ready to launch his Palace of Chance here in Denver.

Serena had pouted a little. Yet Rex Kelly and George Dodds, far from minding a delay, had welcomed it. "We got some unfinished business too," Kelly had muttered savagely. He'd been in a fight, obviously, his lips and eyes showing nasty cuts.

Some private feud, Patterson concluded. He crossed to a window and looked out on Sixteenth. An eight-mule cart moved sluggishly by, the cart loaded bulkily with stone from the Morrison quarry. No doubt for the new Central Presbyterian Church about which Patterson had just noticed a news item. That church stone, the paper said, happened to assay two hundred dollars per ton in silver.

A knock called Patterson to the door. It was the hotel clerk. "You have callers, Mr. Patterson," he announced. "Two ladies. They are waiting in the parlor."

Almost at once Patterson guessed who they were. A sense of guilt had kept them on the fringe of his mind. Who else could they be but Frank Barber's surviving kin? The sister and the niece who were the man's natural heirs! A brief worry shadowed Patterson's eyes. He shrugged it away.

"Tell them I'll be right down."

He stood before the mirror to smooth back the black, crinkly hair which, with the deep, close-cropped sideburns, gave him a look of distinction. He slipped a scarf pin into his cravat, polished his nails. Yesterday he'd provided himself with a handsome broadcloth suit. After a final flick at his boots he went downstairs.

In the parlor were two ladies, one elderly, one young. At once Patterson knew the young one from a photograph on a cabin wall. She wore black with a veil and bonnet, like her aunt, but it didn't keep her from being beautiful. Her loveliness in fact startled Patterson.

The older woman spoke to him. "You're Mr. Milo Patterson? I'm Frank Barber's sister and this is my niece, Faith Harlan. We just stopped by to thank you for a kindness."

"I'm so glad you were with him," the niece murmured, her eyes shining with tears. "I couldn't bear it if he'd died all alone there."

Patterson looked at her and felt an uneasy twinge. For a moment he was tempted to renounce those seven quarts of gold.

But he pushed it from his mind. What was he thinking of? Only a fool would kick away a fortune like that. What they didn't know couldn't hurt them. Expecting nothing, they'd get nothing. Anyway what would two women in a bake-shop do with eighty thousand dollars?

He sat down and made himself sound carelessly self-effacing. "It's not to be mentioned, Mrs. Barnes." He turned earnestly to the girl. "If there's anything I can *really* do for you, Miss Harlan, please command me."

She smiled. "There is nothing, thank you."

"Unless," her aunt amended, "you can tell us how Frank seemed to be getting along up there. Did he seem — I mean except for that last terrible day — do you think he was well fed and comfortable?"

"I'm sure he was," Patterson said glibly. "Snug little place he had. Was it a mining claim he'd staked out?"

"No. There's no mineral sand on it. Frank simply used the cabin as a base to prospect from."

"Did he have any horse stock?"

"No. Only three burros. They're probably grazing near the cabin. And they might as well stay there for a while, since we have no grass down here."

"Your brother had a mining claim, though, somewhere?"

"I don't think so. Many years ago he filed a placer claim on the Tarryall. But after a few months the color played out. So Frank said he'd never file again except in rock. A lode claim, he meant. His idea was that placers are so fickle it hardly pays to file them. If he ever found creek gold again, he told us, he'd just work it quietly until he had it all and then move on."

That, Patterson was convinced, was exactly how the man had amassed those seven cans of dust. At some streak of richly paying gravel on which he hadn't filed, which he'd quickly worked out and whose location would now never be known.

A gay voice intruded. "Oh, here you are, Milo! I've been looking everywhere."

Serena Chalmers came sweeping up as though she owned Patterson. Her eyebrows arched as she appraised the two with him. "Aren't you going to introduce me, Milo?"

He was annoyed. As he hesitated, the unwillingness leaked from his eyes. And instantly Serena knew why. She wasn't a fool. She knew men and their stiff double standards. Her laugh rippled, hiding a bitterness. "I'm Serena Chalmers. Milo and I are old-friends from Santa Fe."

"Mrs. Barnes," Patterson murmured rebelliously. "And Miss Harlan." His face burned. He knew Serena could read him like print. His reluctance was telling her that she, Serena, didn't belong in the same room with these people; that a line of demarcation, uncrossable and as high as the sky, stood between them and women like herself.

Both of them had arisen immediately upon Serena's intrusion. "We only stopped by to thank you, Mr. Patterson. Good afternoon, Miss Chalmers." This from the aunt, and, an impersonal smile from Faith, seemed to dismiss Patterson forever from their lives.

He could have throttled Serena. A sixth sense told him they'd classified her at once. A predatory man might fool them but not a predatory woman. A hundred details, and not just a cosmeticed face and jade earrings, would be as plain to them as spots on a leopard.

"I'll see you to your cab." Patterson turned his back on Serena, knowing she'd make him pay for it; that he'd hear from her later. Gallantly he offered an arm to the aunt.

"Thank you, but we're walking," she protested.

Stubbornly Patterson conducted them out to the street walk, leaving Serena as though she didn't exist. Knowing as he did so that she'd hate this bakery girl, venomously and forever.

It was a morning later when Tony Raegan, prowling for news, ran on to two cowboys in the Grand Central lobby.

Tony hailed them. "You fellows got on anywhere yet?"

Slim Baker shook his head. "If we was miners we could get forty jobs. Or if we wanted to skin a freight team. But bein' just cowfolks, we ain't got a chance."

"Grasshoppers?"

"Grasshoppers. They've et all the cow feed for the past two years. Winter's comin' on and cowfolks are broke. Hay's too high to feed to anything but mules freightin' to the gold camps. Besides, they ain't any hay 'cept in the mountain parks. Here on the flats you can count every rib on every cow. A third of 'em have already been shipped for canners; 'nother third have already starved to death; and the last third's bein' foreclosed by the banks who don't know what the heck to do with 'em. So how's a guy gonna get a job punchin' 'em?"

"If I hear of anything I'll let you know." With a wave the little reporter passed on.

Terry Woodford stood up and slapped on his hat. "Be back by lunchtime, Slim."

With no explanation Terry left the lobby and headed south along Seventeenth. At the Curtis Street ditch he turned east. The gravel walk here was shaded by cottonwoods. His pace slowed as he sighted a neat frame store with a bakery sign over it. The news story about Frank Barber's murder had shocked him for more reasons than one.

What preyed on him now was the memory of his own liquor-inspired tomfoolery under the disapproving gaze of Frank Barber's niece. Not since that moment had he been able to put her from his mind.

He could see that the shop was open for business. Why not simply walk in and offer them, with entire sincerity, his condolences for the passing of a relative?

A bell tinkled as Terry opened the screen and went in. The shop was empty. But a heavenly odor came from the rear. Under glass cases fresh loaves and pies were on display.

It was the aunt who answered the bell. Her hair, contrasting with the black of her dress, looked even whiter than before. Last week's jolly plumpness was gone from her face. She supposed it was a customer till Terry said: "I knew your brother Frank. Just wanta say I'm sure sorry to hear what happened."

She remembered him and smiled. "You were in here one day last week, weren't you?" She seemed vague about it, and for that Terry was thankful.

"Yes'm. I didn't know your brother very well. Stopped overnight with him once, that's all."

"Recently?"

"Only two months ago. Early in June."

"Then you saw him since we did. He wintered with us, you know, and then left us early in May. Too early, I told him. I was afraid he'd catch his death of cold. Was he all right when you saw him, Mr . . ."

"Woodford. Terry Woodford."

"You must tell us about him. Won't you come in, please?" She led him into a small parlor back of the shop. "Faith!" she called. "We've a visitor."

Her niece came in from the kitchen. Today she was dressed in gray with a demure white collar, the mass of her black hair gathered against the back of her head. A

44

question in her eyes at sight of Terry made him flush. It seemed to say, "*You again?*"

"He was with your Uncle Frank in June," the aunt explained cordially. "Far as we know, he was the last visitor Frank ever had." She made Terry take a rocker while she and her niece sat on a sofa. "Tell us how Frank was when you saw him, Mr. Woodford."

"He was feeling fine," Terry said. "I hit there about sundown just as he was taking a batch of sourdough bread out of the oven. Fed me a prime supper and breakfast and wouldn't take a cent for it."

"That would be like Frank," Emily Barnes agreed quickly. "What did he talk about, do you remember?"

"He said he was about to light out for a creek higher in the mountains. Didn't say where it was. Before leaving in the morning I helped him round up his burros."

"Those burros will get along all right, won't they, for the next month or two?"

Terry was sure of it. "A heap better than if they were down here. Grass is plenty high along Elk Creek."

Faith looked at him, and her cool gaze let him know he was still on probation. "You were riding toward Denver?" she asked.

"Yes. I'd just delivered some stock up at South Park."

"Wasn't it awfully cold up there, that early in the season?"

"It was plenty cold in the park, where it's ten thousand feet high. But your uncle's cabin's only eight thousand. Snow was all gone. I remember a coupla white-face heifers were grazing close by, and they looked in right good shape."

The girl looked askance. "Cattle? But there's no ranch near by, is there?"

"No ma'am. Those heifers were strays. Your uncle told me a sort of funny story about 'em. He said late last fall a herd of cattle was driven by there, on the way to stock a ranch the other side of the divide. But two heifers got sore-footed and couldn't keep up. Those rocky trails play whaley with an unshod hoof. So the drovers just left the two heifers right there on Elk Creek. They couldn't afford to be held up by 'em."

"Who took care of them," Faith wondered, "over the winter?"

"No one. They just . . ." Terry stopped, an odd expression creeping over his face. "Your Uncle Frank said they made it through the winter on their own."

"But how could they! Away up there in the mountains in all that snow!"

Terry looked at her, his eyes echoing her question. "That's just what I asked your uncle. We folks down here on the plains always figured a cow'd starve if we didn't get her outa the high country by snowtime."

"And what did Uncle Frank say?"

"He said he was a miner, not a stockman. He didn't claim to know anything about cows. But he said he'd lived in the mountains ever since 'fifty-nine, when John Gregory made the strike on Clear Creek. Sometimes he'd wintered in a high country cabin. And he'd watched the deer and elk. 'When deep snow comes,' he said, 'nobody drives the deer and the elk down to the

46

Denver flats to feed 'em hay. Yet they stay alive all winter, don't they?' He pointed to the two white-face heifers. 'Only way those two ballies could have made it through,' he said, 'was to do just like the deer and elk.' "

"And what do they do?" This from the aunt, Emily Barnes. She'd been hanging eagerly on each word, mainly because it brought to her one last scene in the robust life of her brother.

"He didn't say," Terry answered sheepishly. "And I was too dumb, right then, to figure it out myself. I mean it didn't seem to make any particular difference. Two heifers got stranded in the high country and somehow they wintered there. I rode on down the stage road to Denver and forgot all about it. But now . . ." A subdued excitement gripped Terry. "Now it might be your brother made a strike worth a heap more'n gold!"

Some undercurrent in his mood struck a spark from Faith Harlan. "You mean it would be worth more than gold," she prompted, "to know how cattle could winter in the high mountains?"

"It sure would," Terry said. "Take the way things are right now. No grass or crops down here on the plains. Cattle are skin and bones. Stockmen know there's grass in the mountains. But the cattle are so weak it'd be a tough job drivin' 'em up there. And this being August, in two months snow will fly and they'd have to be brought down again. And nothing to feed 'em when they get here. So why bother with a hard round-trip up-mountain?"

"But if Uncle Frank was right," Faith put in, "they could be left up there all winter."

Terry concentrated on it. "Not all of them," he decided. "Cows due to calf in the spring wouldn't have a chance. Even with the he-stuff and yearlings it would be a big risk. In a normal year you wouldn't want to try it. But this year there's nothing to lose."

"But what good is grass," questioned Aunt Emily, "when it's covered by snow?"

"Deer," Terry said, "get part of their feed by browsing. I mean they nibble tender shoots and buds and twigs from trees and bushes. Elk graze like cattle, pickin' out spots where the feed shows above the snow. On windswept ridges. On the leeside of cliffs. Along running creeks. Here and there near a hot spring or in some sheltered canyon. But most of all both the deer and the elk just drift down-mountain through the season. First snow maybe catches them at ten thousand feet so they drift down to nine; the snow gets too deep at nine thousand so they drop down to eight. And so on through the winter. By January maybe they're clear down to the edge of the grasshopper blight. But they've kept enough flesh to last out a month or two of famine. Then the thaw begins and they shift up to seven thousand, later to eight, to nine, and by June they're back up to their old stamping grounds at ten. The elk do it every winter."

"But cattle," Faith protested, "aren't used to it, like the elk."

"That's right. And they're not as good at pawing snow off grass. So a lot of 'em'd die. Which would still be better than for *all* of 'em to die."

"But wouldn't they freeze?"

"Not as long as they're strong enough to keep moving. The colder it gets, the longer their hair grows. Come zero weather they get right shaggy, cows do."

"So why don't you tell people about this?"

"I sure will," Terry promised. "Likely they won't believe me. But I'll sure tell 'em. You know what? I'd like to prove it to 'em. I mean take a bunch of cattle up there right now. Then just leave 'em and see what happens."

The girl and her aunt exchanged quick glances. The idea seemed to arouse in them some deep personal interest. "You could camp right there in Frank's cabin," Aunt Emily suggested. "No use letting it go to waste. And maybe you could look after his burros. Anyway you'd be mighty welcome, young man."

"I'd be glad to, ma'am."

The tinkling of a bell announced a customer. As her aunt went into the shop Faith remembered something. She smiled. "The croquet set came. The neighborhood children told me to thank you."

The reference to his spree of last week made Terry flush. "We're not always like that," he said earnestly. "I mean Ray Baker and I. Ray'll go along with me if I take some cattle to Elk Valley. We call him Slim."

"My aunt and I," the girl said, "were planning to go by stage to Shawn's Crossing. Just to bring back whatever personal belongings Uncle Frank left in his cabin. But if you're going up there yourself . . ."

"Sure," Terry broke in. "I can round 'em up for you. His clothes and his books and his deer rifle . . . and that picture of you on the wall. Time I'm running along now."

She went to the door with him. There an unanswered question made him linger a moment. Why were they so willing, and even eager, to have him use Frank Barber's cabin? In what did their sudden and personal interest in his idea take root?

When he asked, her response seemed irrelevant. "Do you know what they first named this town? I mean when the first cabins were built here, in 1858?"

Old-timers, in camp and bunkshack, had told Terry about it more than once. "They called it Auraria," he said. "Some folks trekked out here from Auraria, Georgia. A year later another wagon train followed 'em and they started a town. Named it Auraria after the home town back in Georgia."

Faith Harlan smiled. "I was born there. In Auraria, Georgia. I came in a covered wagon to Auraria, Colorado, when I was two years old. So you see, I'm a rugged pioneer."

Terry whistled, grinning. "Gee! You make me feel like a tenderfoot. I only came here three years ago, from Indiana. Let's see 'f I've got it straight. Back in 'fifty-nine this town of Auraria was part of Kansas Territory. A year later some boomers wanted to curry favor with Governor Denver of Kansas. The upshot was Auraria wound up with the name of Denver."

"Three of the Fifty-niners who came here from Georgia," the girl said proudly, "were my father and two of my uncles. Many of the others, like John Gregory, found gold and prospered. But my father and uncles met nothing but disappointments. Year after year they went into the mountains and always came back empty-handed. One by one we lost them. Uncle Frank last of all. But always they had faith in those mountains, Uncle Frank *most* of all."

"Frank most of all," echoed Emily Barnes. She'd joined them unnoticed, and her eyes were moist. " 'It's a strong country, up there.' Frank always said. 'It kills some but it gives strength and life to others. Even the grass is strong. It's like ripe grain, that mountain grass, and if you don't believe it, take a look at my burros.' "

Faith's dark eyes, too, had a shine in them. Terry knew then what they meant and wanted. Presently he was walking down Curtis Street with a purposeful step. The world was suddenly important, with Denver, and the dreams of its pioneers, at the very hub of it. A job? He had two of them now. One was to show Colorado how to save starving cattle; the other was to make Faith Harlan begin liking him.

CHAPTER
FIVE

The vice-president listened with a cool impatience. For an hour he'd let these two denim-clad cowboys cool their heels before admitting them to his sanctum. The country was full of broken-down stockmen who wanted help from banks.

"And will you please explain," he broke in with stern irony, "why this bank should be interested in deer and elk?"

"Because they can live all winter," Terry Woodford maintained, "in the mountains."

"I'm supposed to be impressed?" the V.P. looked at his watch.

"This bank," Terry reminded him, "owns cattle. Cattle too thin to make beef. Cattle fit for nothing but glue and hides if you ship 'em to Chicago. Cattle that'll die if you try to winter 'em here on the plains where there's no grass or crops. This bank has foreclosed 'em from busted ranches. You don't know what to do with 'em, Mr. Thornton. So Slim Baker and I'd like to buy five hundred head."

The banker arched an eyebrow over his plump, tight-skinned face. "And how much, young man, are you willing to pay?"

"One dollar per head over the foreclosure price. Only we can't pay anything down. We'd just give you our note."

"Oh, you would, would you? And adequate security, I presume?"

"Just our note," Terry said simply, "and a chattel lien on the stock."

"And what, may I ask, would you do with these cattle?"

"We'd drive 'em to high pasture. We figure they'd be in good flesh by November. They'd hold their own maybe till January. Then they'd begin gaunting up. Some would die in the drifts. Some would just plain starve. But they'd keep drifting down in front of the snowline, like the elk do, and so by March maybe more'n half of 'em'd be on their feet. And by April we'll have grass again down here around Denver."

Mr. Thornton stood up with a severe stare. "We're bankers, young man. We don't gamble. Good day."

Terry gave a shrug and went out. But Slim Baker couldn't help popping off. "The heck banks don't gamble!" he blurted. "That's all they do. And they do it with other folks' money. When they's a risk, it's us cowfolks that's always got to take it. But this time you're stuck. You know what I hope about them canners you foreclosed on? I hope you have to eat every one of 'em. And without any ketchup, neither. Good day." Slim flipped the snipe of his cigaret at a brass cuspidor. Then he slammed on his brand-new five gallon hat and stalked out.

At the street walk he caught up with Terry. "Huh! Swelled up like a poisoned pup, that guy!"

"Makes three times," Terry grimaced. Both of the other Denver banks had already turned them down.

"So let's kick the dust of this et-out range off our boots," proposed Slim, "and go saddle up for Montany."

"And get ourselves scalped?" Terry quipped. It was only six weeks ago, on June twenty-sixth, that the command of General George Custer had been massacred by Sioux warriors on the Little Big Horn, in Montana.

"I'd a heap rather fight Indians," Slim argued, "than grasshoppers."

Turning in at the Grand Central Hotel they found Tony Raegan waiting for them. With Raegan was a lean, weathered ranchman. "Hi, fellas," the reporter greeted. "Meet Jase Judson of the O Bar."

The O Bar lay along Plum Creek some eighteen miles south. "Jase," Tony explained, "happened to be in the Denver National this morning when they turned you boys down."

Judson nodded. He had a tired, lined face and discouraged mustaches. "Yeah, I heard that spiel you fellas put up." He took a chew of twist tobacco and wiped his lips. "It set me to thinkin'."

"Thinkin' about what?" Terry asked.

"Down at the O Bar, the only thing the grasshoppers didn't eat was my whiskers." Judson stroked them sadly. "So I aim to lay off my hands and ship every hoof to Chicago. You could stand off and count the ribs on that stuff o' mine — but maybe the hides'd pay the freight."

Terry sensed his trend of thought. He broke in eagerly. "Why not sell 'em to us, Mr. Judson? Say at ten bucks a head, on tick. You've got nothing to lose. It'd be better than . . ."

"You don't have to put up no sales talk, young man I've already figgered it out. And you're dead right. I got nothin' to lose. But I still aim to stay in the cattle business, so I wanta keep a half interest in the stuff. I'd sell you boys a half interest, on two conditions."

"Name 'em," said Slim Baker.

"First, I ride up to Elk Valley with yuh and see 'f the grass is as good as you claim it is."

"There's spots," Terry insisted, "where it's stirrup-high to a bronc."

"Second," Judson stipulated, "I wanta look at them two stray heifers you claim made it through the winter. I'd given 'em up for lost, so naturally I wanta see 'em with my own eyes."

O Bar! Now Terry recalled the brand on the two heifers. No wonder the incident had a peculiar interest for this Plum Creek ranchman!

"I sold some stockers," Jase Judson confirmed, "to a San Luis Valley man who drove 'em over the divide. Later he wrote me he got home with all of 'em 'cept two heifers; he said they went sore-footed on him in Elk Valley."

"We can ride up there tomorrow," Terry proposed.

The O Bar man nodded. "Show me high grass; and show me them two heifers fat and sassy; and I'll sell you a half interest in a thousand head, nothin' down."

"Hot zigetty!" Slim gave Terry a thump on the back. "We're in business, cowboy."

"We can handle only he-stuff and yearlings and unbred cows," Terry said.

"Sold!" Judson shook hands with each of them. Cattle deals were commonly closed just that informally. Mr. Jase Judson of Plum Creek then squirted a stream of tobacco juice toward a lobby cuspidor. And with such marksmanship that not a drop touched the rug.

Daylight was breaking as they trotted across the Platte River bridge. Terry, Slim, and Jase Judson. Each man wore a hip gun and each saddle scabbard had a rifle. Terry and Slim, as usual when quitting Denver for a few days, had left their town bags in check at the hotel. On this excursion Slim led a packmare laden with three bedrolls and a sack of grub. "Might take us a coupla days to find those two heifers," Terry said. "For a camp shack we can use Frank Barber's cabin."

"Sure it'll be all right?" queried Judson.

Slim gave a sly wink. "Why wouldn't it be? The kid here's been shinin' up to Barber's niece, they tell me. Just like one of the family."

They struck Bear Creek and followed it to Morrison. Here the range was still grassless. There were a dozen log houses, a store, a stage station and a sawmill. The Leadville stage made its first change of horses here.

Pressing on, the three riders crossed a high, cedar ridge and angled into Turkey Creek. Here there was still no grass. Nothing but dust and red sandstone and the deep wheel-gashes of the trail. The trail climbed steeply to a ridge between Turkey and Elk Creeks and from there they could see the snow-crowned summits which rimmed South Park. Here too the grass began showing. Terry saw a rider approaching, heading toward Denver. A man who sat tall in the saddle of an iron-gray horse and who led a laden mule. And although Terry had never seen him before, the big iron-gray horse seemed vaguely familiar.

He looked like a man of affairs. But not a cattleman, Terry thought. As the man drew opposite, Jase Judson reined to a stop. "Howdy, Milo." Judson hooked a leg around his saddle horn. Travelers rarely passed each other in these mountains without halting for a trailside chat.

"Howdy, Judson." The man on the iron-gray returned the salutation but did not stop.

As he continued downtrail, Judson stared quizzically after him. "Kinda in a hurry, seems like." Then, with a shrug, he continued on with Terry and Slim.

Terry asked, "What was that name you called him by?"

"He's Milo Patterson. Sat in a stud game with him one time."

Terry and Slim exchanged glances. Kelly and Dodds had been waiting to meet a Milo Patterson in Denver. Also the Denver papers had mentioned Patterson as one of two Good Samaritans who'd given first aid to Frank Barber.

Judson bit a fresh quid from his plug. "You fellers know the gent?"

"Heard of him," Terry said.

"We never seen him before," Slim offered. "But we seen his bronc. Remember? That big iron-gray was tied in front of the American House bar day before yesterday."

Terry remembered it. He rode on, idly puzzled. Since the gray was in Denver only two days ago, Patterson had obviously ridden it up this trail no earlier than yesterday. Nor could he have traveled more than fifty miles out of Denver. A packmule couldn't be led farther than that in one day. And since Patterson was now returning toward Denver, he couldn't have remained more than one night in the hills.

Except as a matter of idle speculation, it made no difference. Ordinarily Terry wouldn't have given it a second thought. Or even a first thought if it weren't for the man's connection both with the Frank Barber incident and Rex Kelly.

They angled through the pines and struck Elk Creek on the near side of a grassy valley. Directly at the ford were the corrals, stage depot and saloon-store known as Shawn's Crossing. A sprinkle of rain began pattering as Judson's party drew rein there.

"Pretty near always showers 'bout this time, during August," Terry said. "The grass shows it, too. Take a look."

Judson had already taken many looks. And while grass near the trail was close-cropped, due to the passing of many droves, at a distance it was lush and green. "Higher up we get," Terry insisted, "the better the feed."

"I'm already sold on the feed," Judson conceded. "What I want now is a look at them O Bar heifers."

They dismounted and went into the store. The place had a short, untidy bar. There was a storekeeper with a stained apron over his ample belly. He was shaggy, gross, and with him were two stage hostlers. One of these had a thin, Latin face and was whetting a knife on his boot. The other was a ruddy, thick-necked gringo. He sat on a keg with a mug of beer. Terry noticed he wore two unmatched guns, a forty-five on the right and a thirty-eight on the left. His pants were held up by suspenders.

Judson spoke to the storekeeper. "Seen a coupla O Bar strays lately? Coming-three-year-old heifers. Couple of months ago they were feeding up by Frank Barber's cabin."

"Ain't seen 'em," the storeman said. "What'll you have, gents?" He began swabbing his bar with the skirt of his soiled apron.

"Nothing just now," Terry said. Trash littered the floor and the place was swarming with flies.

Slim bought a sack of tobacco. "They didn't ketch up with Tom Redding yet, did they?"

"Not that I heard about," the storeman said. His bloated face needed shaving. And his quick look at the ruddy, thick-necked man might have been a warning. Terry wasn't sure they didn't know more about Redding than they cared to admit. Or that two prime heifers, August-fat, would be very safe around here.

Judson asked idly, "Did Milo Patterson stop here last night?"

"Nope," the storeman said. "But I seen him ride up the trail yesterday and head back down today. With a pack-mule. Went up empty and came back with a pack. Are you sure you gents don't want no beer? It's plenty cold. I keep the keg in the creek."

"No thanks." Terry went outside and tightened his cinch. Presently the others joined him and they rode on.

The valley was about a mile wide. When they were halfway across it the rain stopped. Wild flowers made color in the meadow. Terry saw lupine and columbine. Clumps of aspen grew here and there.

On the far side of the valley a piny slope rose sharply. Here the trail entered a tributary ravine with a clear brook riffling from it. A little way up it they came to a log cabin.

Dismounting there, Terry saw that the door stood open. His first thought was that vandals might have looted the place. But when he looked in he saw well-stocked shelves. Arbuckle's coffee in pound paper packages and fruit in quart cans. Barber's tarp and blankets were on the bunk. So the cabin hadn't been raided.

A whistle from Slim Baker. "Somethin' sure played whaley with the roof. Take a look."

It had been a flat roof covered with sod. Now the sod was upturned, rudely. Terry's impression was that the upturning had been recent. A spade with fresh earth clinging to the blade lay near by. And leaning against the cabin was a crudely made pole ladder.

"Somebody camped here last night," Judson announced. "Somebody with two broncs."

"How do you know?"

"He grained 'em with oats." Jase pointed to a few grains of moist oats at the base of a tree. Then to a similar sprinkling of oat grains about ten paces away. "He didn't have any nose bags," Jase concluded. "So his broncs slobbered a few grains out on the ground. They'll do it every time when you don't put on nose bags."

"Maybe the posse fed oats," Terry argued. "It came by here four or five days ago to pick up the trail of Redding."

"These oats were dropped last night, son. Or early this morning. Because if they'd been here longer than that, the birds and the squirrels would've cleaned 'em up. Let's go in and see if he made a fire."

They went in and Terry touched ashes in the stove. They weren't quite cold yet. A loose cracker hadn't been carried off by chipmunks — a sure depredation had the loose food been exposed more than a few hours.

Milo Patterson? The man who, a week ago, had watched Frank Barber's last breath? Why would Patterson come back here?

Terry looked in puzzlement about the room. A battered chest was full of Barber's extra boots and clothing. A shelf by the bunk showed a few tattered books. There was a canvas cot. A tobacco pouch and two pipes. A deer rifle offered final proof that no outlaw of Tom Redding's stripe had prowled here the last few days.

Not a thing seemed to be missing. Yet Terry sensed a lack. Something which, in June, had drawn his attention and which wasn't here now. He looked from wall to wall. All at once he spotted it. A frame with a glass front hung from a nail. In June it had held a photograph of Faith Harlan. The frame was still in place. But the face of the girl was missing.

CHAPTER
SIX

Slim unpacked, unsaddled and hobbled the animals. While Jase Judson made supper, Terry assembled what seemed to him worth keeping of Frank Barber's effects. These he wrapped in a pack for transport down the mountain. The night was clear, so they spread their bedrolls under the pines.

During the last hour of twilight Terry found Slim staring up at the disarray of sod on the roof. "Why the heck would anyone want to do that?"

Terry climbed up the pole ladder to the roof. Hardly a single slab of its sod was undisturbed. Much of it was heaped in the center. In spots the clay had been scraped away exposing the horizontal roofing poles. Any heavy rain would leak through.

A small cylinder of white caught Terry's eye. He picked it up, took it down to show Slim Baker.

Slim gave a low whistle. "Candle stub, huh!"

"He wouldn't need it in the daytime, Slim. Means he was up there at night. Turning over that sod by candlelight."

Terry brooded over it during supper. By all accounts Barber had been a poor man. If he'd made any important strike he almost certainly would have confided it to his kinfolks in Denver.

Then a thought jolted Terry. *Maybe he had!* With his dying breath Barber could have dispatched a message to a sister and niece. If so, the messenger would have to be the only person at the bunkside. Milo Patterson!

A certain fact was that Patterson had delivered no such message. Yesterday he'd ridden up this trail with an unloaded mule, and today had returned down-mountain with a load.

A slow red crawled up Terry's neck. Slim noticed it. "Who you sore at, kid?"

"I got a hunch, Slim. That guy Patterson we passed. Maybe Barber had a stash up here and Patterson grabbed it."

Slim wasn't impressed. "No reason to think Barber had anything," he argued. "If any grabbin's been goin' on, I'd rather lay it on them fellas at Shawn's Crossing."

"Plenty of crooks in these hills," Jase added, "without pickin' on Milo Patterson. Jiggers like Tom Redding. He's still on the loose, ain't he?"

Terry had to admit there was no real case against Patterson. Yet the man's name hung in his mind. Two horses, or perhaps a horse and a mule, had been fed oats here last night. Patterson's?

At breakfast they divided the range into three sectors. "I'll scout sou'east toward Buffalo Crik," Judson proposed. "Slim can take the high country nor'west. And Terry, suppose you head straight up the trail to the next stage station. Ask 'em if they've seen two bally heifers."

Terry saddled his bay and rode uptrail. It was a big country, and odds were against stumbling at once on the two heifers.

The trail climbed a ridge known as Crow Hill. From a high bare spot on the summit Terry could see miles in three directions. In a distant glade he saw grazing horses. But no cattle. A nine-point buck posed, forefoot up and high-headed, then broke for downridge timber.

Presently the trail itself dipped sharply downward to the Bailey stage station. It forded North Fork there, and Terry found a wagoner resting his team. A corral full of stage horses flanked a depot and store. Beyond was a bunkhouse where travelers sometimes stayed overnight.

A sunbonneted woman was gathering chips in her apron at the woodpile. Terry tipped his hat. "Mornin', ma'am; do you happen to know Milo Patterson?"

She gave him a puzzled look, nodding. "Why?"

"He stop overnight here, night before last?"

She thought back. "No, he didn't. Last time we saw him was about a week ago when he rode by with Preacher Bell."

"Thanks. You didn't happen to see a coupla O Bar heifers lately? Two-comin'-three ballies?"

She hadn't seen any cows like that. "But you'd better ask the men."

Her husband was in the store. And at the corral Terry found two wranglers. None of them had seen the O Bar strays. "They's a few cattle down. North Fork, though," a wrangler offered.

Terry left the stage trail and rode easterly down the valley. It was fairly flat and open, and Terry came presently to a homestead cabin. The homesteader had a few cattle of his own and a stack of winter feed for them. He hadn't seen any O Bar strays.

It was the same at a miner's shack further down the stream. By now it was past noon and time to begin circling back toward Elk Creek. Terry reined left toward a high bald cone.

A zone of lodgepole pine engulfed him. At the far edge of it the bald cone reared abruptly.

Tethering the bay Terry climbed afoot to the cone's summit. Here was a lookout from which he could see east to the South Platte Canyon and north almost to Shawn's Crossing. A band of elk trotted across his vision and nearer a chunky black bear lumbered out, of sight into berry briars. The moving black shadow came from a soaring eagle.

Terry, shading his eyes, could see no cattle. Nor any camp or cabin. Never had a wilderness seemed so deserted of all but its own creatures.

Before quitting the spot Terry took one more look. East, north and west. This time he spotted one domestic animal Not a cow but a horse. The horse was saddled and about two miles northeast. It was grazing with bridle reins trailing in a small glade tightly surrounded by timber. No rider was near it.

Yet a saddled horse meant a man close by. Perhaps there was a hidden homestead over that way.

Terry slid downslope to his mount. He struck northeasterly through timber, hoping to hit the glade where he'd seen the saddled horse. Ten minutes took him two miles in that direction. It brought him to an open spot in the pines hut he couldn't be certain it was the right one. No horse was there now.

But in the high grass of the glade he found horse sign. A moment later he spotted the horse itself, still saddled. It was a lean-flanked sorrel and was tied by a bridle rein to a sapling. The owner, although not now in sight, had evidently caught and tied the mount since Terry had left the bald cone lookout.

It was a short way into the timber and near by was a pole wickiup slanting from the boles of two giant pines. The rude shelter, or leanto, had its open side away from Terry. Any wandering hunter or prospector might make such a camp. On this side of it were the ashes of a fire with a few coals still glowing. "Hi!" Terry hailed. "Anybody home?"

"Hi!" A voice called back to him from the woods and Terry heard a tread of boots on pine needles. Dismounting he dropped the bay's reins and walked toward the shelter.

Just as he rounded it and looked in, something hard and blunt punched into his back. "That's far enough, brother. Reach!"

The thing in his back was a rifle barrel. Terry didn't argue with it. As he raised his hands ear high, a man back of him snatched the forty-five from his holster. "How many is they of you?"

"Three." Instinctively Terry told the truth and in the same breath wished he hadn't. It would be much more impressive to say ten or fifteen.

"From what county?" the voice demanded.

By now Terry had his wits. "Two from Park and one from Jefferson," he said glibly. "And more on the way."

This, he reasoned, would be the fugitive Tom Redding for whom a posse had last week scoured the hills. Not unnaturally the man would assume Terry to be a posseman. "How *many* more?" the man prodded.

"Plenty," Terry said. "And not too far from here either. Within earshot of a gun, I'd say."

A pregnant silence, while cold steel still punched into Terry's back. "In that case," the man said finally, "I'm putting you to sleep."

The rifle barrel crashed on Terry's head and he went to all fours. A second blow followed the first.

It was sundown when Terry came to with a roaring head. A chill ran up his legs and he became aware that his pants, boots and coat had been stripped from him. Clad only in underwear, shirt, belt and socks, he was propped with his back against a pine.

Seated on a log, about ten feet away, was Tom Redding. Redding had two forty-fives and two rifles. His own and Terry's. Denver papers had carried his picture and so Terry knew him beyond any doubt. This man had been vigilantly hunted since the Golden bank job.

Now he had a two-weeks beard. The hat, coat, pants and boots he wore were Terry's. His own discarded garments lay near by.

"Come dark," he announced tonelessly, "I'm pullin' outa here."

Except for the untrimmed beard he wasn't bad looking. His build and height were approximately Terry's. His eyes had red in them, as though constant fear of capture had cheated him of sleep. Yet just now he seemed fairly relaxed.

"Why," Terry asked thickly from the haze which still clouded him, "haven't you pulled out before?"

"I'd a-been too easy spotted. It'll be different now."

Denver papers had printed descriptions of the man. Particularly as to his clothes and his horse. Last seen he'd worn a black hat with a ragged rim. Quite unlike the fairly new, gray sombrero now on his head.

"In this outfit," the man said slyly, "and forkin' that bay o' yourn, nobody'll stop me on the trails."

Which meant that he had no intention of letting Terry report the change. Having already killed twice, he'd have nothing to lose by killing again. Terry would be left dead here. But why didn't the man shoot him and be done?

His occasional alert glance to right or left gave Terry the answer. Redding was still assuming him to be one of a posse. The only respite was to make him keep thinking it.

"How far back did yuh leave 'em?" the fugitive asked presently.

Terry's head was reasonably clear by now. "See that bald cone about two miles south?" He pointed. "Three of us spotted your bronc from there. I offered to ride here for a look."

"Likely you're lying," Redding said. "But I'm not takin' any chances. So I'll keep you for a pet till dark."

Terry saw the angle. If other possemen closed in, he'd be used as a shield. The outlaw could do his fighting from behind a prisoner who, if the others fired back, would be killed instantly. But only till dark. After that the man would need no shield. With the butt of his rifle he'd brain Terry and fade into the night.

It was well past sundown. An hour or two of twilight was all Terry could hope for.

"You know Frank Barber told on you?" he challenged.

Redding nodded. "I picked up a paper somebody tossed off a stage. It gave what the old coot said." A faint chuckle escaped the outlaw. "He had one thing wrong, though."

"What was that?" Terry prodded. Not that it made any difference. But a thin idea was forming in his head. The man had taken his pants, coat, boots and gun, but a cartridge belt with its empty holster was still draped around Terry's shirtclad waist. It gave him a grotesque look, since below the belt only a shirttail and drawers covered his legs. He hooked his thumbs into the belt as he waited for Redding's answer.

"He thought I was prowlin' that cabin for grub," the man said, smirking. Yet his eyes were alert and deadly.

"And weren't you?"

"Heck no. I was prowlin' for them dust cans he had. Couldn't find 'em nowhere. Accordin' to the papers, nobody else did either."

At once Terry thought of the sod roof. Only night before last someone had dug there. "Dust cans?" he questioned. "You mean placer gold?"

70

"It wasn't nothing else," Redding said. "Dust and nuggets. He was fillin' fruit cans with it when I peeked in through a window."

"The day you shot him?"

"Nope. It was a day before that." The very frankness of the admission meant a death sentence for Terry. "I was lookin' for a blanket. Or a buffalo robe. It was dang cold sleepin' out in the woods."

Twilight deepened. Tom Redding glanced right, then left, alert for the approach of possemen. As he did so Terry Woodford, with a thumb and forefinger of each hand, plucked from his belt two rifle cartridges. His hands closed on them as Redding's eyes swung back. "When you peeked through a window," Terry prompted, "you saw him fill cans with creek gold. How many cans and how big were they?"

"They was seven of 'em," Redding remembered. "Looked like quart fruit cans."

Terry pretended to doubt. "You're makin' it all up," he scoffed. "If you'd seen anything like that, you'd 've held him up right there. Just like you did that bank at Golden."

Again Redding looked left and right; and again. Terry plucked a cartridge with each hand. "Sure I wanted that dust," the man admitted. "But what was the sense fightin' him for it? He had a deer rifle right by him. It was easier to come back when the cabin was empty. In the mornin' I figgered he'd go off pannin' again."

Everything was now clear and Terry asked no more questions. Barber had buried the cans under sod on his roof. Redding, returning next day, had failed to find

71

them. Then Barber had appeared and caught him searching the cabin.

By now Terry had three brass shells in each hand. When Redding again glanced to the left Terry tossed the six shells about five feet to his own right. They landed in soft ashes and sank from sight. Were the ashes still hot? If so how long would it take the brass casings to heat and explode?

Darkness was the deadline. After that Redding would need no hostage. He wouldn't even have to shoot. A blow on the skull would do.

Not for information, but merely to keep the man talking, Terry said: "Those seven cans'd be plenty heavy. More'n you could ride away with on that broken-down bronc of yours."

"Sure," the man admitted. "But I wouldn't need to ride away with 'em. I'd just carry 'em, can at a time, a piece off in the woods and bury 'em." He spat to the left, into what had been his campfire. A sizzle told Terry the ashes were still hot.

On his arrival a few coals had been glowing there. There was no glow now. But ashes stay hot for a long time. And just as certainly Terry knew that heat will explode a cartridge.

Would there be *enough* heat? And enough time? The gray of evening closed steadily in. "You'll head for Utah?" Terry guessed.

"Either there or Peoria, Illinoy." The man's lips jeered.

Again he spat and again the ashes sizzled.

72

A minor hazard occurred to Terry. Minor only when compared to Redding's guns. An exploding cartridge would send chips of brass and ball, like shrapnel, indiscriminately in all directions. If six cartridges went off at once it would be like an exploding grenade. Any human within ten feet could be maimed or killed.

Terry, sitting with his back to a pine, was about five feet from the hazard; Redding was about seven.

But Terry had nothing to lose.

In the half light he pulled up his legs, folding them under him. It was a better stance from which to spring forward. There was only a slight chance that a fragment would hit Redding. But he'd be startled and thrown off balance. Sudden gunshots from his left . . .

They came sooner than Terry had dared hope. Two of them followed by a third; a whistle of ricocheting lead and a whine of brass. Bark flew from a pine and Terry, diving toward Redding, felt a sting at his neck.

Redding had whirled toward the shots. A fourth explosion came almost at once, then a fifth. Redding's guns swung that way just as a human battering ram smashed into his ribs. He went backward over the log with Terry grappling. Convulsively he pulled triggers and both guns roared. The bullets brought a shower of pine needles. Terry clinched, pinioned two arms and made the guns impotent. At the vital instant of impact they'd handicapped, rather than aided, Tom Redding. With one free hand he might have warded Terry off.

Now it was too late. Terry's knees punched into his groin; Terry's fist smashed into his eyes. Redding yelled and dropped both guns. Terry punched him and kneed

73

him and punched again. Bootless, he couldn't kick. But his naked knee battered the breath from Redding. His knuckles rattled Redding's teeth. When the man's hands went frantically to his face, Terry snatched up both guns and backed away with them.

He cocked one of the guns. "Don't shoot!" Redding begged. He lay on his back, doubled up, only a beard and the gloom of night hiding his panic. "Don't shoot . . ."

And Terry didn't. The roar came from hot ashes, where the sixth and last shell exploded. Nothing hit Redding. But since Terry stood over him pointing a cocked gun, his mind felt the shock of a bullet. He fainted in sheer terror.

After cutting strings from a saddle Terry tied him hand and foot. He was impatient to get started. Finding his way to Elk Valley by starlight wouldn't be easy. He didn't bother to reclaim anything except his hat and boots. He put on Redding's pants and coat and, brought up Redding's horse. With the outlaw trussed across the saddle, Terry mounted his bay and, leading the sorrel, set forth to join Judson and Slim.

74

CHAPTER
SEVEN

Milo Patterson rode slowly, cautiously. Slowly Because the mule was tired. Two hundred and fifty pounds had proved too heavy a pack. Time and again the beast had balked; Patterson, tugging and cursing, had had fairly to drag it along.

And cautiously because by now Patterson realized that the very weight of his loot, in relation to its comparatively small bulk, could bring suspicion. It was too heavy to be carried by any one man up to a hotel room. It would need at least two bellboys and if questioned later, they'd remember.

The same would be true if Patterson took it to a bank vault or to any public storage. Seven quarts of gold made a puzzling problem.

Having timed himself to hit Denver after dark, Milo Patterson rode across the Platte River bridge at a walk. The hoofs of his horse and mule clumped on the plank roadway there. This led him to the foot of Fifteenth, and at Wazee he turned west instead of east.

He continued on across Cherry Creek into West Denver. Here was Old Town, originally platted by the Fifty-niners as Auraria. Many of the pioneer log cabins were still here. None of Denver's better hotels or stores were on this side of the creek.

Patterson continued along Wazee to Ninth, turning left there. On the trail today he'd made a decision. Certain encounters had worried him. Curious glances from people he'd passed. If questions were asked, too many people would remember he'd traveled up the trail one day and down the next.

The decision was that he'd better not start cashing in tomorrow. Better to wait at least a week before exchanging gold for money. Otherwise his possession of the gold might seem connected with his journey with a pack-mule into the mountains.

A career gambler, like Patterson, occasionally raked in a jackpot containing something other than chips or cash. More than once, in a poker game, Patterson had won a saddle. This iron-gray horse of his had been won with a pat four aces, in a game up at Leadville. Another time he'd raked in a bill of sale for twenty steers.

Generally Patterson promptly sold such chattel for whatever it might bring. A certain item he'd kept for the reason that it wasn't worth much now but might, in a few years, bring a handsome figure. It was a lot in West Denver with a two-room log house on it. A relic of old Auraria, now unfurnished and untenanted. Denver having passed its log cabin era, the only real value was in the lot. But the doors of the old cabin had stout locks. His present problem, Patterson concluded, made it conveniently useful.

Trailing up Ninth, dark except for a gas street lamp at every corner, he came to the Larimer Street tram track. A vacant lot on the corner had a giant cottonwood, and next to this was the small log house. After first acquiring it Patterson had given it a single contemptuous inspection. He'd never even bothered to record the deed.

Now he rode into its dark backyard and dismounted. There he unpacked the mule. The animal shook itself as the onerous weight left its back; then, perversely, it rolled back its lips and brayed raucously. Patterson cuffed the beast's mouth. "Be quiet, damn you!"

He tugged at the canvas package but couldn't quite lift it. So he rolled it end over end to the cabin's rear door. A key from his pocket fitted the lock and admitted him to a musty interior. At Morrison, Patterson had purchased two candles. One he'd expended on Frank Barber's roof. The other he now lighted to illumine two empty rooms. A ragged quilt had been discarded in one corner. Nothing else was left except a moldy oilcloth on one floor and frayed matting on the other.

Patterson turned back the oilcloth to look for a loose floor board. Failing to find one, he went into the other room and turned back the matting. The flooring was made of crude sawmill slabs with the bark side down. A crack between two slabs offered a pry purchase. Patterson found a bar which had been used for a stove poker.

Patiently, by candlelight, he pried first here, then there. One of the planks gave a little. Presently the plank was off. Underneath were floor joists.

Patterson went outside and opened the pack. One by one he carried seven heavy cans into the rear room. He put the cans in a row under the floor. Then he replaced the plank and knocked the nails into their old holes.

When the ancient matting was replaced, no sign was left of an intrusion. Patterson quit the house, locking the door. He roped the empty tarp back on the mule and led it at a trot down Ninth to Wazee, then east to the Bull's-Head Corrals.

"Return this mule to Pete Young at Morrison," he instructed. "And grain up this horse of mine." He walked stiffly up Sixteenth to the American House and went to bed there.

He slept till noon. He was bone-weary from the trail but after a bath he felt better. Serena, he guessed, would be impatient to know his plans. He'd need to stall her off for a while yet.

She was waiting in the lobby. "Where on earth have you been, Milo?"

"Raisin' some dough." He grinned. "It'll take a few weeks more yet, then we're all set. Get your hat and I'll squire you up to Charpiot's."

Charpiot's Hotel offered the best food in Denver. The heat today was oppressive. Strolling up Sixteenth, Serena protected her fairness with a parasol. She wore elbow-length gloves and a wide hat. "Where's Rex?" Patterson asked.

"He's got a feud on," Serena said. "And Cimarron too. Yesterday they walked the streets all day, spoiling for a fight. I wish you'd make them behave, Milo. They act like this is an Arizona cowtown."

"Who are they mad at?"

78

"They won't say. But someone beat Rex up the other day. He was all cuts and bruises. Oh, look at that gorgeous bracelet!" Serena stopped to gaze ecstatically at a jewelry display.

"Soon as the big deal goes through," Patterson promised glibly, "I'll buy it for you."

All through lunch at Charpiot's she pressed him for details of the deal. Just where had he been these last two days, and why? Her persistence worried Patterson a little. If she were a sheriff, or a shrewd reporter, he'd need a better story than any he'd yet trumped up. He must give thought to it. Although it wasn't likely he'd be questioned, it wouldn't hurt to have foolproof answers prepared in advance.

"You know what I heard yesterday?" Serena chattered. "Mort Jardine wants to sell out and go back to Chicago."

"The devil he does!" Patterson was glad to change the subject. Mort Jardine ran the flossiest gambling resort in Denver. "How much does he want?"

"Ninety thousand for the lease and fixtures, I heard."

"I could swing it," Patterson brooded. "And it might not be a bad idea. It'd kill off just that much competition. We could redecorate it — put in a new bar and trimmings."

"Why don't we?" Serena enthused over it. "Building from the ground up would take too long."

She was right. And delay irked Patterson no less than Serena. What with the new strikes at Leadville, Denver was full of sucker money and more pouring in every day. Why, Patterson wondered, was Jardine selling out?

His Silver Club was worth any gold mine in the state. "Won't hurt for me to drop in and have a talk with Mort."

A waiter brought the check. Patterson reached into the inside breast pocket of his coat for the billfold he always carried there. It was a broad, capacious billfold, appropriate for a gambler who rarely carried less than a thousand in currency. A miscellany of papers and accumulated memoranda was also there; and the edge of one item caught the eye of Serena Chalmers. She couldn't see all of it. Patterson, selecting a bill for the waiter, exposed no more than an inch of what to Serena looked like the photograph of a girl.

Instantly she was alert, militant, determined to get the truth of it. Patterson dropped the bill on a salver, restored the wallet to his pocket. Waiting for the change he rolled a cigaret.

"Make one for me too," Serena coaxed.

"Here?" Patterson looked at her in surprise.

"Of course not, stupid." A woman, naturally, couldn't be seen smoking in the dining room of a reputable hotel. "But we can go into the parlor. No one will be there in this beastly heat."

Patterson nodded amiably. The change came and he left a tip.

Serena devised a quick strategy. Entering the dining room she'd carried a purse and a parasol. Leaving it she had only the purse.

They crossed a lobby to a small parlor, dim and stuffy, furnished with a green velvet divan and rockers to match. It was deserted.

Serena sank into a rocker. "Gosh! I'm roasting. Fix me a smoke, Milo. Then peel off your coat and be comfortable."

Patterson was quite willing to shed his coat. He tossed it on the divan, sat down and made the cigaret for Serena. As he held a match to it she exclaimed: "My parasol! I left it in the dining room. Would you mind getting it for me?"

He grimaced. "You'll lose your head some day." But he went on the errand.

The instant he was out of sight Serena pounced upon his coat and took out the wallet. She opened it, found what she wanted. A girl's photograph! She was that bakery girl! It made Serena's mouth hard and bitter. She was even more amazed than furious. Amazed that Milo could get so far in so short a time! She stared critically at the picture. Pretty enough, she admitted, to turn a man's head. Even a hard-shelled sophisticate like Milo.

Serena put the picture back in the wallet and restored the wallet to the coat. Under her skin she was seething, but she'd only make a fool of herself by upbraiding Milo now. She knew something he didn't know she knew. It was knowledge, and sometimes knowledge was power. More than anything else Serena wanted power, and particularly power over Milo Patterson.

When he returned with the parasol she smiled sweetly. "Thanks, Milo. Now we can relax and talk about buying out Mort Jardine."

After dropping her at the American House, Patterson walked up to Holladay Street and turned left on Red Light Row. Along this nearly every door opened to a dive of some kind. Saloons, dice joints and dance floors on the street level; bawdy shops above stairs. By nightfall the Row would be roaring; but this early of a hot afternoon it was quiet enough. An occasional piano twanged beyond shuttered windows. Two women, their cheeks a bright red even through veils, came out of a doorway and got into a two-horse hack.

A sardonic smile came to Patterson's lips. Holladay Street, boldly operating only a block from Denver's most exclusive shops and hotels, never ceased to amuse him.

Directly off it on Eighteenth he came to the Silver Club. Patterson had often played there. The uniformed doorman knew him. "Most of the games haven't opened yet, Mr. Patterson."

"Suits me, Chester." Patterson flipped him a quarter. "Just dropped by to see Mort. Is he in?"

"In his office upstairs."

Patterson took a look in the barroom on the off chance that Rex Kelly might be there. Kelly worried him a little. Always feuding with someone, that fellow. Patterson needed his dealers to be tough, but he didn't want them to be loose-triggered rowdies.

Only a ruddy, tall-hatted cattleman stood at the bar. He was the Britisher Patterson had seen emerging from a bank, recently, whose ranch was up Golden-way.

Archie Tomlinson was his name. The man looked up and gave a genial wave. "Join me?"

"Another time," Patterson said, and went on upstairs.

The main gaming room had every variety of wheel and card layout. Only a few tables had customers; at small stakes, judging by the bored expressions of the dealers. The murals were too gaudy, Patterson thought, but if he took over the place he could replace them. Two solid arguments weighed in favor of buying Jardine out: the Silver Club had a reputation for square games, a definite asset for its successor; and Jardine, except for a hostess, had never employed any women. Unlike many of its competitors, the Silver Club had no dark-curtained archway leading to vice other than its own.

Mort Jardine, a cheerful, chubby man with a gold pince-nez over his buttonlike nose, was bending over accounts. He looked up, smiling. "Where've you been all summer, Pat? We've missed you."

"Leadville," Patterson said. "What's this I hear about you selling out?"

Jardine lighted a cheroot and puffed broodingly. "It's mostly," he admitted, "on account of Lily and Iris."

Patterson knew that Lily was his wife and that the Jardines lived in a mansion on Colfax Hill. Few men in the state could match bankrolls with Mort Jardine.

"Iris," Jardine explained, "is my daughter. She's enrolled at Wolfe Seminary."

Wolfe Seminary was an exclusive school for girls up on Champa Street. "But what's that got to do," Patterson prodded, "with your selling out?"

"They just can't take it any more. Lily and Iris."

"Can't take what?"

"Snubs. Blank stares. Cold shoulders. Look, Pat. There are just two kinds of women in this town. The kind that show up when Lily throws a party, and the kind that send regrets."

Patterson gaped. "But heck, Mort. They've no right to hold it against Lily just because . . ."

"Lily," Jardine broke in bitterly, "is a lady. She's never been on Holladay Street in her life. But her husband has. He runs the Silver Club. And that brands her. It even brands Iris. The other girls at Wolfe Seminary wouldn't chum up with her."

Somehow it angered Patterson. "Why don't you tell 'em their own fathers and brothers and husbands are your best customers?"

"Two good reasons, Pat. A gambler never tells on his clients. And even if he did, it's no disgrace to *patronize* a house like mine. The disgrace comes when you *run* it; when you put your name over the door."

"You've always banked a square game, Mort."

"Sure I have. But I'm daubed, just the same. There's a line right down the middle of society and I'm on the wrong side of it."

Patterson stared. "It doesn't make sense, Mort. I've seen governors and I've seen Congressmen bucking your wheels."

"Sure. You can find kings at Monte Carlo. But only as customers. It boils down to this, Pat. One side of a faro table is respectable and the other side isn't. That's why I'm selling out. I'll move to Chicago and play the wheat pit." Jardine laughed bitterly. "That will make ladies out of Iris and Lily."

Patterson shrugged. "Well, it won't hurt me any. I'm single."

Jardine looked at him with a wise smile. "You're young, Pat. Let me give you some advice. If you ever open a place like this, incorporate. Keep ninety-five percent of the stock but keep it out of sight. Let someone else have five percent to run it for you. Use dummy stockholders. And don't put your name over the door."

"And if I do?" Patterson challenged.

"If you do, some day you'll ask a nice young girl for a date and she'll say no. A girl from the other side of the line, I mean. That kind might flirt with our kind once in a while, from a safe distance, but when it comes to getting married they'll pick a hardware clerk every time."

Patterson went down to the bar and bought a drink. Something disturbed him, made him take a photograph from his wallet and stare at it. It was hard for him to analyze why he'd stripped it from its frame in a mountain cabin. Having robbed this girl of her heritage, by all logic he should put her from his mind.

Why didn't he? Certainly he wasn't in love with her. In person he'd only seen her once. Why was he keeping her picture?

Maybe it was because she was a symbol of something he wanted fully as much as he wanted wealth and power. It wasn't the girl herself. Probably he'd never see her again. What he wanted was a passport to her side of the line. A ticket of eligibility. Jardine was right. A girl like the one in this picture wouldn't go for Patterson of Patterson's Palace. To bring such a girl into his life he must take Jardine's advice. The right woman, this one or one like her, must know him only as a merchant or miner or rancher . . .

A rancher! Patterson thought of the Englishman who'd stood at this bar a while ago. Archie Tomlinson. With a ranch up Golden-way. The banks, rumor said, had already taken over Tomlinson's cattle. All the man had left was land and buildings. Not much land. But the buildings had class. The main house, of cut stone, had the look of an English manor. An atmosphere of gentility unmatched on the Colorado range. And Archie Tomlinson himself, who'd only missed a title by the accident of being a younger son, was the idol of Denver society.

As Patterson sipped his drink, a gleam came to his eyes. He put Faith Harlan's photograph back in his wallet. A vague idea was taking shape. A way to use Archie Tomlinson and his genteel background as a front, a badge of respectability, a passport to the other side of the line.

CHAPTER
EIGHT

At nightfall Milo Patterson went to the livery barn and saddled his gray horse. At the rear of the place he picked up two empty grain sacks. He made a tight roll of the sacks and tied it to his saddle strings.

Riding uptown he picked Fourteenth Street because it was darker, quieter than the others. At Champa he turned left and rode four blocks to Eighteenth. His hat was pulled low over his eyes as he dismounted by a half-finished stone building. The outer walls were up, the floor in place, the window frames set. A pile of quarried stone lay on the lot, awaiting the masons' trowels. The sky was overcast and Patterson could hardly have wanted a deeper gloom for his purpose.

He tied his horse by a mortar box and unrolled the two grain sacks.

This was the Central Presbyterian Church whose stone, brought from a quarry near Morrison, was reputed to assay something like two hundred dollars per ton in silver. The richness of it was entirely accidental, having been discovered only after the beginning of construction.

It was easy for Patterson to pick up a few broken fragments. In dumping the stone from wagons, an occasional chunk had been cracked off. And the masons themselves, laying stone on stone, had used mallets to true the surfaces.

In a very brief time Patterson had fifty pounds of stone fragments in each sack. He tied the sacks together, balanced them across his horse. Mounting he rode down Eighteenth Street to Abe Grossman's assay office just off Larimer.

Grossman's office was locked and dark. But the man had quarters at the rear and Patterson's insistent knock summoned him. The assayer appeared half dressed with a lamp in hand. "Why the heck," he growled, "can't you fellows do business in daytime?"

Patterson tossed in two sacks of what seemed to be ore. He gave his name. "See if it's worth anything, will you? I'll come by in a day or two for the report."

Patterson's next stop was at the *Rocky Mountain News*. At the desk there he paid for a short, classified advertisement. "Put it in the personal column," he directed, "and run it every day for a week."

When the assay report was made, it showed silver to the value of $166.50 per ton. Patterson was looking at it when a boy came through the American House lobby shouting an extra. "Outlaw captured! Read all about it!"

Patterson bought a copy and settled himself to read. This was the *News*, and the by-line was Tony Raegan's. By the end of the first paragraph his pulse was pounding . . . "Tom Redding, fugitive bank killer who recently murdered Frank Barber in Elk Valley, has been captured after a desperate life-or-death struggle with a cowboy named Terry Woodford. Heaping sensation on sensation, it appears now that Frank Barber buried seven quart cans of free gold on the sod roof of his cabin — gold which seems to have disappeared in the direction of Denver."

With goose flesh tingling at his spine, Patterson read to the end. Every link was given except one: there was no mention of his own name. Two sheriffs, Rankin from Jefferson County and Brewster of Arapahoe, were collaborating on the case. Rankin had jurisdiction, but Brewster was co-operating on a theory that the gold had been packed into Denver.

Patterson read it through twice. The story gave not a hint of his own guilt — unless it was in the phrase "in the direction of Denver." He could now thank his stars that he hadn't yet tried to exchange any of the gold for cash.

No one knew he owned that West Denver shack. Nor would they be likely to know, since he'd never recorded the deed.

"You're Milo Patterson?" The voice at his elbow was respectful. Patterson turned and saw three men there. "I'm Chet Brewster," one of them announced amiably. His vest showed a badge of office.

Patterson kept his poker face. "Yeh, that's my name. What can I do for you, sheriff?"

Brewster looked youngish and capable. He presented an older man with a red mustache and bristling eyebrows as Sheriff Rankin from Golden. The pale, thin-chested young man Patterson had seen before. A reporter from the *News* named Tony Raegan.

The three men pulled up lobby chairs and Rankin took over. "We just been to see that preacher, Jethro Bell. He says Barber didn't make any mention of gold in tin cans."

Patterson smiled. "I wouldn't know what you're talking about, sheriff, if I hadn't just read this paper."

"After Bell left," Rankin resumed bluntly, "Barber was alone with you for an hour or so till he died. Did he say anything about having some gold around?"

"No. If he had, I would have reported it to his sister and niece."

"We've just found out, Patterson, that you went back up there a few days later. With a pack-mule. You went up one day, empty, and came back the next, loaded. That same night someone stopped at the Elk Valley cabin. Somebody with two animals. Was it you?"

"It was not."

"You couldn't have got much farther than that. You passed Shawn's Crossing but you didn't get to Bailey."

"That's right." Patterson gave him a cool, level look. "If you want to know just where I went, and why, ask Andy Brown and Abe Grossman."

The sheriffs exchanged glances. Raegan scribbled in his book. "Everybody knows Abe Grossman," Chet Brewster put in. "But I don't seem to place Andy Brown."

"Yeah," Rankin growled, "who's Andy Brown?"

"An old mountain rat of a prospector," Patterson told them. "It happens I grubstaked him at Leadville.

Later I ran on to him in Fairplay. Asked him if he'd hit any pay. He said he'd found a ledge where the rock has silver in it; but so high and hard to get at that unless the stuff assays at least three hundred a ton, it wouldn't pay to haul it down. I suggested he fetch a sack to Denver for an assay. Too long a trip, he said. But he offered to bring it halfway. So I agreed to meet him at a certain time and place — at the top of Crow Hill just beyond Elk Valley."

Rankin pulled at his lip. His gaze searched Patterson. Brewster asked, "You mean that's where you went? To meet Andy Brown on Crow Hill?"

Patterson nodded, holding a careless light to his cigaret. "He was there with two fifty-pound sacks of ore. I brought 'em to Denver and had 'em assayed by Abe Grossman. Here's Abe's report." Calmly Patterson produced an assay report, dated yesterday, and handed it to Brewster. The test showed silver to the value of $166.50 per ton.

Rankin and Raegan leaned forward for a look. Brewster seemed convinced and apologetic. Rankin didn't. "Where," the Jefferson County man demanded, "could I find this Andy Brown?"

"Pecking at rock," Patterson grinned, "somewhere between here and the divide."

"Just where *is* this silver ledge of his?"

"He didn't say. All he said was he didn't want it if the assay is less than three hundred per ton."

"How you gonna let him know what the assay is?"

"He told me to put a classified ad in the *News*. Personal column."

Rankin stared. "You gonna do that?"

Patterson's smile mocked him. "I've already done it. Take a look." He tossed his own copy of the paper to Rankin. "A bundle of those papers go west on the Leadville stage every day. Andy'll get hold of one, somewhere. Anything else you want to know?"

There was a brittle silence. Patterson looked calmly from man to man of them. Although his story could be doubted, it could never be disproved. The mountains were full of nameless wanderers, wilderness rats who came and went, some of whom in the end disappeared mysteriously and forever. Who could say whether Andy Brown was or wasn't a reality?

"Hello, boys!" Serena Chalmers appeared among them. "What's all the excitement, Milo?" She'd just come down the stairs to find two sheriffs and a reporter grouped about Patterson. She smiled coaxingly at Chet Brewster. "Has he been misbehaving himself, sheriff?" To Patterson her tone was lightly chiding. "I *told* you to keep off of Holladay Street, dear."

It annoyed Patterson. Tony Raegan handed her a copy of the *News*. "Read all about it, lady."

Her eyes swept the headlines. She turned to stare, lips parted, from sheriff to sheriff.

"Somebody," Rankin told her bluntly, "copped a cache o' gold off a dead man's roof. We're just trying to run it down."

Brewster added a word and so did Raegan. Quickly Serena's sharp wits had the whole story "But why," she demanded, would Milo know anything about it?"

92

"Because he passed there about the time it happened." Rankin turned to Patterson with a last challenge. "You're sure you didn't stop in? You went right on up the trail to the top o' Crow Hill?"

Patterson nodded. "Andy Brown was waiting for me there. We camped all night on the hill. At daybreak we transferred the ore samples from his mule to mine and I headed back to Denver."

Chet Brewster got to his feet. "I guess that about washes everything up. Let's be on our way, Rankin." With a nod to Serena he moved toward the street door.

Rankin and Raegan followed him. But at the exit Rankin stopped, as with an afterthought, and he came back to face Milo Patterson. "One thing we didn't mention," he said. "In addition to seven cans o' gold, seems like the raider also copped a photograph off the wall. A picture of Frank Barber's niece."

For the first time a real fear shot through Patterson. That photograph was in his billfold right now. And burning a hole through it! If this red-mustached sheriff should search him, his whole pack of lies would be exposed. He'd sworn to passing by on the trail without stopping. But the photograph would definitely prove he'd stopped in.

Nor did he like the way Serena was looking at him. Her gaze was narrow and penetrating; her beautiful blonde head nodded ever so slightly, as though with a dawning conviction.

Yet Patterson, still a poker player, merely raised his eyebrows questioningly.

"Any ideas about it?" queried Rankin. However, on this issue he seemed confused rather than suspicious.

Patterson closed his eyes for a thoughtful half minute. Then: "Only one, sheriff. There's a rough crowd hangs out at Shawn's Crossing. Only two miles this way from that cabin. Any one of those toughies could know as much about Barber's gold cache as Redding did. And raid it. If he had an eye for a pretty face, he'd pick up that picture."

Rankin stood tugging at his mustache. "That," he admitted, "is the way Brewster sizes it. Me, I dunno. Guess I'd better ride up and have a talk with those Shawn's Crossing fellas. So long, Patterson."

When he was gone, Patterson braced himself for an outburst from Serena. At least she should deluge him with comment and questions. Over and beyond the photograph angle the event bristled with sensations. Gold on a roof! Patterson passing by about the time it was stolen. Patterson, who alone could have received a deathbed confidence from Frank Barber!

A million questions would occur to Serena. And what frightened Patterson, far more than anything else, was that she spoke none of them. She'd seated herself on a lobby divan and was looking at him. Her eyes narrow and knowing! Staring at him with the infernal prescience of a witch. As though she knew exactly what he'd done and could even prove it.

Prove it? But how?

"Well?" he rasped. "What's on your mind?" But still Serena only looked at him. And suddenly it occurred to Patterson that if she knew he had the photograph

94

he'd be completely in her power. Never again would he dare to cross her. A word to the sheriff . . .

"It's beastly hot!" Patterson said jerkily. "Guess I'll go take a bath." Abruptly he went up to his room.

There he took the photograph from his billfold, held a match to it. As it burned to an ash he remembered the other time. When he'd burned a dead man's last message.

CHAPTER
NINE

That pale little newshawk worried Patterson. Tony
Raegan. His was the by-line under which the story had
broken. His therefore was the phrase — "gold which
seems to have disappeared in the direction of Denver."

The sheriffs had offered no evidence to that effect.
Therefore the assumption must have derived from the
mind of Tony Raegan. Being on his toes, that fellow by
now would have interviewed the bakery women. Had
he hinted at Patterson's guilt?

Speculation would be rife. Some would believe and
some would doubt the fabrication about Andy Brown.
Right now the sheriffs had two theories: that Patterson
had taken the gold; that toughies from Shawn's
Crossing had taken it. Why not give them a third? That
the three cowmen had taken it! Judson, Baker and
Woodford.

It would hold water, Patterson reasoned. Woodford
captures Redding. Redding tells about gold. Woodford
returns to cabin where he and his friends move gold
into the woods and bury it.

What did the girl think? Faith Harlan!

To find out, Patterson groomed himself for a social
call. When presently he went out through the lobby,

Serena wasn't in sight. A hack was rattling by and Patterson hailed it. "The Home Bake-Shop on Curtis," he directed.

Up Sixteenth the cab went, twisting through traffic and dust. It drew up by a cottonwood-shaded ditch.

Only a white-haired woman was in the shop. Her face had a flush of excitement as she recognized Patterson. "I thought maybe you'd come around!" she exclaimed. "Everybody else has. You've heard about it, of course!"

Patterson, hat in hand, nodded gravely. "The whole town's talking about it, Mrs. Barnes. It's hard to believe, isn't it?"

Her eyes saddened. "Imagine Frank grubbing years and years for it; and then for it to disappear that way!"

"He was saving it for you," Patterson said earnestly. "You and your niece. And you know what, Mrs. Barnes? I'm burned up about it. I'd sure like to get my hands on whoever took it."

The woman's response surprised him. "That's what Mr. Woodford says. It's nice of you men to take so much interest in us, Mr. Patterson. Mr. Woodford's here now. He's in the parlor with Faith. Let's join them."

She led him back to a little parlor and there were Faith Harlan and a sunburned cowboy. The cowboy was tall, lean at the hips and wide at the shoulders. Except for a gun he wore full range rigging. His denims were dusty and his light, brownish hair disheveled. A saddle-weary look about him meant that he'd rushed right here after reporting to the sheriffs.

He stood up as Patterson entered. And the relaxed cordiality of Faith's greeting meant that no seed of suspicion had yet been planted here. "Oh, it's you, Mr. Patterson!" she exclaimed. "This is Terry Woodford. You read about how he captured the outlaw?"

"Met you on the trail, didn't I?" Terry's voice was casual. He didn't offer a hand. In a corner of the room Patterson saw a tarp-covered bundle.

"He brought us some of Uncle Frank's things," Faith explained.

"Sit down, Mr. Patterson," Emily Barnes insisted. And to Terry: "I didn't know you two had met before."

"I just happened to pass him," Patterson said carelessly, "on my way back from meeting Andy Brown on Crow Hill."

He expected this to draw a challenge. But it didn't. Terry, re-seating himself by Faith, said nothing at all. It was the girl who prompted, "Isn't Crow Hill just beyond Uncle Frank's cabin?"

"That's right." Patterson glibly gave them details of his rendezvous with a prospector and his return to Denver with ore samples. Cannily he watched Woodford. But the cowboy didn't even raise an eyebrow.

In fact Terry let Patterson do all the talking. He made no comment when Patterson suggested the potential guilt of hangers-on at Shawn's Crossing.

Faith listened to Patterson's smooth voice with half an ear, the rest of her attention on Terry's oddly wooden expression. Some undercurrent disturbed her — some sixth sense which warns a woman of an impending clash between two men. It made her seize upon Patterson's first pause.

"Terry and his friend Slim Baker," she broke in, "are taking some cattle up to Elk Creek. They're going to try something new. Tell us about it, Terry."

Terry grinned. "It's a case of choosin' between grass with snow on it and no grass at all. So we're gonna try grass with snow on it."

"You're starting right away, aren't you?"

"At daybreak tomorrow," Terry said. All the while his gaze had been fixed with an odd speculation on Patterson. Something about his expression made Patterson think of Serena's in the hotel lobby, when mention had been made of a stolen photograph. Patterson had the feeling of being accused and it brought a tinge of red to the back of his neck.

He'd meant to do some accusing himself. He'd come for that very purpose, to hint broadly at guilt of Shawn's Crossing toughies and less broadly at guilt of the Woodford-Baker-Judson group at the cabin. But now Patterson couldn't. The other man's silence disarmed him. Advancing any hint of Woodford's guilt would put himself in a bad light with the girl.

It must be done some other way, and with finesse. You couldn't walk into a girl's parlor and accuse a guest already there.

Patterson stood up and took his hat. His bow to the ladies was cavalier. "Like I told your aunt, Miss Harlan. I'm going to try to catch up with whoever pulled that job."

Terry also stood up but he did *not* reach for his hat. "Now that I think of it," he remarked pleasantly, "I met a coupla your friends the other day, Patterson."

"Yes? What friends?"

"Rex Kelly and a man they call Cimarron George." Cautiously Patterson asked: "Yeah? When was that?"

Terry named the exact day. "It was at the Interocean Hotel. Room 206. If you see 'em, say howdy to 'em for me."

No hack was in sight when Patterson got to the street. He walked with impatient strides down Curtis to Sixteenth and down Sixteenth to Blake. The Interocean! Patterson recalled an odd detail now. One day last week he'd seen two cowboys examine the hoof of a roan horse in front of the Interocean bar. And then go inside. It was the date just mentioned by Terry Woodford.

So instead of entering the American, Patterson went diagonally across the intersection to the Interocean. At the lobby desk there he thumbed back through the registry book. On the date in question he looked to see who'd been assigned to room 206.

To his shock, opposite that number he saw his own name. Milo Patterson in a forged writing! But why?

He must find Kelly and get the facts. Then he recalled another remark of Serena's. That Kelly and Cimarron usually patronized the Interocean bar because drinks there were a dime cheaper than at the American.

100

Patterson went into the hotel's taproom and surveyed the crowd. Customers were the usual mixture of mining men, cowmen, boomers, merchants and a few Chinese.

In a moment he spotted Rex and Cimarron in an alcove. Patterson went there and slid in beside Cimarron George.

Kelly still had a sullen look and the cut under his lip was an angry red. "What's the idea," Patterson jeered, "letting those guys beat you up?"

Kelly's pride wouldn't let him admit it. "Let who beat us up?" he challenged. Like Cimarron he was heeled with a forty-five and his belt bristled with brass shells.

"You're not fooling anyone," Patterson said with a wise smile. "Coupla punchers named Woodford and Baker. They suckered you birds up to room 206 and then beat hell out of you."

Kelly erupted. "Braggin' about it, are they? Wait till I find them bozos! I'll fill 'em so full o' lead they'll . . ."

"Bragging their heads off," Patterson confirmed. "All over town. I'm surprised you fellas let 'em get away with it."

"Where'd yuh see 'em?" Kelly demanded. "Lead me to 'em. They robbed me, the dirty thieves. Batted me down from behind and then grabbed seventeen bucks and a half."

Patterson didn't bother to inquire about the seventeen dollars. All that mattered was for these men to be in a homicidal mood.

"Okay, Rex. Feed 'em all the smoke you want. But don't be a sap and do it right here on Sixteenth Street.

101

First thing you know there'd be six in the fight — you and them and a coupla of cops. Use your head and you won't get in any jam."

"You mean ketch 'em out on the range sometime?"

Patterson leaned across the table and lowered his voice. "You can do it better than that. Listen." He gave the highlights of the-seven-quarts-of-gold story. "Now look. We don't know who swiped that gold. But it could have been Woodford, or Baker, or Judson, or any two of them, or all three of them." Patiently he outlined the logic by which such guilt was possible.

"Nobody'd believe it," Kelly scoffed, "seein' as they back each other up."

"Do like I say," Patterson argued, "and plenty folks'll believe it. Right now, suppose you and Cimarron make a round of the bars. Each of you by himself. You take one side of Holladay Street and let Cimarron take the other. At every bar you'll hear people talking about Frank Barber's gold. You join in and say, 'That ain't the way I heard it!' And then you spill this theory about maybe Woodford himself has got it buried in the woods. Time each of you've done that at about ten bars, it'll spread all over town. And nobody'll know who started it."

Kelly wasn't very much impressed. "So the sheriff maybe picks Woodford up. But he can't prove nothin' so he lets him go."

Patterson let himself look pained. "You're dumber'n I thought, Rex. Listen. Nobody picks him up. It's just bar talk. Just a theory with nothing to back it up."

George Dodds gave a bleary stare. His mouth hung open. "What you cookin' up, Milo?"

"It just happens," Patterson told them, "that those two cowboys are driving some O Bar cattle up to Elk Valley. They'll camp in Frank Barber's shack and keep an eye on 'em. Suppose those cowboys disappear! Along with their broncs and saddles. Just fade into thin air nobody knows where!"

Kelly was the first to get it. He smiled thinly. "You got a head on you, Milo. They ride into the woods and never come out. Them or their broncs."

"So what do folks think, Rex?"

Kelly's smile widened. "I'm 'way ahead of you, Milo. First, seven cans of gold disappear. Right at that cabin. Two punchers move in. Then they do a fade-out. Even Cimarron here could figger that one."

It dawned on Cimarron. He slapped his leg and laughed. "It figgers easy. Folks'll think they lit out for foreign parts."

Patterson beckoned a waiter and ordered drinks. "Take all the time you need," he advised. "And don't let anyone know you'll be going up there."

"Leave it to us, Milo." Kelly winked slyly at Dodds. "We can give out we're headin' back to New Mex. 'Stead of that we'll be campin' upcountry somewhere." An afterthought made Kelly throw a suspicious look at Patterson. "How come you want them fellas knocked off?"

"I don't," Patterson denied hurriedly. "Dead or alive they're no skin off my neck."

"Then why you passin' out all this free advice?"

"To keep you hotheads outa jail, that's all. You've been gunnin' for those cow hazers, all primed to shoot it out with 'em on sight. Right on a sidewalk in downtown Denver. With a cop on the next corner, maybe. You could get away with it at Leadville. Or Alma. But here on Sixteenth Street you'd be taking a chance."

They admitted he was right. Nor would Patterson let them discuss details in his presence.

"Better get busy right now," he advised, "and plant that idea about what maybe happened to the gold. Folks'll forget it, then remember it later when those ginks disappear."

He paid for the drinks and they went outside. "I'll work the hotel bars," Kelly said to Cimarron, "and you take the dives on Holladay."

The two separated, each going his way. Milo Patterson crossed to the American House and picked up a later edition of the *News*.

The main spread was about the capture of Tom Redding and the sensation of gold in quart cans. A follow-up editorial caught Patterson's eye.

The surest way to catch the thief, the editor advised, was for sheriffs to watch all markets where cash was traded for gold. The government mint in Denver. All banks. Bars, large supply stores and gambling houses. These should be ordered to report any transaction where the seller couldn't clearly explain how the gold had come into his possession.

It put Patterson on guard. He'd have to let the quart cans stay hidden in the West Denver house for a longer time than he'd planned. Nor could he risk anyone following him there even on the darkest night. The reporter, Tony Raegan, worried him. A "lunger," by the looks of him, out here for the high altitude cure. His eyes, Patterson remembered uneasily, had fixed on Milo Patterson with an absorbed speculation. Much as had Terry Woodford's in the bake-shop parlor.

Kelly would take care of Woodford but he, Patterson, must take care of Raegan.

Right now he'd better go tell Serena they'd have to mark time for a while.

He called a boy and ordered a tray of drinks carried to her room. When Patterson knocked there she let him in. She'd just put on a black evening dress, off-shouldered, her high-coiled golden hair giving a startling contrast. It brought an involuntary gasp from Patterson. "You're stunning, Serena!"

"You like it?" She whirled with her arms outspread. "I was just trying it on. Direct from Paris, they told me at Joslin's." She took his cheeks between her hands and kissed his lips. "Shall we dine at Charpiot's, lover?"

He closed the door. "First, Serena, I've got some bad news. We'll be held up a month or so. Getting things started, I mean. It'll take a little longer than I thought to raise the money."

"Okay, Milo. A month or so won't matter." She took two highballs from a tray and handed him one. The other she lifted gayly to her lips. "Happy days, man of mine!"

A chill pierced Patterson. Yesterday she would have protested, or pouted, at delaying another month. The fact that she didn't now could only mean she'd expected it; as though she knew exactly why he must wait. He remembered her oddly prescient stare down in the lobby, when a girl's photograph had been mentioned. How much had she guessed? How much did she know?

She seemed now to radiate a new self-assurance and power. As though she owned him, and from this minute on could control him at will.

CHAPTER
TEN

The drive dragged slowly up Bear Creek, sluggish, under conditions painful to both brutes and men. A thousand head of O Bar cattle; and, like Slim Baker said, you could stand off and count every rib.

The pitifully weak stragglers, and the plaintive bawlings even from those in the lead, depressed Terry Woodford and almost made him wish they hadn't started. He loved livestock and it hurt him to see cattle in distress. Hides and bones on four legs, this O Bar stuff. The mature she-stock had already been shipped as canners. Here were the mature steers and yearlings and young heifers. Getting them across the South Platte yesterday, at Littleton, had been an all-day job.

Grass there was none. Nothing but a few quick-sprouting weeds along the creek and along the berms of ditches. Not that there were many grasshoppers on the range now. They'd come and gone, this year just as last. Forage which had sprouted in the spring had been ravished to the roots. The insect horde had swept on, then, leaving only bleak earth in its wake.

"We can get 'em to Morrison," Slim predicted. "But it'll sure be a trick to get 'em up Turkey Crik hill."

Terry couldn't doubt it. Here the trail was almost level and the drive could be bullied along. But the ridge between Bear and Turkey was cloud-high and the trail to its summit steep. The Leadville stage made it every day — with grain-fed horses. But how could starving, staggering cattle climb that grade?

"Anyway they're all our'n." Slim grimaced.

"Half ours," Terry corrected. Jase Judson, too stubborn to quit the cattle business entirely, had retained a half interest. A bill of sale for the other half was in Terry's wallet. They'd given their note plus a chattel lien on the stock.

Judson was helping them make the drive. Also he'd brought along two saddle-colored sons of his O Bar cook.

One of the Mexican boys had been scouting ahead. He came loping back with a glowing face. "We have luck, *compañeros!*" he shouted. "Ahead we have found tumble weeds. The wind has tumbled them against a fence."

They'd be last year's tumble weeds, Terry thought, brown and bleached and full of stickers. Generally at a hedge or fence one found a few of them. Only desperately famished cattle would touch them at all. Even the grasshoppers had passed them by.

Still, it was tumble weeds that got them to Morrison. At twilight the herd bedded wearily down back of the sawmill there. Terry looked hopelessly ahead at tomorrow's trail. The precipitous climb began only a mile or so farther on. "They'll never make it," he fretted.

He rode to a fire where Judson was boiling coffee. "Look, Jase. You sure nobody around here's got a stack of hay?"

The old cattleman looked up with a shrug. "Hay's gold, son, this season. If a fella had a stack of hay he could retire." He waved toward the wide sweep of the Bear Creek meadows. "Hay started growin' in May, all right, but before it got high enough to mow along came the grasshoppers."

"You asked everywhere?"

"I sure did, son. What crop they put up's already been fed or sold, except what's being kept to winter a few milch cows and horses."

The buildings of a farmstead lay about a mile away, across the valley. Terry pointed. "Isn't that a haystack I see over there?"

Judson peered in that direction. "Nope. That there's Cass Purdy's place. All his hay got grasshoppered out, same as mine did. What you see is just a mound of old spoiled timothy left from two years ago."

"How badly spoiled?" Terry persisted.

"Cass told me it got rained on in the shock. He turned the shocks over and they got rained on again. It bleached black, that timothy did. Wasn't much good in the first place, 'cause it was mixed with foxtail and weeds. After it spoiled no cow would eat it. If a horse tried to eat it he got the heaves. So Cass just forked it up on a shed roof and it's been rotting there, come two years."

"How much," Terry wondered, "does he want for it?"

"I asked him that, son. And believe it or not, he wants thirty dollars a load. So I told him to go jump in the crik. Trash, that's all it is."

Terry brooded on it that night, rolled in his blankets under stars.

At breakfast he brought out a ten dollar bill. "Match me, you fellas," he demanded. "I need thirty bucks." He kept coaxing until Slim and Jase each gave him ten dollars.

"What you figgerin' to do with all that money, son?"

"You guys just push the stuff on as far as you can," Terry evaded. "Maybe you can get 'em to the foot of that steep grade. Chances are you won't see me again till sunup tomorrow."

Jase shook his head sadly. "One load o' spoiled hay won't do us any good," he argued. "Throw it on the ground and they'd trample each other to death, fightin' for it."

Terry, looking mysterious, made no answer. He tossed a saddle on the bay and rode toward the Cass Purdy homestead.

Jase, Slim and the two boys tried to get the herd up and started. Getting the weaker ones on their feet took half the morning. By noon they'd made only a mile. And there the trail began standing on end, climbing steeply toward a cloud-high skyline.

The drovers shouted, bullied, whirled ropes. They coaxed and cursed. It was no use. And at midafternoon Judson gave up. "You'll never get 'em up there," he

110

muttered, "without you hog-tie each crittur and haul it up in a wagon."

"They just ain't got the legs for it," agreed Slim.

"Might as well camp right here," the older man sighed, "and wait fer Terry. Him and his load o' spoiled hay."

"Even if it was *good* hay," Slim gloomed, "you couldn't feed a thousand head with one measly load."

Twilight came on and they made supper. Sheer weariness, that night, made Slim sleep soundly. Wagon wheels awakened him. And the bawling of cattle. But the lowing had a different note; a note of eager hope — a mad hysteria for some prize almost, but not quite, within reach.

Slim scrambled to his feet and rubbed his eyes. Day was just breaking. Up the trail went a hay rick pulled by four stout horses. Cass Purdy was driving. On the rick was about half a ton of hay so aged and mouldy and fouled with dust that Slim could smell it even from here. Terry Woodford rode at the wheel.

"Come and get it!" Terry yelled.

One thousand starving cattle came to get it. Jase Judson appeared in the half light, hooking on his suspenders. "What the heck does that kid think he's doin'? Divide among 'em it'd be only a pound apiece. Not fit to eat at that! And they'd trample each other gettin' at it."

On went the wagon, not stopping. On up the steepness of the Turkey Creek trail. And on went the cattle, bawling, crowding each other to be the first back of the load.

Suddenly it dawned on Jase. Sheepishly he rubbed his stubbled chin. "Well I'll be dogged! He don't aim to toss off that hay. He's just baitin' 'em with it. Lurin' 'em up the hill."

It worked just that way. And even the weakest heifer trailed along, staggering, stumbling up the grade. Not one of them cared to be left behind. In plain sight, ahead, reared a load of hay. Or what looked like hay. The older steers remembered winters when they'd been fed daily from a hay wagon. Surely this one would soon begin throwing off hay. So up they went, one mile, two, three . . .

Toward a high paradise which grasshoppers hadn't defiled!

They didn't need to be driven. The wagon of hay *led* them. Slim Baker rode back of them with his mouth hanging open. Ahead of him the long line of red and white, amidst a chorus of moos, went plodding steadily on and up. "Yesterday they couldn't make it!" Slim marveled. "And look at 'em now!"

Jase, riding stirrup to stirrup with him, bit off a chew. "Cows are like folks," he concluded. "Hang the right bait in front of 'em and I reckon they'll go anywhere."

Not a pound of that mouldy, smoky load was ever fed. Straight up the mountain Cass Purdy drove it, his four Percherons humping their broad backs at the steepness. Cedars closed in on the trail, and then pine. At the summit was a park of red sandstone in grotesque shapes and columns, hemmed in by an evergreen

112

forest. And still the wagon moved slowly on with the O Bar cattle strung out behind.

No grass yet. For even here there'd been grasshoppers. Presently the trail began angling into a new watershed. By hugging the sidehill it kept a fairly even contour.

In the early afternoon the wagon dipped into Turkey Creek Canyon and moved up it, the drive spreading out a little as the width permitted. Another mile and Slim noticed a cessation of sound. The cattle had stopped lowing. For about here the grass began showing. Not much of it, for even here the hoppers had invaded. But here was a mountain climate which occasionally brought early afternoon showers. A drop spanked Slim's cheek. It was cool here, in this piny canyon, cool and moist. He saw a steer desert the wagon to pounce on a clump of greenness.

The farther upstream they went the more frequently they found grass. Some of the older steers trotted forward, actually by-passing the wagon in eagerness to find forage farther on.

Cass Purdy pulled to one side and stopped. Three hours ago the herd would have stormed it. But now it lost interest in the wagon and moved on, sensing a more succulent lure ahead, the sweetness of mountain grass.

Terry gave Cass Purdy fifteen dollars. "You can go home now," he grinned.

Cass drove back down the old stage road with his load intact.

"Here's your change, pardners," Terry announced. He gave a five dollar bill to Judson and another to Slim. "I didn't buy that load o' hay. I only rented it."

Jase cocked an admiring eye. "How come you thought of it, son?"

"I got to cogitatin'," Terry told them, "about a story I learned when I was a good little boy and went to Sunday School. All about the feedin' of five thousand people with five loaves and two fishes. So I thought maybe if we tried hard enough, and prayed hard enough, we could feed *one thousand* cows on what you might call nothing at all."

All they did that night was make sure the cattle didn't wander back down the creek. In the morning Jase sent the two Mexican boys back to the O Bar.

No cattle were in sight. Slim, up earlier than the others, reported that during the night they'd drifted higher into the timber. "Grass ain't nothin' to brag of yet. But compared to what they've had, it's heaven."

"We'll get 'em a mile or two off the stage road," Jase said, "on the high side. Then we'll rest 'em a day. They'll find water grass along the creek, and ferns and a blade o' bluestem here and there. There oughta be some other way over to Shawn's Crossin' without usin' the road. We could find a game trail or two, maybe."

Slim cocked an eye up at an aspen ridge which walled them from the Elk Creek drainage. "Give 'em half a bellyful and they'll make it all right."

Jase, in a mellow humor, heated water for coffee. Later he went up the creek with a string and penny hook and came back with three fat trout. "Fat as them two heifers we left at Barber's cabin," he chuckled.

It was Slim who'd found the long-lost heifers. He'd returned to the Elk Valley cabin with them in midafternoon, Judson not appearing there until sundown. Terry Woodford, encumbered with Tom Redding, hadn't arrived till past midnight. "We sure thought you'd fell in the creek, son," Judson chuckled.

The reminder sobered Terry and veered his mind back to Faith Harlan. And to a vandal who'd robbed her of a fortune in gold. Patterson? Terry, idling a day on Turkey Creek while the herd rested, had time to think about Patterson. And the man's glib story of a trip with a pack-mule to Crow Hill!

CHAPTER
ELEVEN

A few at a time, some on this game trail and some on that one, the cattle were pushed to the divide between Turkey and Elk creeks. The route of drive was well to the right of the stage road. Only faintly could they hear the rumble of wheels or the pop of a muleteer's whip.

A gentle shower was pattering when they came down to Shawn's Crossing. Here, at eight thousand feet above the sea, was grass. Not the slim pickings they'd found thus far, but grass lush and cured. Paradise for this famished O Bar drive.

It splashed across the riffles just above the stage station and soon was spread out across the valley. No bawling now. Every head was down, nosing the goodness of this land. Terry looked at Jase and saw moistness in his eyes. The old rancher had suffered with his cattle, this season and last.

A light warm rain was still falling. Terry and Slim hazed the last straggler across the creek and then joined Judson at the stage-road ford. "Good thing they're too skinny to make beef," Judson muttered, thumbing toward the Shawn's Crossing store.

The two stage-horse hostlers sat on a bench, sheltered from the rain by the store eaves. The same ill-mated pair, Terry noted. The thin-faced Mexican was again whetting a knife on his boot. Beside him sat the ruddy, thick-necked gringo with suspenders supporting his baggy pants. And again this man was wearing two guns, a forty-five on the right and a thirty-eight on the left. He was chewing a straw as he cocked a speculative eye at the O Bar herd.

In the open doorway stood the fat, aproned storeman with his bald head oily and shining. Terry waved a hand. "Hi, neighbors."

The storeman gawked at the cattle. "Takin' 'em up to South Park?" he yelled.

"Nope. Only a piece above here," Terry said.

But when they tried to resume the drive very little headway was made. The stock wouldn't stop its greedy grazing long enough to take more than a step between bites.

"Jase is right," Slim said. "No danger of those bums rustlin' this stuff till it puts some tallow on. Let's leave 'em right here."

The shower was over and sunlight broke through the clouds. Terry took off his slicker, tied it in a roll back of his saddle. The others did the same and they rode through the spread-out cattle to the far side of the valley. There, where a branch riffled out of a tributary ravine, they came to Frank Barber's cabin. It was just as they'd left it. The bedrolls and duffel they'd brought on the earlier trip hadn't been disturbed.

"And look!" Slim exclaimed. "There's those two bally heifers. They ain't hardly moved outa their tracks since I rounded 'em up the other day."

Beyond, in the pines, Terry glimpsed one of Frank Barber's burros and knew the other two weren't far off.

They unsaddled the horses, turned two loose and hobbled the other. Jase took over as camp boss. "Slim," he ordered, "you rustle some firewood. Terry, fetch me a bucket o' water and I'll start supper."

Terry took a bucket and walked toward the ravine brook. Halfway there he crossed the stage road. Moving on to the creeklet he dipped water from the riffles. In the soft loam at the stream's edge he saw tracks which told him two horsemen had forded here. They'd come down a rocky slope on the other side, forded the riffles and then, a few yards farther on, had turned up the stage trail. Terry thought nothing of it beyond noting that the riders had passed less than two hours ago. He could be sure of it because no rain had fallen on the hoof prints.

He set the bucket down and rolled a cigaret. The stream sang to him. Leaning against a split fir he considered the O Bar battle, now half his own and Slim's, and wondered how they'd fare through the winter. This was still early August; so by the end of October they should be in good flesh. November would bring snow but probably not too much; then . . . Terry's eye caught something which checked his thought abruptly.

He kneeled for a better look. Then he cupped hands over his lips to yell: "Slim! Come arunning, Slim!"

Chaps flapping, Slim came striding through the trees. Terry was still on his knees at the water's edge. "Take a look, Slim."

What Slim Baker saw was the left hind hoof print of a shod horse. The shoe had no cleat.

"Only that *one* shoe's a flatty," Terry exclaimed. "Two broncs. The one that crossed upstream has four good shoes. This one has three with cleats and one flatty."

After a look Slim nodded slowly. "Just like them other two broncs," he muttered.

"Could it happen twice, Slim?"

"Maybe it could and maybe it couldn't. My money says it's them. Looks like they're still gunning for us, cowboy."

The hoof marks couldn't be followed farther than the road. There they mingled with innumerable other prints from wheel and hoof. "All we can do," Terry concluded, "is keep eyes open and guns loaded."

At midnight Milo Patterson walked west along Larimer to the Cherry Creek bridge. Beyond here the bright lights petered out. After Tenth Street there was only a gas lamp on each corner. Patterson glanced warily over his shoulder to make sure he wasn't followed.

One lot short of Ninth Street a low log house loomed on the left. A house put up seventeen years ago by a Fifty-niner. Patterson circled it and let himself in at the rear.

When he emerged his pockets were nearly four pounds heavier. Only that much of the gold could he risk taking. The rest he must leave under the floor. What he carried now was two buckskin dust-bags each containing about thirty ounces. No particular risk in that. A miner, coming to Denver for a night's play, commonly brought with him a thirty-ounce pouch of dust or nuggets. Patterson knew of half a dozen games where, at this very minute, such stakes were being pushed across the board.

He hurried straight to Mort Jardine's Silver Club and looked the crowd over. At one big stud table two miners were betting chips purchased with raw gold. Patterson drew up a chair and sat in. He played till the miners left the place. Then Patterson, yawning, quit the game himself. He went to the cashier's cage and tossed in a thirty-ounce pouch. "This wasn't their night." He grinned.

The cashier was used to it. He weighed the pouch and passed out six hundred dollars. Knowing the miners had been in possession of free gold, he presumed Patterson had won it in the game.

Patterson's next stop was at 1451 Blake Street, a place called the Palace Theater. Actually its all-night burlesque show was mainly a blind for sky-limit gambling. For three years it had been one of Denver's hot spots, and now, an hour after midnight, it was going at full blast. Patterson idled by the cashier's wicket till he saw men buy chips with gold. He followed them to an upstairs balcony which had private, curtained rooms with a view of the stage. No show was on just now. Each of the balcony rooms had a game going. Wine girls in short skirts flitted back and forth with trays. When a show came on they'd lay aside the trays to don tights in a high-kicking chorus. All the customers were men. Raw and barbaric was the Palace, a theater in name only. A society of Denver ladies, primly determined on reform, in a current crusade were publicly proclaiming it "a death trap to young men, a foul den of vice and corruption."

Even Milo Patterson, inured to the rawest dives of the gold camps, preferred to do his gambling in less tawdry atmospheres.

This night he made short shrift of it. Twenty minutes in one game, thirty in another, and he was through. "Looks like this was my night," he joked to the cashier as he offered a thirty-ounce pouch of dust.

In the morning he deposited twelve hundred in cash at the First National Bank. For a long time he'd kept an account there. Other accounts in his name were at banks in Leadville and Central City. These were balances which he must fatten considerably before he could deal with Mort Jardine.

That night he stayed away from the Silver Club and the Palace. Instead he chose the Ophir Bar and the Oriental. Night after night Patterson repeated the operation. A furtive visit to his cache for sixty ounces; a few sit-ins for the sake of appearance. And no great risk, since gold buyers were only required to report transactions where the seller couldn't explain the source.

Patterson worked every dive in Denver where mining men habitually bought chips with gold. The Crystal Bar; the Sawdust Corner; the Paradise; the Come One Come All; the El Dorado. The cache at the log house shrunk; the balance at the First National grew.

Once, at the Ophir, he turned to see a thin, pallid young man watching his cards. Raegan of the *Rocky Mountain News!* Odd that he'd be here at two in the morning. It made Patterson uneasy, cautious. Leaving the place he offered only chips to the cashier.

Had Raegan been shadowing him? It wasn't likely. But to play safe Patterson passed up the Denver clubs for the next week. With a heavy suitcase he took a narrow gauge train to Central City, putting up at the Teller House there. Here, in a cloud-high settlement strung for miles along Gregory Gulch, was where Colorado had really been born. Although past its peak now, time was when the town's summer population had vastly exceeded Denver's. Here had been spawned the first gold fortunes of the Rocky Mountains. Even now the opera house and hotel here quite overshadowed anything in Denver. "The Kingdom of Gilpin," men called this gulch. Here a nugget was legal tender and here whisky was still a "pinch" a drink, the bartender taking as much as he could pinch, from a dust pouch, between thumb and finger.

Here, and at the outlying camps of Blackhawk, Mountain City and Nevadaville, Patterson bought chips for six straight nights. When he went back to Denver his suitcase was twenty pounds lighter and his Central City bank balance had increased by six thousand dollars.

In Denver he resumed his schedule of two clubs per night. The Leadville Club, the Arcade, the Gates Club, the Capitol, the Jockey and the Pioneer on Holladay. No one questioned him, not even Serena. Serena seemed resigned to waiting, indefinitely, as long as he wined and dined her and let her shop merrily at Joslin's.

On the first day of September Patterson stepped into the saddle of his iron-gray gelding and cantered mountainward across the Platte River bridge. The bulk of his stake was still in the log house, but enough cash was banked for his immediate purpose. Angling slightly north of west he struck Clear Creek and followed it toward Golden.

Here lay a fertile chain of meadows, now brown and barren, but potentially a verdant garden. A gate on the left side of the trail had a sign over it: CROSS T RANCH —GALLOWAYS —ARCH TOMLINSON.

Patterson turned through the gate and crossed a grassless pasture. After topping a rise he could look down into a cottonwood rincon, a narrow tributary valley set against juniper foothills. A group of buildings there had stone walls and gabled roofs. An imposing layout, Patterson thought, compared with the run of western ranches. Trust an Englishman, whose home was always his castle, to build like a gentleman.

In the foreground were cows. Black, shaggy, hornless cows that Patterson knew were purebreds from Scotland. And though Arch Tomlinson had spent his last dollar shipping in hay for them, they were lean and ribby now. The gauntness made their black heads look grotesquely oversize. And yet stubbornly the Britisher hung on to them. His pride and his innate love of fine stock wouldn't let him ship them to market as canners.

All this Patterson knew. He'd made a point of looking into the current standing of Arch Tomlinson. The man was bankrupt. His credit was exhausted. He'd laid off every Cross T employee except a Chinese cook. The banks had foreclosed all his grade cattle, leaving him only three hundred head of purebred Galloways. They were about to foreclose his land and ditch right. Patterson could see the ditch now, bankful as it circled by the house. And he sensed that a single good season would put the ranch back on its feet.

He rode to the main house and tied his horse. When he knocked, an elderly Chinese admitted him.

"Is your boss home? Milo Patterson calling."

He waited in a living room of quiet distinction, with a stone hearth and a high, beamed ceiling. A portrait hung over the hearth. It showed the calm, firm face of a woman; her name was Victoria and she was queen of England.

Which reminded Patterson of another Victoria, an older sister of Tomlinson's who lived here with him. Once Patterson had seen her at a theater and had been a little awed by her. He'd come here today with an offer; and it was the sister, rather than the brother, who was more likely to say no.

Arch Tomlinson came briskly in, a tall, spare man in tweeds, ruddy, blond, clean-shaven except for a thin mustache. "What, he, Patterson?" he greeted. "Down, Nigel."

A Great Dane had followed him in; it now moved obediently to the hearth rug and settled there with

124

paws outstretched, red tongue panting. Patterson spoke his purpose without preamble. "I like this outfit of yours, Arch. I wouldn't mind buying a slice of it, if you're interested."

The Britisher blinked. Then he waved Patterson to a seat. "Chan," he called. "what's holding us up?"

The Chinese servant came in with whisky and soda. Tomlinson mixed the drinks and passed one to his guest. "Didn't know you had a turn for ranch property, Patterson."

"I've some loose cash to invest. Ten thousand dollars." Patterson paused for it to sink in. Ten thousand would save the Cross T. Nothing less would. With it Tomlinson could ship in feed to winter his Galloways and have enough left to pay interest on his notes. "I'd give that much, spot cash, for a third interest in the ranch."

Tomlinson sipped his liquor. Over the glass he looked critically at Patterson. And Patterson, knowing him well, accurately read his thought.

To forestall it Patterson said: "I wouldn't intrude here at the house, Arch. It would still be your private home. You have a small guest cottage, I believe. That could be assigned to me for quarters whenever I happen to be on the property."

Clearly the proposition tempted Tomlinson. No less clearly it distressed him. Pride of race was strong in him. His eyes flicked toward the portrait of his queen over the mantel. "Sort of bowls me over," he murmured. "You're a . . . er . . . I mean . . ."

"You mean I'm a gambler. That's why I'm making this offer. You don't have to say yes or no right away. I'll hold it open."

"I'll talk it over with my sister." The Britisher's tone was dubious.

Patterson finished his drink and picked up his hat. "You can find me at the American."

Tomlinson went out to the gate with him. And Patterson, riding away, felt anger stirring him. It was noon, and if he'd been anyone else Tomlinson would have made him stay for lunch. Anyone else would have been presented to the sister. Mort Jardine was right about it. A professional gambler was sure to be snubbed by women like Victoria Tomlinson.

Twisting in his saddle he looked back at the lean Galloway cows. Sight of them was reassuring. The Tomlinsons wouldn't dare turn him down. Passing up his offer would mean losing every hoof and acre. However much they might wince at being contaminated socially, they couldn't afford to say no.

Arch Tomlinson appeared at the American House soon after banking hours the next morning. "We're taking you up, old chap." His surrender was none too cheerful and Patterson smiled as he handed over the check.

"Never mind a receipt, Arch. Your word's all I need. Tell your lawyer to send me a one-third interest deed. Let's go into the bar and I'll buy you a drink."

When the man left him Patterson ordered his horse. In his room he put on a green silk shirt and silver spurs and riding gauntlets and a high-crowned cattleman's

126

hat. Later, riding up Sixteenth, he looked every inch a ranchman.

He hitched under a cottonwood on Curtis, in front of the Barnes bakery. A bell tinkled as he went in.

Faith Harlan was back of the counter. "Hello," she greeted; and although her tone was unaffectedly cordial, something about him seemed to puzzle her a little. "We thought you'd forgotten us, Mr. Patterson."

He wondered why he was so powerfully attracted to her — why he had such an overwhelming desire to make her think well of him. She wasn't as beautiful as Serena — well, maybe she was in her clean, clear-eyed way. Her hair was so soft and so carelessly lovely. When she offered to call her aunt he said quickly: "Don't bother. Just happened to be riding by and thought I'd ask if anything's turned up. About those cans of gold dust, I mean."

"Not a single thing, Mr. Patterson." She smiled ruefully. "People are beginning to think it's a hoax; that Tom Redding just made it all up."

"Might be," Patterson agreed soberly. It would suit him for people to think like that.

"But Mr. Raegan," she went on, "won't give up. He's a reporter on the *News*. He's sure a thief took the gold and hid it somewhere."

Raegan! With an uneasy shrug, Patterson shifted the subject. "I've been out of touch with it myself. Got tied up in a cattle deal."

"Oh!" She looked at him with a new interest. "I didn't know you were a rancher."

"Happens I am," he said carelessly. "Cross T out by Golden. Most folks know it as the Arch Tomlinson place. Arch and I are partners."

Patterson left her gracefully, conscious that he'd scored. Confident that any talk she'd heard to the effect that he was an adventurer, a gold camp gambler who lived by his wits, would now be brushed from her mind. A partner of the Tomlinsons! No name in all Denver society carried more prestige. No dinner guests more popular than Archibald and Victoria of the Cross T.

Riding down Curtis, Patterson turned to look back. Faith stood framed in the bakery door. With a gallant sweep he waved his high-crowned cattleman's hat.

CHAPTER
TWELVE

The deal with Mort Jardine took even less time. Patterson faced the man across his office desk. "You say ninety thousand, Mort, for the lease and fixtures. I'll take over on a few simple conditions."

"Which are?"

"That my name doesn't appear. You sign everything over to a corporation. I'll call it the Columbine Club, Inc., and I'll retain ninety-five percent of the stock."

Jardine, chewing his cigar, gave an understanding nod. "What else?"

"I know your floor manager, Whitey Dall, and your cashier, Lew Goodson. They're square shooters. You persuade them to stay on here and I'll issue each of them one percent of the stock."

"I see. You want 'em for directors in the corporation."

"That's right. Dall can be president and Goodson secretary. The third director'll be my hostess, Serena Chalmers, who gets three percent of the stock."

"You're smart, Pat, keeping out of it yourself. Anything else?"

"Not a thing, Mort."

"It's a deal." Jardine reached a plump hand across the desk. His grip sealed the sale. No one had ever known Mort Jardine to welsh on his word.

Patterson wrote a check for twenty thousand. "Just for a binder, Mort. You'll get another twenty thousand when I take over; then ten thousand a month for five months."

The terms suited Jardine and he took Patterson down to his bar for drinks. A dozen customers were there and two of them, at the far end, were in a heated argument. A glance told Patterson they were gun-slung cowboys who'd been imbibing too freely.

He paid them no further attention until he heard one of them bawl out, in high-pitched temper, "Here's what I think of *your* man!" The cowboy pulled his forty-five and began shooting. He pumped six fast shots into a wall opposite the bar.

"And here," bellowed his companion, "is what I think of *yourn!*" He too pulled his gun and fired six times. After which each cowboy sheathed his empty gun and took a swing at the other.

The man who appeared from an anteroom might have been a department store floor-walker. He wore an Ascot tie, and a gardenia adorned the buttonhole of his impeccable Prince Albert. In build he was a giant nearly seven feet tall; all Denver knew him as Alfred, Jardine's genteel bouncer.

He took each of the cowboys by an arm and led them firmly but quietly out. Rowdyism at the Silver Club had always been handled that way.

Patterson was gazing at a bullet-riddled wall. With customers in both political parties, the Silver Club had tried to show its impartiality by mounting twin campaign posters on its bar wall: one a likeness of Samuel J. Tilden and the other picturing Rutherford B. Hayes. The national election was only two months off. Each portrait, Patterson noted, was now punctured with six slugs.

"That's the trouble with politics," the bartender complained. "It gets folks all het up." He swabbed his bar sadly.

Mort Jardine chuckled. "Reminds me of what happened up at Central City three years ago. President Grant paid a visit there and the Teller House laid silver bricks from his cab to the lobby so he wouldn't get snow on his boots. Then a couple small boys spoiled everything."

"What'd they do, Mort?"

"They threw snowballs at Grant's plug hat."

Serena listened with mixed emotions when Patterson told her about his deal with Jardine. Getting three percent of the stock elated her. But Patterson's concealment of his own connection gave her an opposite reaction.

"Using me for a front, are you, Milo? I'm to be the naughty underworld while you're the hoity-toity man about town! Look, Gentleman Jim. I've known you to wear holes in the knees of your pants, shooting craps down in Taos."

Temper sparked his eyes. "I'm dealing this hand. You'll pick up your cards and play 'em, or else get to hell out. And if you want to know why, go ask Lily Jardine. She'll tell you fast enough."

Serena had already asked Lily Jardine. And Lily had made it quite clear. The known owner of a dice house couldn't run for Congress and he couldn't make love to upperworld girls. But Serena smothered her resentment. After all she was getting a block of stock; and without further waiting she'd be queen of the flashiest resort in Denver. In the end, because of what she knew, she could always crack a whip over Patterson.

"Sorry I popped off, Milo." Serena turned gracious and mixed him another drink. "The Columbine Club? I like it. So refined! You'll visit us sometimes, I suppose? Or shall we just mail you the dividends?"

It gave him a half sheepish grin. "I'll be your best customer, Serena."

Later Patterson bought copies of the *News* and *Tribune*. He skimmed through them for a story he expected to break. About the mysterious disappearance of one, or two, or three men from a cow camp near Shawn's Crossing.

But there was no mention of anything like that. It puzzled Patterson. Those three should be riding daily through the woods, keeping an eye on their cattle. Generally they'd ride separately. Picking them off, one at a time, should be easy for snipers with the talents of Cimarron and Rex Kelly.

132

★ ★ ★

Circling buzzards drew Terry and Slim to a wooded ravine off Elk Creek. By now the cattle had spread far and wide. A few had drifted to the top of Crow Hill. All of them, as far as Terry knew, were above Shawn's Crossing.

"Maybe one of 'em just laid down and died," Slim surmised. He cocked an eye at the soaring vultures.

They turned up the ravine and there Terry spotted the tracks of a wagon. A spring wagon, by the narrowness of the tires.

Terry sniffed. He looked at Slim. A rancid odor made them spur farther up the draw.

Two huge black birds flapped awkwardly away from a lump of fresh, carrion. Only the head, horns, hide and offal were there. The tire tracks came this far and then swerved back toward the stage road.

"It's one of them two fat heifers." Slim looked pretty grim about it.

"Jase won't like it," Terry said.

"Reckon somebody got tired of venison, so he butchered him a beef." Slim's eyes took the general direction of Shawn's Crossing. Those two shifty hostlers there were capable of it. None of the thousand head of lean stock, just arrived, would make beef. So the petty rustler had picked one of the two plump heifers.

They lost the tire tracks at the road. Yet without hesitation Terry loped on toward Shawn's Crossing. Slim came pounding after him. "Let's take a look in their meat-house, fella." Each of them had a hip gun and a saddle rifle.

As they pulled up at the store-saloon, the outbound stage was there changing horses. It was a Concord stage with high boots, front and back. Its four jaded horses were being led to a corral by the ruddy, thick-necked wrangler who worked here. The man still wore his two mismatched guns. His helper, the thin-faced Latin, was tossing harness on fresh teams.

Terry and Slim stopped by the stage. "We'll wait till it pulls out, Slim, before we jump 'em."

Slim hooked a leg around his saddle horn and rolled a cigaret. "Hi, Slim. Hi, Terry." A familiar voice hailed them. "How come you guys are still outa jail?"

It was one of the stage passengers — a cattle hand named Brad Bixby who a season ago had worked for the Cross T on Clear Creek.

"Howdy, Brad," Terry greeted. "Who you riding for these days?"

"Nobody. The Cross T laid everybody off 'cept the cook. Me, I'm headin' for the San Luis where there ain't been no grasshoppers."

An English outfit, that Cross T, Terry remembered. "I sure hate to hear it. I kinda cottoned to that fella Tomlinson. The banks cleaned him out, did they?"

"Everything but his purebred Galloways. He saved them by sellin' a third interest to a gent named Patterson. This Patterson put up enough *dinero* to ship in roughage from Kansas."

Slim cocked a curious eye. "You mean Milo Patterson?"

"That's the gent. Know him?"

134

"Heard of him. Didn't know he was a cowman." Slim tossed Brad Bixby the makings.

After rolling one Bixby veered back to his first question. "I wasn't kidding," he grinned. "How come you guys are outa jail after this song and dance about you stealin' gold by the quart?"

An undertone alerted Terry, "What song and dance, Brad?"

"Ain't you heard? It's bar talk goin' up and down Holladay Street. Nobody knows who started it, but I heard it myself twice."

"Heard what?"

Bixby chuckled. The skit is that you guys maybe found them gold cans yourself after Redding tipped you. And then buried 'em in the woods till it's safe for a fade-out . . . Now hold on, Slim. Don't go on no prod! I said it was a song and dance, didn't I? Nobody believes it. It's a cinch the sheriffs don't or they'd 've been up here shakin' you down."

"All aboard!" the stage driver shouted. His fresh horses were in the traces and ready to go.

Brad Bixby climbed in. "So long, fellas." Off went the stage toward the next station along its route to Leadville.

An Indian squaw appeared at the store door and rang a bell. As the hostlers headed that way, Terry nudged Slim. "Make out like we're not interested till they go inside."

They rode a little way up the creek, halting back of willows. Slim's face wore a storm cloud. "Who you reckon started that talk?"

"Nobody's mad at us," Terry brooded, "'cept Rex Kelly and his playmate. Wonder what those guys were doing up here!"

For days it had puzzled them. The print of a cleatless shoe made by a left hind hoof.

"Funny how we keep runnin' into the name Patterson," Slim muttered. "He's tied up with Kelly and Cimarron, someway."

"The stage wranglers'll be eating dinner by now," Terry said. "Let's look the place over."

They rode back to the station corrals and in a shed there found a rickety spring wagon. Slim leaned over its bed and sniffed. "It's hauled fresh-butchered beef, last day or two," he concluded.

Terry was less certain. One of the wranglers could have shot a deer, dressed it and hauled the meat here. "Isn't that a dugout cellar, Slim? Let's take a look."

The dugout had a mound of clay over it and steep steps leading down to an underground door. The door had a padlock. It was a typical provision cellar and on the hottest day would always be cool.

"Wait a minute, Slim." Terry went to the sheds and came back with a short iron bar. He went down the steps and slipped an end of it into the padlock's staple.

When he heaved mightily the staple came out. Terry kicked the door open. Everything was dark till he struck a match. Slim peered over his shoulder and they saw beef suspended from rafters. Four quarters. Three were intact while one of the quarters lacked six or eight pounds at the loin.

136

They closed the door and went grimly up the steps. Terry had shopped several times at the store, buying tobacco and staples. "The room they eat in," he remembered, "is between the bar and the kitchen. You go in the back way, Slim, and I'll take the front."

Terry circled the main building and entered the store room. It was empty. From beyond it came a clash of forks on plates. He crossed to a door, opened it, and stepped into the presence of three men and a woman.

The men were eating; the woman, an Indian, was serving them. Each man was squared in front of a prime sirloin steak. Beyond them Terry saw Slim peer in from the kitchen.

The Mexican wrangler had a forkful halfway to his mouth. His black eyes narrowed as he held it suspended there. The other wrangler jumped to his feet red-faced and angry. "What's the idea bustin' in here like that?"

Slim Baker's ironic response made him whip around toward the kitchen. "We just wanted to find out how you like O Bar beef."

The fat storekeeper sat gaping, his bristly, bloated face losing color. The Indian woman backed to a wall and stood motionless.

No gun could be seen on either the storekeeper or the Mexican. Because the ruddy gringo wore two, Terry and Slim gave him their main attention. The Mexican, in spite of his shifty eyes, had a smoothly polite voice. "I am Manuel Lopez," he announced. "Of what you speak I know nothing. This is meat which my *cuñado* hauled yesterday from Tarryall."

137

The storekeeper found voice. "He sure did. What the heck'd we wanta butcher one of them skinny O Bar steers for? Me an' Brockmeyer ain't left this station for a week, have we Brock?"

It kept the eyes of Terry and Slim on the ruddy man, Brockmeyer. Giving Lopez his chance, and a knife came whizzing. Terry shifted in time to make it miss his throat. The blade stuck quivering in the wall back of him.

At the same time Brockmeyer drew two guns. Before he could cock the hammers a shot from Slim broke his arm. The man dropped both guns. Terry plowed a slug down the dark, tangled hair on the head of Lopez. Pink appeared in a groove there. The Mexican clapped a hand to it and the hand came away smeared. He sank to his knees in terror. "Please do not kill me, señor."

The storeman stood with his hands stretched upward. "I didn't know they stole it, honest I didn't. I'll see they pay for it," he bleated. "I'll make the stage company take it out of their wages."

"Get some rag's and patch those fellas up," Terry ordered. He turned to the squaw. "You rustle some hot water. Fix 'em up for a ride to Golden."

Mention of the county seat added to Lopez's panic. "Please do not take me there, señor!" The frantic pitch of his plea gave a hint that this wouldn't be the first time he'd been yanked in front of the sheriff at Golden.

Slim advanced to pick up the guns dropped by Brockmeyer. He looked at the man's bleeding arm and grimaced. "Always was too soft-hearted! Why didn't I put one through your wishbone? Wrap 'em up, Terry, and let's snake 'em down to the sheriff."

"Please no, señors!" Again came a desperate plea from Lopez. Fright mottled his sharp, swarthy face as he turned it to Terry. "If you will let us go, señor, I will tell you of a great danger of which you know nothing. To know will save your life, perhaps. I, Manuel Lopez, swear it is true."

"Pay no attention to him," Slim derided. "He's just tryin' to beg off."

But Terry caught something earnestly convincing in the man's voice. "Spill it," he demanded.

"If it saves your life, you will let us go?"

"If it saves my life, and you pay for the beef, and I don't ever catch you wearing a knife or gun again, I'll let you go."

"It is at noon yesterday," Lopez divulged eagerly. "You ride to the top of a small red sandhill and look in every direction, to observe your cattle. I am far away, señor, but I see plainly."

Terry thought back. It was true that at noon yesterday he'd ridden to the top a red sandstone hillock. "So what?"

"I see a puff of smoke. It comes from the creek brush perhaps two furlongs away from you, señor. Then I see two men there. One has just fired his rifle. But he has missed. So they ride quickly away."

At once Terry knew it was true. He recalled a detail which had puzzled him. Chips of bark flying from a pine bole about fifty yards upwind. Cascades of the creek, back of him, had kept him from hearing the shot.

There was an easy way to check the story. "You say you saw two men ride away. On what color horses?"

"One of them, señor, is on a buckskin. The other rides a blue roan."

Kelly and Cimarron! It was all too pat to be doubted. "You'll guide us to the spot," Terry said. "If we find a forty-four rifle shell there, like one we found in the willows below Denver, you and Brock won't have to go to jail."

The empty shell was there, in creek brush by a roaring waterfall which would smother the sound of a shot, and Terry kept his word to Lopez. No complaint was made on the rustling charge. Charley Grimes, the Shawn's Crossing storeman, paid cash for the heifer. Terry and Slim crossed the valley to join Jase Judson.

From that moment each of them rode tight-lipped and constantly alert. The bole of any tree could hide Kelly or Cimarron. Twice they'd fired to kill, from ambush, and would surely try it again. "They're huntin' us like rabbits," Slim muttered.

"Looks like we'd better do a little hunting ourselves," Terry concluded. "We got to find those birds and find 'em fast."

"Fast and first," Slim agreed.

CHAPTER
THIRTEEN

In the gathering dusk Serena Chalmers, with a cape over her head which hid most of her face, stood on the walk at the corner of Fifteenth and Curtis. Directly across from her was Guard Hall, sometimes known as Governor's Guard Opera House. Bitterness seethed inside of her as she watched a crowd over there. Cabs and carriages arrived in endless procession, discharging gallants and ladies to an event which was highlighting the Denver season. Gentlemen in top hats and derbies and sombreros; in swallow tails and corduroys; ladies in feathered hats and sweeping gowns. What infuriated Serena was that she wasn't one of them.

Soon Denver would boast an opera house the equal of Central City's; but at present the best it could offer was Guard Hall. There was the Palace Theater, of course; and a nameless place at Eighth and Wazee where shows of a sort were staged. But neither had a reputation which would permit a lady to appear there. Nor would a world-famous actor, presenting *A Midsummer Night's Dream*, choose either of those tawdry settings as a background for his talents.

The play had run before packed houses up at Central City, cloud-high gold town in the Kingdom of Gilpin.

On the way out, as an afterthought which stung Denver's pride, it was making a one-night stand here at Guard Hall. For a week posters had advertised it in every lobby. For days every seat had been sold out. Not to attend meant that one was of no social importance whatever.

Naturally tickets had been on sale at the American House desk. And Serena had caught Milo Patterson buying three of them. Why three? Asked, he'd as much as told her to mind her own business.

But now she'd know. It was nearly curtain-time and he'd have to arrive soon. Serena watched every cab and carriage. When at last she saw him her jealousy made a burning flame. That chit from the bake-shop and her aunt! Serena saw Patterson hand them to the walk and dismiss his carriage. The women were dressed plainly, in bonnets and dark capes, and no doubt it was the first time they'd gone out since the death of Frank Barber. In the gloom Serena couldn't see the girl's face. But she could see that it was upturned to her escort as she chattered excitedly, with a hand on his arm.

How devilishly clever he is, Serena thought bitterly, taking the aunt along too! First get in solid with the aunt; the cozy twosomes could come later.

They entered the foyer and disappeared from Serena's sight. Her first fierce impulse was to rush after them and take him away. She could if she liked. She could snatch him from that bakery girl, or any other woman in Denver, any time she wanted. All that consoled Serena, now, was the certainty of her power to do just that.

142

How? She could merely appear at his elbow and smile sweetly. And whisper in his ear: "Shall I tell her about the photograph, dear? The one you took from her uncle's wall while you were stealing the gold?"

No doubt by now he'd burned the photograph. So it would only be her word against his. But he wouldn't dare let the issue even come up. He couldn't risk arousing even the whisper of suspicion — not while he was courting the girl. Nor could he risk having a sheriff shadow him by night. Surely there was a cache somewhere to which the law might trail him.

A mere threat to expose Patterson would bring him to heel.

Reluctantly Serena decided against doing it now. Tomorrow three percent of a corporation's stock was to be issued to her. Best to get her hands on it before starting a fight with Patterson.

And after all she didn't need to worry too much about that bakery girl. Milo had taken a shine to her, yes. But maybe he'd get over it. And if he didn't, what about the girl herself? Surely she'd learn, in time, that Patterson was a professional card and dice man. And girls like Faith Harlan didn't marry card and dice men.

At best, Serena reasoned, he'd only get himself turned down. Good enough for him, too! After which she, Serena, would gather him in on the rebound.

Sustained in part by this conclusion, she walked back to the American House and retired to her room there. Tonight she'd need her beauty sleep, anyway. For tomorrow the Columbine Club opened, amid a grand fanfare and free champagne, with Serena presiding as hostess.

As she sat beside Patterson in Guard Hall, a single columbine was pinned to Faith's blouse. A lovely flower white in the center, and with five deeply spurred petals on the outside. It was past the season for mountain columbines and Patterson had brought this one from a hothouse operated by a man whose hobby was Colorado wild flowers.

"'A little western flower,'" Patterson had murmured, presenting it to Faith when calling for her tonight.

"It's beautiful!" She'd held it against her cheek before pinning it on. His spontaneous "And so are you!" had echoed her. How thoughtful he was! And how nice that he'd insisted on taking along Aunt Emily!

And how handsome! Glancing sidewise at his profile she couldn't help comparing him with other men in the hall. Hardly a one looked as distinguished as Milo Patterson. Many of them she knew by sight or reputation.

There were Governor and Mrs. Routt only two rows ahead of her. To their left she glimpsed the Chaffees: Mr. Chaffee was running for the United States Senate in the coming election. So was Mr. Henry Teller from Crystal City but he didn't seem to be here. Guard Hall had no gallery or boxes. Its single floor had seats for eight hundred people, all of them filled now. Turning her head this way and that Faith saw the Pitkins, the Joslins, the Doolittles and Mr. Daniels who was building the beautiful new store on Sixteenth.

144

Many of the men, she noticed, wore dress suits. She was grateful that her own escort wasn't wearing one. Maybe he'd guessed that she and her aunt didn't have evening gowns; and so had appeared informally himself, even wearing his tall and wide cattleman's hat.

Later, while the play was on, he turned to her and glanced down at her columbine. "'A little western flower,'" he murmured again.

And suddenly the same words from the stage made her know he'd chosen both the phrase and the flower with aforethought. For Oberon, king of the fairies, was saying to Puck:

". . . a little western flower,
Before milk-white, now purple with love's wound,
And maidens call it, Love-in-Idleness.
Fetch me that flower, the herb I show'd thee once:
The juice of it on sleeping eyelids laid
Will make or man or woman madly dote
Upon the next live creature that it sees."

Faith stole a quick glance at the big rugged man by her. He loomed in a new light, now, a hard-riding plainsman with a flair for the classics — else how could he have known such a line? Every element of this exciting night, all the beauty and chivalry of Denver close around her, the soft orchestral music, the romantic theme of the play itself — all of it made her pulses pound and her cheeks flush.

During applause as the curtain dropped at the end of the scene, she saw Patterson nod to some acquaintance in the audience. Her eyes followed to the Tomlinsons, brother and sister. The one blond and rubicund, with a small yellow mustache; the sister older by ten years and with a spinsterly austerity. "My partners on the Cross T," Patterson murmured.

Seated nearer to them Faith noticed a thin, pale young man and remembered that he'd interviewed her following the sensation of Uncle Frank's lost gold. He was watching them, she noticed, or rather his stare was on Milo Patterson with what seemed to be a quizzical challenge. "A reporter for the *News*, isn't he?" Faith whispered.

"I believe so." Patterson hurriedly turned her attention to more important people. "There's General Larimer who laid out East Denver. And there's General Palmer of the D & RG narrow gauge. We owe a lot to those fellows."

He spoke of them as boon companions although actually he only knew them by sight. And when he saw how the names impressed this young girl, certain of his own private ambitions expanded within Patterson. Long ago he'd steeled himself to become not only the richest but the most powerful figure in Colorado. His code and his creed assured him that money could buy power; that the quickest way to get money was to have stupid men bring it to him; and that once he had it a few generous campaign contributions could buy him any nomination he wanted. Four years should be long enough; the tide of fortune ran fast on the frontier. So what was to prevent him, by the year 1880, from kicking the dust of this cowtown from his boots and moving to Washington?

Yet by now Patterson also knew he'd need something else besides money. He must have the respect of top-layer citizens. He must wear a badge which stamped him as one of them; and such a badge, the young, lovely girl at his side, he was wearing tonight. She'd raised him, this past hour, to a level he'd never known before. A hundred glances cast this way had told him that. Arch Tomlinson had blinked twice, then whispered to his sister whose cool level gaze had seemed to say: "Perhaps we've misjudged him, Archie. Maybe he isn't quite the bounder we thought!"

No less had Aunt Emily, seated at Patterson's left, proved to be a badge of distinction. Coming in through the crowded foyer a matron of wealth and social prominence had not only called Aunt Emily by her first name but had greeted her with an impulsively affectionate kiss. For a moment it had puzzled Patterson. Then he'd realized that both Aunt Emily and the socialite were Fifty-niners. So too was Faith Harlan. A definite conviction struck Patterson: that in the end social rank in the west would be gauged not by wealth but by pioneering seniority. Which meant that Faith Harlan, who as an infant had traveled by covered wagon from Auraria to Auraria, would bring to the man she married, and hand down to her children's children, a priceless heritage.

Patterson knew now that he needed this girl and her atmosphere, far more than she could ever dream. A pleasant glow settled over him as the play went on.

Driving home in the carriage, he was shrewd enough to give most of his attention to the aunt. "Do you live out on your ranch?" she asked.

He laughed. "It's just partly mine, Mrs. Barnes. No, I only stay out there when I'm needed. Like today. A car of roughage came in from Kansas and I had to help Archie unload it. Look!" He spread his hands to show the blisters.

"I wonder," Faith exclaimed, "how Terry Woodford is coming along with *his* cattle. You heard about his experiment? He plans to hold cattle all winter in the mountains."

"They'll get buried in snow," Patterson predicted.

"The deer and the elk don't," Faith chattered. She spent the rest of the way home discussing Terry's venture. An undertone of vivid personal interest annoyed Patterson. Almost it spoiled his entire evening.

At their door Emily Barnes thanked him graciously. "We can make a pot of tea, Mr. Patterson, if you'll come in?"

Although tempted, he decided against it. "It's late," he pleaded. "Don't forget I'm a hard-working ranch hand."

"It's been a wonderful evening, Mr. Patterson." Faith's voice was warm and provocative, like the touch of her fingers.

At the American House he dismissed the carriage and hurried up to his room. It was nearly midnight and there was work to do. He must sit in at a club or two and get rid of another sixty ounces. Half the stake still lay hidden under a floor in West Denver. To complete cashing in Patterson must keep eternally at it.

He changed to corduroys and boots, buckled on a gun belt. In certain of the Wazee and Holladay street dives where men gambled, a player could command more respect with a gun at his hip. It made losers less inclined to argue.

A half hour past midnight, Patterson walked up Sixteenth to Larimer. He hurried west along Larimer, past an occasional cantina, a gas lamp glimmering at each corner. He crossed the Cherry Creek bridge and found no life beyond. West Denver had gone to bed. At Ninth he crossed a vacant lot to the backyard of his own log cabin.

He unlocked it, went in and lighted a candle. Practice had quickened his operations here. Rolling back a matting took less than a minute. The nails of a floor board were loose and came out smoothly. Three of the quart cans had been emptied and thrown away. From one of the remaining four, Patterson filled two thirty-ounce bags.

After replacing the board and matting he blew out the candle. Tonight there was no moon and as he left the house Patterson made no more than a silhouette. He locked the rear door.

"Ho there, Patterson!"

The voice shocked him, made him whip around with a gun in his hand. A slight figure in the yard was too dim to be recognized. But he knew the voice. The reporter, Tony Raegan!

Raegan had shadowed him here! The entire business was exposed unless ... panic, rather than any calculated intent, had jerked the gun from Patterson's holster. Panic — a sweep of overwhelming terror — pulled the trigger. He heard the roar of his gun and he smelled its smoke; he saw Raegan crumple.

Patterson's impulse to run lasted hardly a second. A body found here would cost him the gold. Police would find it inside, once their attention was drawn to the cabin. Having reasoned that far, Patterson became cool and practical. He went back into the cabin and came out with an old mildewed quilt. He wrapped it about the dead man and heaved the burden to his shoulder.

Ninth Street was black, deserted. Patterson crossed it and ducked down the alley between Larimer and Lawrence. He followed the alley to Eighth, then to Seventh. There he dropped Raegan. He took a wallet from Raegan's pocket, removed the money and tossed the wallet away. Police would call it a holdup by some back street thug. Denver was full of them. Hardly a night passed without someone running afoul of a footpad.

Patterson took the quilt with him. Blood was on it, so he carried it gingerly. He dropped it in Cherry Creek where Curtis crossed it.

An hour later Patterson was at the Jockey Club cashing thirty ounces of gold.

CHAPTER
FOURTEEN

High in the mountains the first chill of fall was in the air. Terry and Slim sat their saddles in a copse of aspen above Lost Creek. Here they were screened from any distant view. It was the third day they'd waited in this shelter, alertly observant. Nothing had happened, and Slim was getting discouraged. "Maybe we figgered 'em wrong, kid."

"They picked this spot *once*," Terry argued.

This side of the creek was steep and timbered. Only a hundred yards downslope a waterfall made a never-ending monody of sound. The other side was a flat open meadow except for a sandstone knoll a little way beyond the falls. It was the same brush-bound waterfall from which a sniper had fired at Terry Woodford.

A well-chosen ambush, because the roar of the falls would keep a shot from being heard. "They don't know we know they tried it," Terry argued. "They do know I use that knoll for a lookout point. So why wouldn't they try again?"

Slim shifted his weight to the other stirrup and hooked a leg around the horn. His gaze picked up a few red and white spots in the meadow beyond the creek. "They're beginning to put on tallow."

O Bar yearlings, knee-deep in cured grass over there, made a sight to warm a stock-lover's heart. "Just like Frank Barber said," Terry commented. "Lots of strength in this high country feed. Gets a head on it like grain. Skin and bones, those ballies were only a month ago. And look at 'em now!"

"Jase sure is tickled!" Slim grinned. "He'd give that stuff up for buzzard bait 'bout the time we made the deal with him."

The O Bar stuff wasn't fat. In fact it was still lean. But it was no longer weak on its legs. A man could no longer count ribs. "Might even make late fall beef," Slim predicted, "if we're lucky enough not to get any snow till November."

"Sh!" Terry cautioned. "They're comin'."

He'd glimpsed horseflesh moving upcreek through the brush. A moment later he saw it again. A blue roan. The man astride of it was Rex Kelly minus his fancy vest. Camping in the hills had given him an unkempt look. If Terry hadn't been watching for him, he might not have recognized him at all.

Trailing him came George Dodds who, habitually bearded, showed less change. He rode a buckskin and carried a rifle across his saddle pummel. Presently they drew up by the waterfall and went into patient ambush there.

Slim nodded grimly. "You sure doped it right, kid."

"How'd we better take 'em, Slim? Afoot or asaddle?"

152

The older cowboy gazed speculatively at the enemy. They'd tied their horses out of sight in the brush. Kelly now sat on a rock while Cimarron squatted with his back to a pine. Kelly said something but his voice, smothered by the waterfall, didn't carry this far.

Slim chuckled. "They don't figger we're in miles of 'em."

"Seein' as they're afoot, Slim, let's not take any unfair advantage." Terry stepped from the saddle, tying his mount to an aspen. Slim Baker did the same.

"You take a long gun, Terry. I'll take short'ns." He reached for the forty-five Terry handed him, wedging it in the left side of his belt. Terry took the carbine from his saddle scabbard and both men moved afoot downslope.

Creek sounds blotted out the crunching of their boots on gravel. Terry carried his rifle at trail; its chamber had one shell and its magazine five. With a long gun he was slightly more accurate than Slim; but with holster guns Slim had few equals. The ambushers were equipped with both, making the odds even. "They been lookin' for a fight, kid, and they sure found one."

"Which one do you want, Slim?"

"Kelly. You take Cimarron."

They were at the foot of the slope and on grass now. The ambushers, their backs this way, had no inkling of an approach. Kelly's rifle leaned against the rock he was sitting on. A cartridge-studded belt girded him, weighted with a hip gun. Cimarron, squatting at the base of a pine, held a rifle across his knees. He spat into

153

the creek and turned toward Kelly. "Reckon he'll show up, Rex?"

Kelly shrugged. "If one don't, another of 'em might. Any one of 'em 'll do, providin' we don't leave anything to show." Terry was near enough now to catch some of the words. He moved forward a few paces more, Slim flanking him. The gap narrowed to twenty yards; fifteen; ten; and still the two men didn't see them. Terry wished now he had a short gun; the range was too close for rifles.

Seven yards from Kelly's rock they stopped. Slim gave voice loud enough to be heard above the waterfall. "You birds waitin' of anybody?"

A whip cracked at his head wouldn't have brought Kelly quicker to his feet. He whirled with a hand on his gun. Sight of Slim and Terry froze him; he didn't draw. His startled whirl dislodged his rifle, toppling it to the sand.

Cimarron was up, eyes popping. Both hands held to his rifle but he didn't bring it level. His lips moved. "Talk louder," Terry suggested pleasantly. "We don't want to miss anything."

Terry's rifle was still at trail, barrel at a downward angle. He watched Cimarron's. To his left Slim Baker, to show his contempt, was giving Kelly better than an even break. Kelly's hand was on his gun butt and Slim's wasn't. Slim's thumbs were hooked in his belt, well to the front.

"Waitin' for anybody?" Slim repeated.

Cimarron licked his lip. "We was just deer huntin'," he said.

154

Slim laughed. "Hear that, Terry? If you go over on that knoll be careful you don't hold up nine fingers. They might think you was a nine-point buck."

Not a move from Kelly. Terry couldn't see him because his own eyes were on George Dodds. Both men, he sensed, were weighing chances. They'd pull if they thought they could get away with it. Or Dodds would whip his rifle level and let fly. Terry saw the muzzle of it move an inch. "I wouldn't do that," he cautioned, and let his own barrel come up the same inch.

Kelly spoke for the first time. "It's a free country, Baker. We got just as much right here as you have."

Slim grinned at him. "How you like my hat, Kelly?"

The man's face blackened. His gaze flicked to Terry and then back to Slim. "We folks don't like bein' shot at," Slim remarked easily. "Do we, Terry? Not from a gulch I mean, or a patch of willows. On the other hand if you wanter do it right out in the open, like we are now, we don't mind so much. Start shooting any time you feel like it, Kelly."

Kelly drew. A double fusillade broke out at Terry's left but his own attention was straight ahead. Flame spouted at him from Cimarron. Terry tipped his rifle level and began triggering it. He didn't bring it to his shoulder or even to his hip. Smoke and flame licked at him and he gave in kind, the carbine level in his hanging hands. Unbuttressed, it kicked and bounced there, and later he knew that all but one of his shots missed.

A waterfall and four guns roared and one man pitched forward. He was Rex Kelly with five slugs in his stomach. The very first of them had spoiled his aim and Slim Baker wasn't touched. Slim's voice spoke out of the smoke. "They'd ortern't 've done that, kid. They sure ortern't 've done it."

In near-by willows Terry heard two horses snorting, pulling at reins. He looked down and saw Cimarron jack-knifed against the pine. The man didn't move. Presently Terry knew he was dead.

Jase went as far as the stage station with them. It was after sunset and Terry was impatient to get finished with an unpleasant errand. It was a long way to Golden, the county seat, and the dead men must be delivered to a sheriff there. Rankin, Terry remembered.

Shawn's Crossing, its man-made structures in shabby contrast to the grandeur of its mountain forests, seemed entirely deserted. Slim and Jase led two horses to the corral and tied them to the endgate of a spring wagon. It was the same wagon which had hauled rustled beef. The bodies were unroped from their saddles and laid in the wagon's bed. Jase covered them with a tarp.

A squaw came trudging upcreek. Although she had no visible tackle, she carried seven trout on a forked stick. How Indians could do it had always been a mystery to Terry. Some said they used horsehair nooses. "Where's your menfolks?" Jase questioned.

"I go catchum." She went into the store with her fish.

Presently Grimes and Brockmeyer came out, rubbing their eyes. They'd been asleep. "Where's Lopez?" Terry demanded.

The storekeeper blinked blearily. "Manuel? He's around somewhere." The man raised his voice. "Manuel! Come arunnin'."

No response from Manuel Lopez. Slim went through the store and outbuildings but Lopez wasn't there. "His bronc ain't in the corral," Brockmeyer offered. "Must've rid off somewhere."

Terry herded Grimes and Brockmeyer to the wagon and turned back the tarp. "Ever see 'em before?"

Grimes stared. "No," he said hoarsely. "Who are they?" The look of puzzlement on his face was matched by Brockmeyer's. "Don't know 'em from Adam's off ox," Brockmeyer swore.

Slim took over. "Your pal Lopez said he saw two guys pot at Terry with a rifle. Up at the Lost Creek waterfall. Are these the same guys?"

Grimes gaped again at the dead men. "You'll have to ask Manuel," he said. "It was *him* saw 'em, not us."

Terry shrugged. "Okay. We'll ask Manuel. Meantime loan us a team for this wagon. The county'll pay you for it."

The station man was agreeable and a team was hitched to the spring wagon. "I'll hang around here till Manuel shows up," Jase said. "Then I'll snake him down to Golden and have him identify those buzzards."

The roan and the buckskin were left at the station corral. Terry tied his bay to the endgate and mounted the wagon seat. He flicked the whip and was off at a trot, Slim riding at the wheel. It would take most of the night, getting down to Golden.

In the morning Ray Rankin, sheriff of Jefferson County, approached his courthouse office to find a spring wagon tied there. Two sleepy cowboys were sitting on the steps. One of them, he remembered, had brought in the outlaw Redding. Since then Redding had been tried and was now awaiting execution.

"Hi," Rankin greeted. "You fellas been raisin' any more hell?"

"Not any more'n we could help," Slim said.

"Coupla guys laid out in the woods for us," Terry said. "Finally they caught up with us."

"That so?" Rankin asked idly. "Know where they are now?"

"Sure." Terry pointed to the wagon. "Right there under that tarp."

The match the sheriff was holding to his cigar went out. He walked to the wagon, raised the tarp, took a startled look, then came soberly back to the steps. "You mean you gunned it out with 'em?"

"I mean they tried to drygulch us," Slim said. "Once they put a slug through my hat. 'Nother time they missed Terry about this far." Slim held up two fingers. "Got kinda monotonous, dodgin' slugs allatime."

A deputy appeared and Rankin gave terse orders. The deputy drove the wagon to the morgue. Rankin took the two cowboys to his office while the county attorney was sent for. Presently he arrived, a chubby little lawyer with a gold-toothed smile.

158

"Begin at the beginning," Rankin said to Slim.

Slim told about being a witness in a Taos murder trial and about Kelly's threat after the acquittal. Then about a bullet fired through his hat from willows along the Platte River. At that point Terry took up the story and told frankly about the incident at the Interocean Hotel.

Here Rankin broke in. "You admit you tricked 'em to a hotel room and beat 'em up?"

"Call it that if you want," Slim said. "Next we heard of 'em was at Shawn's Crossing." He relayed the testimony of Manuel Lopez.

When the complete account was given Rankin looked rather grave about it. But the county attorney, Showalter, took a liberal view. "If it was like you say, I can't see what else you could have done. You naturally wouldn't want to let them keep potting at you, day after day. You say the witness Manuel Lopez is on the way?"

"Jase Judson," Terry said, "promised to bring him right here."

"Fine." The attorney gave a cherubic smile. "If Lopez will tell me he saw one of them snipe at Woodford from ambush, and if he'll identify either of these dead men as the sniper, we'll drop the matter right there. You, the hunted, simply turned on the hunters in reasonable self-defense. All I ask is that you don't leave town until I have a chance to question Lopez."

"We'll hang around," Terry promised.

Wearied by the all-night ride, they went to the Golden Inn and slept the clock around.

The hand that wakened them was Jase Judson's. Jase sat on the edge of the bed with a dour look. "Shuck on your duds, cowboys. We got trouble worse'n grasshoppers."

Terry winked the sleep out of his eyes. "What kinda trouble?"

Jase waited till they'd pulled their boots on. "Lopez," he announced, "has vamoosed. Bag and bronc. Nobody knows where he went."

"So what?" demanded Slim.

"Leaves us minus our only witness," Jase said.

Rankin and Showalter were waiting for them at the courthouse. The sheriff's chin looked aggressive. But Showalter smiled and his tone was apologetic. "We hate to do this," he began, "and we won't if you can dig up just one witness who'll testify that Kelly was out to get either of you two men." The prosecutor put five plump fingers against five and went on judicially. "I mean all you need to do is show homicidal hostility, or threat thereof, on Kelly's part. Right, sheriff?"

Rankin nodded. He shoved a paper toward Terry — a warrant for arrest, charging fatal shootings of Rex Kelly and George Dodds. "Do that," Rankin growled, "and I'll tear this up."

A dull anger filled Terry. "The way you talk, sheriff, you'd think *we* were the drygulchers, 'stead of Kelly and Dodds."

"Look at the facts," Showalter placated. "By your own admission you tricked those men to a hotel room and beat them up. By your own admission you waited for them by a waterfall — waited three separate days for

160

them. When they appeared, by your own admission you slipped up on them from behind. By your own admission they said they were there deer hunting. By your own admission you killed them."

"Killed 'em in a grudge fight," Rankin put in stonily. "Leastwise that's the way it looks to me."

"You're crazy!" Terry exploded. "What would you want us to do? Just stand there and let 'em fill us fulla lead?"

"You knew where the county seat is. If you thought they were layin' for you, you could've reported it to me."

"Nuts!" derided Slim Baker. "Since when did self-respectin' cowhands begin beggin' chair-warmin' sheriffs to protect 'em? Terry and me had a notion we was big enough to protect ourselves."

"Come now," purred Showalter. "Let's have no name calling. Unfortunately we can't find the man Lopez. If we do, and he identifies Kelly and Dodds, we'll release you at once. Or if any other witness turns up to convince us those men were the aggressors."

Rankin stood up and waved his warrant. "I'm serving this." He walked over to Slim and took his gun. Terry had left his at the inn. "This way." The sheriff stalked into a corridor leading to the cells.

Jase saw rebellion on Slim's face and interposed hastily. "Go along with him, boys. He's crazy as a coot but buckin' him'd only getcha in worse. Let him lock you up. I'll go dig us up a lawyer."

Showalter rubbed his hands, beaming. "Excellent advice, Mr. Judson."

Terry went bitterly along in the sheriff's wake. Slim followed with his face blood red. Rankin slammed a cell door on them, turned a key.

The cell had double-deck bunks. Slim sat down on one of them, started to say something, cut it to an explosive "Damn!" He stared through bars into the next cell.

A man lay on a cot there, snoring hoggishly. He was the condemned killer, Tom Redding.

CHAPTER
FIFTEEN

An amiable jailer came with a tray of food. A glare from Slim made him protest: "Don't look at me, cowboy. All I do is shag grub to the boarders. You got any troubles, tell 'em to your lawyer."

To prove his good will the jailer gave them a copy of yesterday's *Rocky Mountain News*. A headline caught Terry's eye. It was a follow-up story on the mysterious killing, last week, of Tony Raegan.

The shock turned Terry's mind to troubles other than his own. "Look, Slim. Somebody gunned Tony Raegan. After midnight, it says, over in West Denver."

"Footpad, they say," the jailer offered. "Nice feller, that reporter boy. Everybody liked him. The papers are raisin' heck about it. They're buildin' a fire under the sheriff over there, Chet Brewster. And under the Jeff County sheriff, too, seein' as we're just across the river. Gun killin's 've got to stop, they say. We're a state now, the *News* says, so we got to be civilized." The jailer lowered his voice. "Just between you 'an me, that's why Rankin cracked down so tough on you boys. It'll show 'em he's bearin' down, see?"

With a knowing smile the man shuffled out with his tray.

Tony Raegan! Terry read the account from beginning to end. "Remember the last thing he said to us, Slim?"

Slim couldn't remember.

"He was talking about Andy Brown," Terry said. "Said Andy Brown sounded fishy to him; meaning he figured Patterson made Andy Brown up out of whole cloth."

"If Patterson made Andy Brown up," Slim agreed, "he had a reason for it. Like explainin' what he had on the pack-mule."

"I'd bet on it, Slim. Means Tony suspected Patterson of copping those cans of gold. And I'll bet on something else. From that minute Tony tried to keep an eye on Patterson. My money says he was doing it when a slug stopped him, in a dark alley over in West Denver."

Slim grimaced. "So here we are in jail in the next county. Like mutton on ice! Where we can't do nobody any good, includin' ourselves."

Terry brooded over it. "Look, Slim. Know what I'm gonna do? Soon as I get out of this deadfall, I'll take up the trail right where Tony Raegan left off. Right in that West Denver alley."

"*If* you get out," Slim corrected gloomily. "We killed two guys, remember. We beat 'em up in a hotel room, then we sneak up on 'em in the woods. Coupla nice, peaceful deer hunters settin' on a rock. Manuel Lopez knows it ain't so. But nobody else does. And where the heck is Lopez?"

164

Faith Harlan, at breakfast with her aunt, heard the morning paper thud against the front screen. She went for it and brought it back to the table. "See if there's anything new about Tony Raegan, Aunt Emily, while I warm the coffee."

Emily Barnes unfolded the paper. The feature story had a Golden date-line. "How awful!" Her eyes widened as she read a little further. Then she sighed. "And he seemed like such a nice young man!"

Faith, looking over her shoulder, almost dropped the coffee pot. Terry Woodford in jail at Golden! A grudge fight, the paper said, in which he and Slim Baker had killed two enemies near Shawn's Crossing.

"I don't believe it!" Faith gasped.

"According to the paper," her aunt said, "he admits it."

Faith read the account through. "He says they were hunting him, Aunt Emily. They'd shot at him twice. They were waiting there to waylay him again."

"I hope it's true. But after all," the older woman admonished, "don't get too worked up over it, Faith. You don't know him very well."

"Well enough," Faith protested in a tight voice, "to believe he's telling the truth."

She took the paper to her room and read it again. At the end was a statement by Jefferson County's prosecutor. "We hope that some witness will come forward to convince us the self-defense plea has substance in fact. If so we'll be disposed to drop the charges. Especially since one of the defendants, Terry

Woodford, recently did us a good turn by bringing in Tom Redding."

All morning Faith tried to discipline her mind and think straight about it. What did she really know of those two cowboys? First she'd seen them shooting bullets through croquet balls in alcoholic glee. Later one of them had come back, a few times, using as a card of admission a passing acquaintance with her Uncle Frank. In return for using the Elk Valley cabin as a cattle camp he'd gathered up some of Uncle Frank's things and brought them to Denver.

What else? Nothing at all, really. He'd come into her life as a rowdy and now he was leaving it in the same role, or worse, a gunman killer.

Faith tried to drop it right there. Somehow she couldn't. Her woman's sixth sense kept whispering, telling her there was something else, a good deal else she must admit about Terry Woodford. *You like him. You believe everything he says. You like him better than Milo Patterson.* As far apart as two poles, those men. Terry reckless and loose-triggered; Patterson restrained, correct, romantic, gallant. And yet — she liked and she trusted Terry Woodford. His compliments came the hard way, as from one who deals in deeds and not in words. Patterson's came with the ease of long training in flattery.

A bell tinkled at the front. Her aunt's voice called, "A visitor, Faith."

She fluffed her hair a little, then worked on her face till the taut look was gone from it. Intuitively she knew it was Patterson calling, and somehow she didn't want to see him. Every day of late he'd rung the bell and each time she'd hoped it would be Terry. Today the hope was dead. Terry was in jail for murder.

As she entered the little parlor the immaculate perfection of Patterson's attire affronted her. Gray cords tucked into half boots, yellow silk shirt, wide filigreed belt. He was spurred and gauntleted. She thought of a young cowboy crushed and brooding on a jail cot. Her tone was a little brusque as she noticed a paper in Patterson's hand. "You've seen what it says about Terry and Slim? What do you think?"

He didn't hesitate. "I think it's a rotten shame, Faith, jailing him like that. What did they expect him to do, stand around and let 'em shoot at him?"

The quick reaction of her eyes told him he'd scored.

"You really think it wasn't his fault?" An unconscious concentration on Terry made her use the singular pronoun.

"I don't think he'd lie about it," Patterson said. "Woodford, I mean. About the man Baker I can't say. Don't know him."

His gray stood in front, reins hanging. "Can't stop but a minute, Faith. What about supper at the Broadwell, this evening? A famous violinist'll be there and he'll do a number or two."

"Of course, Mr. Patterson." She said it under the impulse of the quick, warm gratitude she felt for his magnanimous attitude toward Terry Woodford.

"I'll be around at seven, then." With a wave of his big rancher's hat he was gone.

Riding down Curtis Street Patterson smiled to himself. How well he knew women! She'd sensed he was Woodford's rival and she'd expect him to crow a little, or be covertly pleased, at the cowboy's predicament in Golden. So praising Woodford had been a neat gesture. Instantly his stock had gone up. Actually he'd helped himself and not Woodford. A few more passes like that and she'd tumble into his arms.

Riding on to the American he told the clerk to order him a carriage for seven o'clock.

Serena Chalmers saw the carriage arrive. She didn't know it was for Milo. She herself had just dressed for the evening. Habitually she dined at Charpiot's and from there took a cab to her evening duties. She liked it at the Columbine Club. The miners and cowmen and boomers were giving her a big play, spending money like water. They weren't as gallantly picturesque as the customers she'd had at Santa Fe, but they had fatter wallets. Everything was perfect except for Milo's aloofness.

He appeared at the Columbine nearly every night, always as a customer and always at a late hour. And always he made up to important people, especially to big name politicians. He was building himself up with them. Only herself and two directors knew that he really owned the club. Serena smiled. Except for one flaw, Milo's masquerade rather amused her.

The flaw was a black-haired girl up on Curtis Street. Milo seemed to be getting serious in that direction. Until now Serena hadn't worried too much, being confident the girl would turn him down. But today's news gave the matter a new angle. A boy named Woodford had gotten himself jailed for a killing. The law was taking a tough attitude, calling it a grudge fight, using Woodford as an example to cool off other gunmen in the clean-up campaign launched after the murder of Tony Raegan.

They were making it look like Woodford and his friend had picked the fight. All of which could easily disillusion Faith Harlan. If she believed the charges she'd be revolted. She'd turn away from Woodford, perhaps, and Milo Patterson might catch her on the rebound.

The possibility worried Serena. And just as it occurred to her, Milo came down into the lobby. All dressed up in his lady-killing best, with a boutonnière in his lapel. Serena hid her pique and called out in a gay banter: "Hello, Milo. Who's the date?"

With a wave and an evasive grin Patterson passed on. She saw him go out to a carriage, dismiss the coachman, take the reins himself. Off he went at a smart trot, south along Sixteenth. Faith Harlan, Serena remembered, lived in that direction.

Serena had a grim look as she called a cab and rode to Charpiot's. She dined bitterly alone. Patterson was out with the Harlan girl somewhere, wining and dining her while Serena had to pick up her own check.

To cover her fury Serena used a light tone as she paid the cashier. "Where *is* everybody, Pierre? It's like a morgue this evening."

He gave a Latin shrug. "They desert us for the Broadwell, mam'selle. Because of a great violinist who plays there tonight."

The Broadwell was only half a block east, with arcades over both the Larimer and Sixteenth Street walks. Carriages and cabs, arriving in unusual numbers, meant that Pierre was right. Tonight the Broadwell was a hub of attraction.

Serena entered its lobby and from there could see into the dining room. The place was crowded. By a grand piano a man with a Vandyke beard was playing a violin. The customers, in general, were of a type alien to Serena's world. In Denver it was said that big money went to the American, big appetites went to Charpiot's, and fine artists went to the Broadwell.

Serena quickly spotted them, Milo and the girl. Faith Harlan, all her attention on the violinist, had a rapt look; but no more rapt than Milo's whose entire attention was on the girl. Tonight she was beautiful enough to make Serena hate her more acridly than ever.

Not to be caught spying, Serena went out and took a cab to the club. Her entrance there was as poised as usual; she seemed irrepressibly gay as she crossed the main gaming room, exchanging pleasantries with the men who swarmed about her. All evening she danced with them, played with them, fascinated them. But every minute of it she was planning reprisal against Patterson.

Early in the morning she left town in a fast livery rig. "The courthouse at Golden," she said to the driver.

Wheeling up the Clear Creek road, she rehearsed what she must say to the sheriff there.

As for those two cowboys in the Golden jail, they could hang from the highest scaffold for all Serena cared. But something must be done to checkmate Patterson. Patterson was having too clear a field. From the first Serena had sensed a triangle there, with Terry Woodford as the third corner. Young, clean-cut, buoyant — Serena saw him as a more natural choice for a girl like Faith. At the very least a girl would think twice, with a boy like Woodford in the offing, before letting herself be swept off her feet by a man like Patterson.

But Woodford under the cloud of a rowdy grudge killing was no help. So the cloud, Serena decided, must be brushed away.

Well before noon the rig rolled into the little foothill county seat of Golden. Serena told her driver to wait. She crossed the courthouse yard and saw an elderly stockman sitting dejectedly on the steps. "Where," Serena asked him, "can I find the county attorney?"

"I'll show you, miss." Jase Judson led her to an office where Showalter was conferring with Sheriff Rankin.

"I'm Serena Chalmers of Denver," she announced. "I've just read a news account about Rex Kelly and George Dodds and I feel duty-bound to tell you what I know."

Jase was quickly alert. Showalter sprang to his feet and drew up a chair. "Sit down, Miss Chalmers. You say you know something about Kelly and Dodds?"

She accepted the chair graciously and raised her veil. "I'm hostess at the Columbine Club in Denver. A year ago I had a similar position in Santa Fe. Kelly and Dodds were faro dealers there. So I knew them casually, although I never liked them. They were ruthless, dangerous, spiteful. They left Santa Fe and I didn't see them for months. Then I came to Denver and found them registered at the American House. Why, I don't know."

She'd agreed with Patterson that now, Kelly and Dodds being dead, it was best to disclaim any professional connection with them.

"You spoke to them?" Rankin questioned.

Serena nodded. "Knowing them, I couldn't very well avoid it. One afternoon I saw them come out of the Interocean Hotel and cross to the American. I was in the lobby when they came in — Kelly had bleeding lips and a black eye; Dodds looked like he'd been in the same fight. 'Who beat you up, boys?' I asked, just to be friendly."

"Did they say?" prompted Showalter.

"Not by name. But Dodds was so mad he blurted out: 'I'll fill them guys so fulla lead the buzzards won't eat 'em.' Kelly also was too mad to keep his mouth shut. 'I missed him once, but I won't miss him next time.'" Serena looked Rankin in the eyes. "That's what they said, sheriff. So when I read yesterday's papers I thought you ought to know."

Showalter, tremendously impressed, wrote it all down and made her swear to it. The old stockman standing by no longer looked dejected. "You said one

172

witness was all you needed!" he chortled. "And you sure got her."

Serena went out to her rig and was driven toward Denver. She was barely out of sight when Terry and Slim emerged from the jail, free men.

CHAPTER
SIXTEEN

They wasted no time puzzling over their release. "Let's saddle up for the high country, Jase," crowed Slim.

"I'm rarin' to ride, son. Wanta see how much tallow them O Bars've put on."

Presently Jase and Slim cut south toward Morrison, there to take a steep uptrail for Shawn's Crossing. Terry himself headed straight for Denver. The brutal midnight shooting of Tony Raegan was goading him.

Terry jogged by a ranch gate and saw a name over it. CROSS T RANCH — GALLOWAYS — ARCH TOMLINSON. So this was the place in which Patterson had bought an interest! Terry puzzled over it. He couldn't quite see Patterson in the role of a cattleman.

The pasture beyond the gate was grassless. Nor did any green show in a distant meadow dotted with black cattle. A full ditch told Terry the place had a first-rate water right. He looked again at the barren meadow, eaten to the roots by grasshoppers in spring and early summer. A timothy meadow, probably; or perhaps native vega. Suddenly a remark of Slim Baker's came back to Terry. Slim had been telling about the hay meadows down in New Mexico; meadows irrigated and harvested by Mexicans for generations. Those people had learned things about the climate of the west, and about hazards to crops, that gringos still didn't know.

The thought absorbed Terry as he rode on. Ideas were like seeds; the winds blew them from one range to another. They drifted in the minds of cowboys like Slim Baker — Slim who'd drifted from the old Spanish culture of the Rio Grande to the banks of the Platte, where Johnny-come-lately gringos had lacked both the patience and the experience to really learn the secrets of this western land.

One of those secrets took root, now, and sprouted in the mind of Terry Woodford. According to Slim, the Mexicans of New Mexico never worried much about grasshopper blights. And they'd been down there a long, long time!

In Denver Terry stabled his horse and put up at the Grand Central on Larimer. He'd left a bag stored there. After a bath and a quick supper, he set out to see Faith Harlan.

Faith's greeting had reserve in it but no surprise. The news of his release had already reached Denver and no doubt she'd heard it. Aunt Emily had gone to midweek prayer meeting and the shop's kitchen, usually so humming and hot, was cool and calm. A measure of naturalness came to them as Faith made coffee.

"You'll be going back to Elk Valley?" she asked.

"Not right away. Jase and Slim went back up there." He'd never before wanted to talk about himself and his troubles. He was used to carrying his own saddle. But

175

now it was different. Here was this girl — what did she think of him? He wanted to know. He *had* to know.

"Look, Faith . . . You know what happened up there . . . Do you blame me?"

"No, I don't blame you." Her eyes, with a disturbed look, searched him. "Not for what happened by the creek. But the other time — why did you have to beat up those men in the hotel room?"

"I guess we were wrong that time." His tone was contrite. "They'd just put a bullet through Slim's hat and we wanted to stop it."

"You could have gone to the police. Why didn't you?"

"All we could show the police was a hole in Slim's hat and the print of a flatty shoe. They wouldn't call it proof." Terry looked at her and went on earnestly: "But there was another reason. Saddle hands, like Slim and me, kinda get used to mendin' our own fences. We just don't go crybabyin' to the police every time somebody gets funny."

She smiled at his earnestness. They carried the coffee to the parlor. "What," she asked, "are you going to do now?"

"Next I'm starting right where Tony Raegan left off. In a West Denver alley. To find out who killed him and why."

"They think a footpad did it. His purse was gone."

Terry started to say something, but didn't.

"You don't think it was like that?" the girl prodded.

"No. I think he was shot by whoever stole seven quarts of gold from your uncle."

Her stare was incredulous. "But if he knew who did that, why didn't he tell?"

"He had suspicions but no proof."

"Suspicions of what?"

"Of that cock-and-bull story about a prospector named Andy Brown." The name boiled out of Terry before he could stop it.

Suddenly she was cool again. He hadn't mentioned Patterson's name. But if Andy Brown didn't exist, then Milo Patterson was a liar. And if a liar, a thief.

Faith said nothing. Her chilly silence was all the answer needed.

It angered Terry and he plunged on. "You asked what I think and I told you. If you want it a little plainer, I think Tony followed Milo Patterson to a cache. And got shot for it."

"How can you say such things!" Faith burst out. "When *you* were under suspicion, Milo Patterson stood up for you. He wouldn't believe you were guilty and he told me so right in this house. He gave you the benefit of every doubt!"

Terry gave her a long, level look and shook his head. "I hate to see you get taken in like that. The man's a fake. Riding around like a big-time cowman! He's no more a rancher than a jaybird, He's a professional gambler using a ranch for a front, that's all."

She stood up, her face flaming. "I think you'd better go now." She said it very quietly and he knew she meant it.

"Listen. Why don't we . . . ?"

"Please go." She cut him short. "Milo Patterson has been very nice to us. My aunt and I trust him completely."

Terry picked up his hat and went to the door. "You'll find I'm right," he said stubbornly. He tried to smile but it was a forlorn effort. He opened the door and went out. She heard his spurred boots click on the gravel walk.

For the first few blocks, as he strode away, Terry was too mad to care, *To hell with her.* His mind kept saying it over and over. *To hell with anyone dumb enough to fall for a guy like that!*

Later that night Terry stopped in at the Columbine Club. Fast play was on at faro tables, roulette, monte and dice boards. Every type of patronage was there, from socialites in patent-leather shoes to muckers in brogans. A bland giant in a Prince Albert seemed to be a house man. "You the manager?" Terry asked him.

"My name is Alfred, sir. My duty is to keep order here, nothing else." Alfred wore striped pants and had a gardenia in his lapel.

"Who owns the joint?"

"A corporation, sir," said Alfred, parroting instructions. "Mr. Dall is president and Mr. Goodson is secretary. Our hostess, I believe, holds a small block of stock."

"Milo Patterson in on it?"

"Not that I am aware of. Occasionally he plays here, but only as a customer."

Terry looked up the hostess. She was dazzling in an off-shoulder gown of green. When Terry appeared she

178

brushed off her man of the moment and reached out a jeweled hand. "Hi, cowboy. Glad to see you out of jail."

"I owe it to you, don't I?"

"Why not?" She tucked the hand in his arm and led him toward a bar. Not the main bar, but a small private one for select friends. "Maybe you can do me a favor some time."

It puzzled Terry. Twice he'd seen her at a distance, dining or shopping with Milo Patterson. But how could she know *him*? And what could be her interest? "Where's Patterson?" he asked casually.

"How would *I* know?" Her indifference seemed overdone.

In the morning Terry's question was answered by the clerk at the American House. "Mr. Patterson is out at his ranch, sir."

After lunch Terry saddled his bay and took the Golden road. A forty-five weighted his holster and the brass caps of forty shells gleamed at his belt. He hadn't made up his mind just what he'd say to Patterson. But he was impatient and frustrated and tired of running into blind alleys. The truth, he felt sure, was known by Milo Patterson. And by him alone. An hour with Serena last night had convinced him she wasn't in the man's confidence.

A face-to-face challenge of Patterson might gain nothing. But at least Terry could find out how the man stood with the Tomlinsons. Terry had met the Englishman and his sister once, when delivering horses

179

to the Cross T. It was hard to imagine them teaming up with Patterson.

He passed through a gate and crossed a barren pasture. From a swell in the land he saw the house, a brimful ditch circling its meadow. A timothy meadow, Terry noted, but producing not a spear of hay this season. In the distance he saw Galloway cattle, purebreds. No grade stock was in sight; nor any ranch hands. Baled hay stacked in a pen meant the place had been shipping in feed.

Terry tied his horse at the corral and walked to the house. Its air of exclusiveness made him wonder again why Patterson would be accepted here. A white-coated Chinese answered his knock.

"I'd like to see Mr. Patterson."

The servant stepped out on the porch and pointed. "He lives there, please." His finger indicated a guest cottage some two hundred yards down the ditch.

"Thanks." Terry walked there and found no one at home. But the cottage door stood open, suggesting that its inmate intended to return soon. The open door showed a snug little parlor with reed furnishings and Indian rugs.

Patterson had nothing to hide here, Terry thought, or he wouldn't leave the door open. Why not go in and wait?

Terry stepped inside, took off his hat and sat down. Since he'd been directed here by a servant he could hardly be accused of prowling.

A magazine lay on the table — a late issue of *Potter's American Monthly* published in Philadelphia. Near it lay a scrap of paper. It was a receipted bill from Joslin's, the item being a lady's evening wrap. The lady, Terry concluded, would be Serena Chalmers.

But Terry saw nothing else which even vaguely suggested a connection with Serena and the Columbine. A ditch gurgled pleasantly by the door. From the corral came the plaintive bawl of a calf; the single protesting note of a calf not yet adjusted to weaning.

Terry rolled a cigaret, lighted it. He was still puffing it when the calf bawled again.

He thumped the snipe into the fireplace and tried to summon just what he'd say to Patterson. He might trip the man up with a question about a camp on Crow Hill. At nine thousand feet above the sea, two men wouldn't camp overnight without a fire. Yet Terry had searched the top of Crow Hill a day later without finding the ashes of a fire.

A footstep on gravel. The doorway darkened. The tall figure of Patterson loomed there. His hip was holstered with a gun.

A cross between fear and hate flashed over the man's face before a smile made it suave again. Then Patterson came inside with a purred greeting. "Sorry I kept you waiting, Woodford. Been here long?" He held out a hand.

The brash hypocrisy sent a wave of fury through Terry. It brought back something Faith had said — "He stood up for you . . ." The generous, magnanimous Mr. Patterson! Double-talking pretense it was, and because it had deceived Faith, Terry impulsively took the opposite tack. Instead of double talk, he'd give straight talk. Rather than probe with sly questions, as he'd intended, he'd attack straight from the shoulder with the truth about Tony Raegan's murder.

"You killed him, Patterson."

The man stiffened, dropped his hand.

His retort came cautiously. "Don't be stupid. Redding killed Frank Barber and he admits it."

"I was talking about Tony Raegan. You hid the gold in West Denver. Tony followed you there, after midnight, and you gunned him."

Patterson stood quite still, his face a shade darker. Terry knew he'd scored.

Patterson turned, closed the door, bolted it from the inside. "What's to keep me," he said quietly, "from gunning *you?*"

From the corral a calf bawled. Terry stood up before he answered. "Go ahead, if you feel like it." Alertly he watched the man's right hand. This was a showdown and he knew it.

Patterson went on in the same low, cold voice. "It's not big enough for the two of us."

"You mean this room?"

"I mean this range. All of Colorado's not big enough. Only one of us is going to walk out of here, Woodford."

He thinks I really know something. Nothing less, Terry reasoned, would make the man force a gunfight here and now. *He thinks I've found something and he has to shut me up. I was right about West Denver and he's scared.* Aloud Terry said: "Okay, Patterson. Start shooting any time you feel like it."

182

The man's eyes fixed contemptuously on the butt of Terry's gun. Complete confidence was there — an arrogant sureness that he could beat Terry to a draw. "Go for your gun," he ripped out.

"That's right sporting of you," Terry said, "giving me an even break like that." The calf again bawled from the corral. "Too bad Slim Baker's not here. He's chain lightning. I'm not. Shall we set a signal? All we need is someone to drop a hat. Or wait a minute! That calf'll do it. He bawls for his mammy every minute or so. Next time he bawls, we go for guns."

"Suits me," Patterson agreed. And Terry was fairly sure he'd wait for the signal. He'd wait because he was fast and was confident he could draw first. Also it would give a color of truth when he claimed, later, that he'd fired to save his life.

Half a minute dragged by and the calf didn't bawl. The gaze of each man fastened with intense concentration on the other's right hand. Terry heard an inexorable ticking from the mantel clock. Then Patterson's voice. "You asked for it," he jeered.

Terry didn't answer him. His ears strained for a signal from the corral. The calf was overdue to bawl. A single plaintive cry from the beast and then two gunshots. A roomful of smoke with only one man on his feet, the other dead. A miss was unthinkable. The range was point-blank, less than three paces.

The sound which came startled Terry. Almost it deceived him into making a draw. He saw Patterson react with shock, then half turn toward the door. The sound came again. A polite tap there.

Tomlinson! Who else, Terry thought, could it be? With a gesture of annoyance Patterson unbolted the door and threw it open. The Chinese servant from the main house bowed, grinning.

"The honorable lady sends compliments," he chanted. "She serves tea in the drawing room, if you please. Mr. Patterson and his guest are invited."

The mantel clock said four o'clock. An hour when any English household might serve tea. Yet to Terry the interruption seemed too pat. As though the Tomlinsons sensed a hostility here and wanted to break it up.

He looked at Patterson and saw surprise, plus something else, on the man's face.

Actually Milo Patterson was shocked almost to petrifaction. Until this moment the Tomlinsons, socially, had entirely ignored him. Not once had he been invited into the house. Why now?

With a nod of acquiescence, Patterson walked out. Terry followed. The Chinese stood aside to let them pass, then trailed in their wake.

As they stalked by the corral, the weaning calf there belatedly bawled.

In the ranch home of the Tomlinsons, only the sister was waiting for them. Victoria. She sat in queenly poise back of a silver tea service. Tightly stayed, with a high lace collar, she looked hardly less imperious than her namesake over the mantel. Her head inclined slightly toward each man as he entered. "Mr. Patterson, I believe. And you're Mr. Woodford, aren't you? So nice of you to come. Archie's in town and I was lonesome. Won't you sit down?"

She waved them to seats. Then, with an amazing composure, Victoria Tomlinson poured tea.

"Sugar, Mr. Woodford?"

"If you please, ma'am."

"We don't have cream this year," she explained. "Or anything else much, because of the grasshoppers. And you, Mr. Patterson?"

"None," said Patterson. He was stiff and nervous and suspicious.

She handed their cups in turn to the Chinese who passed them on to the guests.

"And how is your great experiment coming along, Mr. Woodford? This idea of yours that cattle can keep alive all winter in the mountains."

Terry grinned. "It's not quite winter yet. So we don't know. I'll tell you all about it in the spring."

"Be sure to. But I can't imagine their surviving in the snow."

"Some won't," Terry admitted. "But if any at all pull through we'll be just that much ahead." He drank his tea a bit gingerly. Java in a mug was more in his line. A man could easily crush this fragile cup between two fingers.

"Our timothy crop," she sighed, "used to see us through the winter. But for two years now the pests have taken everything."

An idea which had been fermenting in Terry burst forth into speech. "I got a friend named Slim Baker. Slim's lived most of his life in New Mexico. He says the hoppers never clean 'em out down there."

"They don't!" exclaimed Victoria. "Why?"

185

"Because the Mexicans always put their meadows in alfalfa. It makes three cuttings — in June, August and October. Along comes a hopper year. The hoppers eat the June crop to the roots. The hacendados irrigate and the second crop starts growing. Maybe the hoppers gobble up that one too. But they don't get the third one — the October cutting."

"And why," questioned the lady, "don't they eat the third crop?"

"Look outside," Terry said. "You don't see any grasshoppers. This is September and they all left us in August. After hoppers clean out a range, they move on to another one."

"I see." A gleam came to Victoria's eyes. "If our meadow were in alfalfa, instead of in timothy, we'd have lost two crops. But the third one would be spared and we could harvest it next month."

Terry nodded. "That's what the Mexicans found out, years and years ago. Trouble with us gringos, we come out here from Ioway and Illinoy and try to farm the same hay crops they do back there. Timothy, red top, clover. It's awful good hay, but it only comes up once a year."

He finished his cup and accepted another one.

"What a sensational idea!" exclaimed Victoria. "Three crops in the same meadow each year. Two for the hoppers and one for the cattle!"

After his second cup Terry decided it was time to go. He took his hat and stood up. "Thanks, Miss Tomlinson. Guess I'll be ridin'. Be dark, time I hit Denver."

"You must come again, Mr. Woodford."

Patterson tried to follow Terry out but the hostess called him back. "I was wondering if you'll go over some accounts with me, Mr. Patterson."

Terry went on to his horse and rode away. A smile lighted his face. A sharp woman, Vic Tomlinson! *And nervy, too! She guessed I was sittin' on a powder keg, so she bit off the fuse.* If she'd kept her eyes open, Terry reasoned, and read every scrap of news and gossip about gold in quart cans, about the killing of Tony Raegan and the jailing of Terry Woodford, and above all if she'd sensed a rivalry for Faith Harlan, Victoria might easily be disturbed to have the rivals meet in her guest cottage.

So she'd served them tea! And now, quite plausibly, she was holding one man while the other rode safely away.

CHAPTER
SEVENTEEN

Faith found herself restless, dissatisfied, uncertain.

Just now she was shining the glass showcase with such energy that Aunt Emily pushed her "near" glasses up and regarded her with puzzlement. "You've been shining that showcase for twenty minutes, honey. Is something troubling you?"

"Oh no . . . I was just thinking . . . It's a nice day and I think I'll go out for a while."

But she *was* troubled. Terry Woodford and Milo Patterson! What did she really know of either man? One said the other was a professional gambler; that his role of a ranchman was only a masquerade.

A whisper or two to the same effect had reached Faith from other sources. They troubled her. She didn't believe them, and she wanted to refute them once and for all. Who would know? She knew no gamblers. But she *did* have one close friend whose father ran the biggest gambling club in Denver. Iris Jardine was her name. Faith had been a schoolmate of Iris' at the Wolfe Seminary. Other girls at the school had snubbed Iris. But Faith, scorning such snobbery, had befriended the outcast. From her father Iris could find out the truth about Milo Patterson and pass it on to Faith.

They lived, Faith knew, in the finest mansion on Colfax Heights. She went out and walked a block south to Eighteenth and Champa. A horse tram ran on Champa Street. When a car came along, Faith paid her fare and got a transfer. At Sixteenth she changed to a southbound tram and rode this to a wide dirt road called Broadway. Getting off there she walked briskly up a hill into a neighborhood of expensive homes. Denver's rich lived here, and a rumor ran that some day the state capitol would be built on this hill.

The Jardine house was a tall brownstone surrounded by a cast-iron picket fence. A winding brick walk led to its door.

Faith tapped with the brass knocker, waited for a moment, then noticed the place had a deserted look. Window shades were drawn. A gardener was trimming shrubs on an adjacent lawn. He yelled to her, "The folks there moved away, miss."

"You mean the Jardines?"

"Yep. Moved to Chicago. Sold the house furnished but the new people ain't moved in yet."

It meant she couldn't see Iris. Faith was passing out through the iron gate when a horseman dismounted in front. He took off his big cowboy hat and looked at her, a bit awkward and embarrassed. "Mornin', Faith. I didn't expect to see *you* here."

Her first quick suspicion was that he'd followed her. But a genuine surprise on his face made her know he hadn't. Day before yesterday she'd quarreled with him. She tried to make amends by keeping any trace of unfriendliness from her tone now. "Hello, Mr.

Woodford. If you came to see the Jardines they're not here. They moved to Chicago."

"That so? Then I might as well amble back down the hill." But he didn't remount. "Mind if I walk along with you?"

Leading his bay horse, he fell in step as she moved down the gravel walk toward the tram line. "I just wanted to ask Mort Jardine a question," he explained. "Wanted to know who he sold out to."

"Perhaps the gardener would know," Faith suggested.

"I don't mean the house. I mean his business. They say he sold it to an outfit called the Columbine Club, Incorporated. Thought maybe he might tell me who's back of it."

"Iris Jardine," Faith said, "was a schoolmate of mine. I didn't know she'd left town."

No further explanations seemed necessary. Faith gazed straight ahead at a snow-capped skyline. Terry echoed her thought: "You sure get a dandy view from here!"

Denver lay below them — a frontier trading town now bursting out of its cocoon of log cabins. Still half a cowtown, raw and awkward and growing too fast for its cowboy breeches, its oxcarts tangling with its spangled carriages — yet shooting its brick and stone upward on a dozen swarming streets. Beyond lay the reason, and at this moment both Terry and Faith sensed it with an unerring logic. "Isn't it beautiful!" the girl exclaimed, meaning not the town but the town's majestic backyard. So close and intimate, too, that skyline of

190

spruce and snow. Not only beauty was there, but climate, pure invigorating air, health and strength — strength for both cattle and men.

The thought made Terry say: "Your Uncle Frank was right; it's a strong country up there. And mighty pretty, too, right now. You oughta see the aspen parks up around Elk Valley. Yellower than fresh-churned butter."

They came to the tram track and Faith waited for a car to come along. Terry, standing by his horse, waited with her. She wanted to know how they'd gotten the O Bar stock up the steep grades. He was telling her when the car came.

So he continued telling her after she boarded. Stepping into his saddle he rode along beside the car. It was easy to walk his bay alongside and talk with Faith through an open window. She learned how a load of spoiled hay had been used as a lure.

The tram man took her nickel and gave her a transfer. At Champa she got off to wait for an eastbound Champa Street car. Again Terry dismounted, standing by her on the sidewalk as she waited.

All at once she sensed a tension and saw that he was staring across the street. "Lopez!" he exclaimed under his breath. "And he's all dressed up!"

A narrow-faced Mexican in a gaudy serape and braided trousers had turned off Champa and was heading down Sixteenth. On his head was a bell-crowned velvet hat. His back was toward them as he receded down Sixteenth. "I needed him for a witness," Terry said, "but he disappeared. Looks like he

191

made a raise somewhere, all rigged up fancy that way. I'd sure like to tag along and see where he goes."

"Why don't you?" Excitement tinged Faith's question. She'd read about the Shawn's Crossing witness who'd mysteriously disappeared just when needed to save Terry from being jailed.

"Trouble is he knows me," Terry brooded. "Soon as he sees I'm tagging after him, he'd be careful not to lead me anywhere that counts."

"He doesn't know *me*," Faith offered. "So why don't *I* follow him? I'll have to hurry — if I don't he'll be gone."

Before Terry could stop her she darted across Champa and was off down the Sixteenth Street walk. The seraped figure of Manuel Lopez was nearly a block ahead.

Terry mounted and rode slowly that way. He kept well behind Faith so that the man ahead wouldn't notice him. Traffic thickened after they crossed Curtis. It increased still more beyond Arapahoe. At Lawrence a crowd swallowed Lopez and for a moment Terry lost him.

Then the Mexican leisurely emerged. He'd merely paused to gaze upward at masons laying brick high on the façade of the new Daniels and Fisher store. The man went on to Larimer. On its northwest corner he stopped briefly to gaze into a Brooks-Giddings show window where saddles were on display.

Faith stopped at the southeast corner, under the arcade of the Broadwell House. Terry drew rein some fifty yards back of her. Both of them saw Lopez light a corn-husk cigaret, then take off westerly along Larimer toward the Cherry Creek bridge.

Faith, as she followed warily, kept on the opposite side of Larimer. By the time she got to the *Rocky Mountain News* offices, Lopez, on the other side of the street, had gone on past Charpiot's Hotel. Terry, mounted, turned the corner from Sixteenth in time to see Lopez cross Fifteenth. The man was moving briskly now.

If he noticed a girl paralleling him on the other side of the street she meant nothing to him, since he'd never seen her before. Yet Terry Woodford, a block behind them, began to worry a little. He whistled, hoping to attract Faith's attention and call her back. They were getting into a neighborhood of cheap shops and cantinas.

Manuel Lopez went only a few doors beyond Fourteenth. There he disappeared down steps leading to a basement poolhall — a place with a Spanish name over it.

Faith came to a stop on the opposite sidewalk. Terry caught up with her and dismounted. "Sorry I let you take all that trouble," he said. The poolhall destination meant nothing, since a man like Lopez would naturally frequent such places.

"But thanks anyway," Terry went on sheepishly. "I'll take it from here. First cab that comes along I'll send you home in it. Kind of a tough neighborhood around here."

No hack was in sight. Faith smiled. "Did I do all right? I'm sure he didn't notice me."

Then Manuel Lopez catapulted out of the poolhall as though shot from a cannon. Behind him came another man in pursuit. This one wore his left arm in a sling. A gun roared once, twice, three times. A bullet, barely missing Faith, plunked into an adobe wall at her back.

Lopez was dashing across the street and almost directly toward her. The man chasing him, shooting as he ran, was a ruddy gringo. Brockmeyer from Shawn's Crossing!

Terry picked Faith up and ran a dozen steps east, up the Larimer Street sidewalk. Brockmeyer, ignoring everyone but Lopez, was still shooting. "Hold out on me, will you!" he yelled. A bullet knocked Lopez flat. Terry, now safely out of the line of fire, set Faith down. He turned in time to see Lopez twist to his knees and snatch a knife from his boot. The knife whizzed just as Brockmeyer fired his last bullet. The gringo screamed, collapsing forward with a blade in his throat. He fell between the rails of the single-track tram line. He tried to get up, fell again and lay still.

But no stiller than Lopez who sprawled in the gutter dust, face down and arms outflung.

"Run, Faith," Terry urged. "Get outa here fast. I'll be along later." He went to Lopez to see how badly the man was hurt. A policeman rounded the corner from Fourteenth and came running. Patrons poured from the poolhall. Attracted by the sound of gunshots, people closed in from all directions.

The policeman took charge. For a moment he stooped by Lopez and then moved gravely to

194

Brockmeyer. "Both dead," he announced. "What happened?"

Several of the poolhall patrons began telling him, all talking at once. The crowd grew. Two other policemen and a county deputy appeared. "Who are they?" the deputy demanded. "What were they fighting about?"

The poolhall patrons didn't know. Terry, a short way up the walk with Faith, hadn't yet been questioned. "Guess I'll have to tell them," he whispered. "Other guy's named Brockmeyer. They were stage-horse wranglers at Shawn's Crossing."

Faith looked fearfully at the death scene. Shawn's Crossing! Inevitably she sensed a connection with other tragedies at or near Shawn's Crossing. "You heard what he said, Terry?"

Terry nodded. "Hold out on me, will you!" were the words which had erupted furiously from Brockmeyer as, pumping bullets, he'd charged Lopez. "Looks like they made some kind of a cleanup together and Lopez ran off with it." Terry turned it over in his mind, frowning. "No, that's not quite right. It sounds more like Lopez was supposed to divvy up somethin' with Brockmeyer."

He took Faith's arm and led her to the corner of Fourteenth. There she stopped stubbornly. "I'm not going any farther till I find out why it happened."

"Wait for me in the Charpiot lobby," Terry said. "Soon as I find out about it I'll join you there."

He turned back toward the crowd assembling around the dead men. One of them was on horseback and looked like County Sheriff Chet Brewster. "Don't be too long," Faith said.

She walked on to Charpiot's and turned in there. Impatiently she waited for Terry Woodford.

CHAPTER
EIGHTEEN

An hour went by. Why should it take Terry so long? But he'd promised to come back and so Faith kept waiting.

The second hour was half gone when Terry appeared. His face was troubled as he drew up a lobby chair. "You found out?" she prompted eagerly.

He nodded. "I told Brewster who they were. He searched them. Nothing on Brockmeyer but a few coins. But Lopez had currency — about two hundred dollars. Also he had on brandnew clothes. They found a room key on him. A key to a room at the Plaza Gonzalez, at Eighth and Blake in West Denver."

West Denver! It made her remember Tony Raegan, murdered at midnight in a West Denver alley.

"Brewster and I went to the Plaza Gonzalez. Lopez was registered there as Arturo Sanchez of Pueblo. That's why we couldn't find him last week when we needed him as a witness over in Golden."

She looked puzzled. And Terry could gauge her thought. Since Lopez had disappeared *before* Terry and Slim's gunfight with Kelly and Dodds, how could Lopez have anticipated the law would need him for a witness?

"He didn't," Terry explained. "He wasn't hiding from the law, or from me, but from Brockmeyer. Because when we searched his room just now we found a *poncho* with a canvas bag rolled in it. The bag had a hundred ounces of gold dust — about two thousand dollars' worth."

"Oh!" Faith stared, lips parted. "Do you think . . . ?"

"We think but we can't prove it. The sheriff, the police, the newspaper people — all think it's part of about eighty thousand dollars' worth of gold your Uncle Frank hid on his roof."

Terry brought out the makings and rolled a cigaret. "The sheriff," he went on, "is holding the hundred ounces for evidence. He says if he ever proves it was part of Frank Barber's cache, he'll turn it over to your aunt as the natural heir."

"What," Faith asked excitedly, "do they think really happened?"

Terry gave a cryptic smile. "They're so sure of what happened they want to bet on it. Lopez and Brock, they say, lived only two miles from Frank's cabin. So they had more chance than anyone else to spy on him. So if anyone saw him bury tin cans on his roof, it would likely be those two stage-horse wranglers. After Frank died they went there and took the gold. It was too heavy to carry very far right away, so they just buried it in the woods. Then they agreed to wait till everything was safe."

The logic of it convinced Faith. "But Lopez," she put in, "cheated Brockmeyer. He took it all for himself and ran away."

"That's what they all think," Terry admitted. "I mean the county and city officers and the newspapers. They think Lopez slipped out one night while Brockmeyer was asleep, dug up the gold, moved it as far as he could and reburied it, keeping only what he could ride fast with. He brought that much to Denver, changed his name and bought himself some fancy duds. Brockmeyer came down here looking for him; when he found Lopez, he cut loose."

"Of course!" A superior smile curved Faith's lips. Her eyes had an I-told-you-so look and Terry knew she was thinking of Milo Patterson. "I hope you're ashamed of yourself now," she chided.

Terry grimaced. "If that's the way it happened I'll sure have to eat crow, won't I?" But he was quickly sober again. "Trouble is I don't figure it happened that way at all."

"But how else *could* it be?"

He evaded and looked at the lobby clock. It was past noon. "I hear they serve awful good victuals here. What about us going in to eat?"

"Not," she said sternly, "till you tell me how else it could possibly be. Everything points to Lopez. They found the gold in his room. He was living in West Denver, only three blocks from where poor Tony Raegan was shot. And with his last breath Brockmeyer accused Lopez of treachery."

"Remember the word he used," Terry argued. "'*Hold* out on me, will yuh!' It doesn't fit. If it happened like you and the sheriff think, Brock would say. '*Run* out on me, will you!' That's not all. Slim and Jase and I went by the stage station and tried to pick up Lopez for a witness. We found he'd disappeared. But was Brockmeyer sore about it? It didn't bother him a bit. Which doesn't make sense, unless . . ."

"Unless what?"

"Unless Lopez came to Denver, with Brockmeyer's knowledge, to blackmail a man they'd seen with a candle, at night, digging on a sod roof. At the time they wouldn't know what he was after. But later it all came out in the papers. Seven quarts of gold. They knew who got away with it so they sent Lopez down here to put the squeeze on. The man gave Lopez enough to shut him up. Lopez was supposed to take it back to the Crossing for a divvy with Brock. He didn't. He changed his name and *held out* on Brockmeyer. It fits. Nothing else does. Brock cutting loose on him and yelling, '*Hold out* on me, will you!' "

Scorn was back in Faith's eyes. It wasn't necessary for either of them to mention Milo Patterson. "You'll go to any length, won't you?"

"For what?"

"To besmirch a man you don't like." She stood up and spoke to a bell boy. "Will you call a cab for me, please?"

Terry followed her to the front walk. "You asked what I think and I told you. I've as much right to . . ."

"Yes," she cut in, "you've as much right to be stupid and vindictive as anyone else." She looked him in the eyes. "I'm really sorry for you, Terry Woodford. Sorry you can't be as generous as the man you accuse."

200

A two-horse hack drew up and she got in. Terry took off his hat and stood looking after her, wretchedly and yet bitterly rebellious.

The sensation of the Larimer Street fight monopolized the front pages that evening. It was the same the next morning. And for once the *Herald* agreed with the *News*. Both concurred with law authorities in a solution of the season's most baffling mystery. All guilt, barring Tom Redding's, lay with Lopez and Brockmeyer. The only loose string, now, was to locate the spot where Lopez, after double-crossing Brockmeyer, had reburied the gold. Due to its weight it was probably still in Elk Valley. A check of Denver corrals developed that Lopez had not arrived leading a pack animal.

"It's out in the woods somewhere," Sheriff Brewster was quoted.

The main result was a thorough whitewashing of all other suspects, including Milo Patterson. Even the cynically suspicious Sheriff Rankin, out at Golden, took the popular view. And Terry Woodford, after the cool reception his blackmail theory had drawn from Faith, did not present it to anyone else.

In succeeding days, campaign news took over the front pages. This being October, the first Tuesday of next month would bring a national election. Political talk filled every bar and lobby.

Terry kept aloof from it. A single goal absorbed him, to turn up proof on Patterson. Doggedly he began a door-to-door canvass of West Denver. Beginning at the house nearest to the spot where Tony Raegan's body had been found, he asked over and over again the same question: "Howdy, neighbor; did you see or hear anything unusual that night?"

The starting point was Seventh Street between Larimer and Arapahoe. Homes in this section were shabby. A few were decayed and untenanted. Terry worked his way along Seventh Street to Blake.

"Which night do you mean, señor? . . . Oh, that one?" A Latin shrug. "So far back I cannot remember."

"If there is shooting that night, I do not hear it."

Other responses were just as fruitless.

Yet by day Terry kept stubbornly at it. Evenings he tried to keep an eye on Milo Patterson.

Evening after evening he watched the American House, where Patterson kept a room by the month. Generally the man was out at the Cross T helping Tomlinson feed Galloway cattle.

When Patterson finally came to town it was to take Faith to supper at Charpiot's. Spying on them made Terry hate himself. But he had an idea and he must sink or swim with it — the idea that some night Patterson would repeat the prowl on which perhaps he'd once been followed by Tony Raegan.

After taking Faith home the man went to the Broadwell House for a huddle with two men high in party politics. After conferring with them he wrote a check. Terry, observing from a dim corner of the lobby, saw the two men accept it with thanks. After which Patterson sent for his horse and rode home to the Cross T.

202

It wasn't too hard for Terry to identify the recipients of the check. The chairman and the treasurer of a major party machine. "Ain't the first time," the Broadwell bartender confided, "that he's sweetened the kitty for 'em. Campaign contribution, y'understand. All legal and aboveboard. But they's them that figgers Milo Patterson aims to own that party, some day. The way I hear it, they've already promised him the lieutenant governorship, in 'seventy-eight."

The new angle puzzled Terry. A gambler turned rancher! And now a rancher turned politician!

Terry's own room was at the Grand Central. A letter from Slim reached him there.

... a whole flock of deputies showed up and they sure gave Grimes a going over.

Grimes, Terry remembered, was storekeeper at the Shawn's Crossing stage station. Slim's letter went on:

They thought maybe Grimes was in cahoots with Brock and Lopez. So they worked him over good. But Grimes swears he knew nothing about it. There's not a grain of dust at the store. The deputies figure he wasn't in on it. Jase and I figure the same way. The deputies are scouting in circles now, looking for a cache in the woods.

Slim made it clear he didn't expect them to find one. He leaned to Terry's idea that the two station hostlers had schemed to shake down Milo Patterson, and that

203

one of them, Lopez, had gouged from him about nine pounds of the loot.

What most interested Terry was an account of the O Bar cattle.

You'd never know 'em, kid. They're scattered out all the way from Crow Hill to Buffalo Creek and you can't count nary a rib. Jase and me say our prayers every night asking for a late winter. If we can keep 'em feedin' good till December, we figure to drive everything over two years old down to Denver and ship it for beef. That'd put us out of debt, Terry. And still leave the young stuff up here in the hills.

By day Terry kept up his door-to-door canvass of West Denver. His next sight of Patterson was at a big party rally in Guard Hall. Nor was Patterson alone that night. As the man pushed through the crowd Faith Harlan held to his arm. Her dark eyes shone with excitement, for Denver's' gayest and most prominent were there. A brass band flared forth. Carriages rolled up with celebrities who included candidates for the governorship and for the national Senate.

Terry, elbowing in, managed to find standing room at the back.

His eyes picked up Patterson and Faith. With them were the two high-ranking party wheel horses Terry had seen at the Broadwell. Further back he spotted Serena Chalmers who'd arrived with the Columbine Club's manager. The hostess had a discontented look. Not far from her Terry saw the English ranchfolk, Arch and Victoria Tomlinson.

Patterson, Terry grudgingly admitted, made a gallant figure sitting there beside Faith. The earnestness of his attention to Faith was apparent not only to Terry but to anyone else looking that way. Definitely looking that way was Serena Chalmers.

Her eyes, Terry thought, were shooting arrows of hate.

A pompous voice from the platform broke in on Terry's thought. It introduced the first speaker.

Of that speech, Milo Patterson hardly heard a word. His eyes, meeting Serena's, hadn't missed the bitterness of her smile. A smile with a dagger lurking back of it! And reminding Patterson of certain hints she'd dropped, this past month; hints which, when he analyzed them, sometimes sent shivers up his spine.

Once, referring to Faith Harlan, Serena had remarked with an overdone sweetness: "Such a pretty girl, Milo. But I think she was even prettier with her hair coiled on her head in braids, don't you?"

It hadn't registered immediately. Then, with a shock, Patterson had remembered. The photograph stolen from Frank Barber's cabin had shown Faith's hair in that style. During recent months she'd never once worn it that way. So how could Serena know — *unless she herself had seen the photograph!*

Had Serena pried into his wallet? More than once Patterson had sensed consciousness of power in her manner toward him; at times she'd been almost like a cat playing with a mouse.

Then more recently she'd said to him, purringly: "You'd rather I wouldn't mention Lopez stopping us that night, wouldn't you, dear?" As they strolled down Sixteenth, one evening, in the dusk, a swarthy hand had touched Patterson's arm. "*Una palobra*, señor." For that whispered word he'd drawn Patterson aside; after which Patterson had turned to Serena, his face twitching with fury, and dismissed her abruptly. Off down Blake he'd gone with Manuel Lopez.

Patterson's first impulse had been to take the man to some quiet spot and shoot him. But two of them knew, Lopez said. So disposing of Lopez would still leave Brockmeyer. Murder would need to wait, Patterson had decided, till he could get them both together.

Then the break, a few days later. The pair saving him the effort by killing each other. Merely' thinking about it made the sweat of relief ooze from Patterson. All they'd cost him was the hundred odd ounces he'd paid Lopez. Every shadow was erased, now, except Serena's. Serena with her sweetly bitter smile and knowing eyes!

Those eyes were on him now, warning him. Or perhaps even commanding him. Actually the woman worried Patterson more than all the sheriffs in Colorado.

Beyond her he saw the prim and tightly laced figure of Victoria Tomlinson. She too was looking this way. Her gaze fastened on him with a question, then fixed with what seemed to be a kindly anxiety on Faith Harlan. As though some sixth sense warned her the girl had misplaced her confidence.

206

The speech ended and amid applause Patterson heard Jim Smead, the party chairman, whisper to Faith Harlan. "A big man, the Senator. And he thinks a lot of our friend Milo here. Keep your eye on Milo, young lady. He'll go high and far."

"I'm sure he will." Faith looked up at Patterson with a smile.

Patterson gave her hand a pat. "Don't let him kid you, Faith."

It was a moment later when he saw Terry standing at the rear. Terry too was staring at him. Damn him! Damn everybody! Why couldn't people mind their own business?

He brushed them from his mind — all but Serena. Only Serena, he decided, could really hurt him. And she wouldn't dare. Nor could she gain by it. She had too good a thing at the club.

CHAPTER
NINETEEN

In the morning, canvassing in West Denver, Terry finished Ninth Street. He decided to tackle Arapahoe from Ninth to Cherry Creek.

The first shack was empty. The next had board walls and a tin roof. A Mexican laborer lived there.

The woman who answered Terry's knock had an infant in arms. When he'd patiently asked his question she answered, "I cannot remember that night, señor."

It was reasonable that she couldn't since more than a month had passed since the killing of Tony Raegan. "What about *any* night? Ever notice anybody prowling the neighborhood? Catfooting along by himself late at night?"

She thought a moment. "No one, señor. But once I see a candle burning and I wonder why it is there. It is in a house where no one lives and the hour is very late."

"Where was that?"

"It is across the alley, señor. A house of logs where no one lives for many years. I get up at midnight to fill a bottle for the baby. And I see the glow of a candle at a window."

When Terry coaxed her around to the backyard, she pointed. The log cabin across the alley was very old.

The side this way had a door and two windows. "You never saw anyone go in or come out?"

"Not for many years," the woman said. She shrugged. "Perhaps a tramp breaks in there to sleep. *Quién sabe?*"

Terry crossed the alley, to the cabin's rear yard. Only a vacant lot with a cottonwood tree on it separated it from Ninth Street. In front of it ran the West Denver tram line. Terry circled the house and saw stout padlocks on the doors. The glass windows had no blinds and he was able to peer in. The two rooms were empty of furniture. One floor had an old oilcloth; the other a tattered matting. Corners were filled with cobwebs. Nothing suggested any recent occupation.

Yet the woman had seen a midnight candle here! A parallel recurred to Terry. Another candle had gleamed from the sod roof of Frank Barber's cabin. Perhaps its distant gleam had been seen by Lopez and Brockmeyer, leading them to take a closer look.

In any case here was, or had been, another furtive candle. Terry noted the number of the house. Then he set off at full speed for the county courthouse, on Lawrence Street at Fifteenth.

The county clerk, having delved through records, said: "It's one of the oldest houses left around here. Built in 1860 on the original townsite. Changed hands half a dozen times. Last recorded owner was John Riley, a miner."

"Has he kept up the taxes?"

"He paid last year's taxes, but current taxes are in default."

Terry crossed the hall to the tax collector's office. "You know a miner named John Riley?"

"Know him by sight," the collector said. "He used to live over in West Denver."

"Have you seen him lately?"

"He came in a year ago to pay his taxes. Seems to me he said he was going up to Fairplay, in Park County. I dropped him a card, month or so ago, tellin' him this year's taxes are overdue."

"Hear from him?"

"I dunno. Wait'll I ask my clerk."

The clerk dug through a file. "Can't find anything on it. But you might ask Chet Brewster. Chet knew John Riley pretty well."

The sheriff's office adjoined the collector's and Brewster was at his desk. "John Riley? Sure I knew him."

"*Knew* him?" To Terry the past tense sounded ominous.

"That's right. Riley was killed in a cave-in up near Fairplay, coupla months ago."

"He had a family?"

Brewster concentrated a moment. "Only kin he had, as I recollect, was a daughter up in Greeley. Let's see. Ella's her name. Ella Riley, a schoolteacher in Greeley."

"In that case she inherited Riley's property."

"She should have," Brewster agreed. "Or she will soon as they settle her old man's estate."

Terry rolled a cigaret. "When," he asked thoughtfully, "is the next train to Greeley?"

210

It was only a three-hour run up there. Terry had no trouble locating Ella Riley. She was a stout woman wearing thicklensed glasses. Her cottage wasn't far from the Greeley depot and she'd just come home from school when Terry knocked there.

"Your father had a cabin in West Denver, didn't he?"

"Yes, but he sold it," the woman said.

"Who to?"

"He didn't say. I mean he wrote me from Fairplay about six months before he died. He said he was looking for a farm to retire on and mentioned that he didn't own that West Denver cabin any more. Wait, I'll find the letter."

Ella Riley found the letter and showed it to Terry. The words were just as she had quoted. "So when the current tax bill was forwarded to me recently," she said, "naturally I didn't pay it. I suppose the new owner will, as soon as he gets around to recording his deed."

Terry caught a train back to Denver. He went directly to the West Denver cabin and stared thoughtfully at its padlocked doors. The padlocks were stout, but looked old. Terry considered smashing one of them with a hammer.

It would be an illegal entry and could get him into trouble. Best to have the law do it Terry went on to the courthouse and looked up Brewster.

The sheriff listened tolerantly but wasn't impressed. "You want us to crash in a private house just because a neighbor thinks she saw a glimmer at the window? It would take a court order."

"Okay. Let's get one."

Brewster pulled at his lip. "They's a gas street lamp at Ninth and Arapahoe, ain't they?"

"Yeh. So what?"

"Maybe the woman saw the reflection of a street lamp in a window of that empty cabin. Let's go talk to her."

They went to the Arapahoe Street shack and there Brewster's questions confused the woman. "I have think it is a candle, señor. But it is one, two, maybe three months ago and I do not pay much attention. A gas lamp shines that way, yes. Perhaps it makes a shine on the glass."

Brewster crossed the alley, looked at the padlocks, peered through the dust-encrusted windowpanes. "Before we go crashin' in," he decided, "wait till I hear from the sheriff at Fairplay. I'll write and ask him to see if he can find out who bought this dump from Riley."

Terry crossed the bridge to East Denver and went to his room at the Grand Central. A letter from Slim was there. "It's getting plenty cold up here. Wrap up that heavy wool shirt of mine and ask the stage driver to drop it off at Shawn's Crossing."

Terry Went down to a trunk room back of the lobby. Drummers used it sometimes as a place to display samples. Along one wall was a four-deck rack with open cages each large enough to hold a small trunk. In them were bags, valises, slicker rolls and boxes left in check here by rangemen who expected to register at this hotel again sometime. Each parcel had a tag on it. Terry found a duffel bag with Slim Baker's name on its tag.

He took a woolen shirt out of it, re-tied the bag and left it in its proper niche.

After making a package of the shirt Terry gave it to the hotel porter. "Put it on tomorrow's Leadville stage, Sam." There was no post office at Shawn's Crossing. But a stage driver would always accommodate by dropping off an addressed package.

When darkness came Terry buckled on a gun and walked over to West Denver. Street lamps were flickering at each corner. Terry stood in the Mexican woman's backyard and looked across the alley to the rear windows of the Riley cabin. They were black. The angle wasn't right to reflect a glow from the Ninth and Arapahoe gas lamp.

Terry crossed to the vacant lot and stood under the cottonwood there. On this last day of October most of its leaves had fallen. He leaned against the white bark of its bole and rolled a cigaret. Should he bring Brewster here and prove to him that his reflection idea wouldn't stand up?

Suppose he did! And that Brewster, after getting a court order, should break into the cabin and find evidence! What evidence? The most potent evidence possible would be all or part of seven quarts of stolen gold. Only a thin chance of any such windfall; but even if found here would it convict Milo Patterson?

Terry knew it wouldn't. For Patterson could deny all knowledge of it. It would take either of two things to convict Patterson. Ownership of the house would do it, providing the house held the stolen gold. The other clincher would be for Patterson to be caught entering the cabin with his own key, by stealth at night, and emerging with stolen gold.

The thought made Terry snuff out his cigaret. While waiting for Brewster to hear from the Fairplay sheriff, why not keep a nightly watch here? It would be tedious and exhausting. He'd have to come at dusk and stay till well after midnight, night after night. Was it worth the effort?

Terry thought of Faith Harlan. Faith and her supper dates with Patterson. He couldn't gauge what progress Patterson had made with her. Certainly the man had won her trust and respect — perhaps even more. She was young, inexperienced, would naturally feel flattered by attentions of an important man of the world like Milo Patterson. The hazard disturbed Terry. Every maximum effort, however slim its chance of success, must be made to expose Patterson.

Squatting on his spurs under the cottonwood, Terry settled down for a long, silent watch.

An hour after midnight, stiff from holding one position too long, he went to his hotel and to bed. But a night later he was there again. He'd checked at the American House where they'd told him Patterson was out at the Cross T ranch.

The man might, however, ride in after dark and come straight to this cabin. Terry leaned against the trunk of the old cottonwood, his holster flap open. From here he could see both ways along Ninth; also both ways along an alley. He couldn't see either Larimer or Arapahoe streets except where they crossed

Ninth. At either intersection street lamps would make a target visible.

The long watch passed and nothing happened. An hour after midnight Terry again went home.

It was the same a night later. Patterson, from all information, was still at the ranch. Tuesday, Terry thought, would bring him in to vote. A man in high councils of his party, like Patterson, would hardly miss an election.

Election day came and Terry watched for him. He himself went to a booth and cast a vote for Samuel I. Tilden. It was his first presidential ballot. With only one exception he made crosses after the Democratic candidates. The exception was Henry M. Teller, a Republican running for the U.S. Senate. The man's forthright personality, speaking at a recent rally, had won Terry over.

All day he watched hopefully for Slim and Jase Judson. They might ride down from the mountains to vote. By twilight they hadn't come. Neither had Patterson. Then it occurred to Terry that Patterson and Arch Tomlinson would vote at Golden, the Cross T being near there.

By dark Denver was in an uproar. All day the politicians had been standing treat at the bars: Cowboys and miners had swarmed in to vote and many were imbibing too freely. More than once during the early evening Terry heard gunshots. Ranch hands galloped up Holladay Street shooting into the air. On occasions like this policemen usually looked the other way.

Soon after dark Terry went to his post in West Denver. Streets on that side of the creek were deserted. All Denver was concentrated tonight in the hub of excitement, east of Cherry Creek, where the first results would be announced. Many would haunt the depots to catch telegraphic reports from the east. It would be a neck-and-neck finish, the papers said.

Brass band music, from far up Larimer Street, came down the night wind to Terry. Both sides were planning victory parades and maybe one of them had started already. Surely, on a night like this, Milo Patterson would ride in. He'd backed one of the campaigns with real money. But if he did come in he might be too busy for any side issues. He'd more likely go straight to one of the hotels for a huddle with party leaders.

Terry almost dozed. Tonight it was hard to take his vigil seriously. From a distance came the chimes of a belfry bell and he counted them. Only ten o'clock. A cigaret would taste good but he put away the temptation.

Just after eleven he did doze for a minute. He shook himself, walked twice around the tree to get up his circulation. A baby wailed in a shack across the alley. A light came on over there and the window showed a woman pouring milk. For minutes more the baby cried; then the window went dark and presently the child was quiet.

Clouds had overcast the sky and not a star was in sight. The night was like a black fog and except in two directions Terry could see nothing. Two street lamps, one at the Larimer corner and one at Arapahoe, gave him two lanes of vision. The log house itself, although a bare dozen paces away, made only a dim silhouette.

An owl hooted from a grove down by the river. Terry thought he heard a trotting horse, heading this way up Ninth. The sounds stopped more than a block away; then a long quiet, broken only by a donkey braying from the Bull's-Head Corrals.

Squatting on his spurs, Terry picked up sand to sift it idly through his fingers. A roar crashed on his eardrums and pain knifed through him. The roar came from behind and he twisted around in time to see a second flash — gunfire not fifteen yards away. He whipped his own gun out and fired back. Again a flash from the dark and again he gave in kind, shooting at the flash. He could see nothing else.

The pain dizzied him but he knew it was Patterson. Patterson was pumping lead from the dark. The man's fourth shot was a hit and Terry bumped to his knees, still firing. Blood ran from his scalp and across his eyes. A fifth bullet came at him and through him, killing him with pain; but somehow his head was clear enough to know why and how the man could hit him, in the dark, with nearly every shot.

He could do it because Terry was neatly between him and the Ninth and Arapahoe lamp post. The man had maneuvered himself to that position before opening fire. He himself stood flattened against the black façade of the cabin. Again he fired and this time Terry fell on his face. Dizziness swamped him; in any case he was helpless, his gun empty.

So was Milo Patterson's. But Patterson, on his feet and unhit, reloaded. He took three steps forward to finish Terry, in case a breath of life were left there. He aimed with deliberation, began tripping the trigger, pumping still more lead into Terry. Then across the alley a window sash flew up and he heard a woman scream.

From the distant dark a police whistle blew. Patterson didn't dare wait longer. He holstered his gun and ran, dashing across Larimer and north along Ninth. In mid-block he came to his horse. Tonight he'd ridden a bay instead of the gray, and for that he was thankful. He raced off down Ninth to the river bottom, thundered across the Platte River bridge and took the Golden road.

Beyond the North Denver settlement he pulled off the trail and raced on across sod. He couldn't risk meeting anyone. At the Cross T they thought he was in bed. If he emerged from his cottage at daybreak, his alibi would be perfect.

Indeed he'd intended to stay there all night. At nine o'clock he and Arch Tomlinson had returned home from Golden where they'd gone to vote. Arch had stopped for a while at Patterson's cottage, for a drink and to speculate on the election. He'd left Patterson on the point of retiring. Later Patterson, restless, had felt a call from the fleshpots of Denver. There was still one full can of gold at his West Denver cache, plus an inch in another. Tonight, he'd thought, would be a good chance to get rid of another sixty ounces. At the same time he could pick up some easy money at the clubs.

218

Election bet winners would be flush and stakes would be high.

The full quart plus one inch, now, was lost forever. Police would find it there and take over. The luck of Patterson was that he wasn't, by any record, tied to the cabin. Some bump of discretion had kept him from recording the deed. The records would show the owner was a man named Riley, and Riley was dead.

Riley had signed a deed in a smoke-filled room one night at Fairplay, in a game where liquor flowed freely, and had tossed it into a jackpot. Just who'd won that jackpot even Riley might not have remembered a few weeks later. A West Denver cabin so old it needed to be torn down — nothing to cry about on Riley's part, or to be put with a rush on record by Patterson.

So he'd lost a quart of gold plus one inch, and plus the hush stake he'd paid Lopez, and an old log cabin. In return he'd rid himself of Woodford. Patterson cursed Woodford, slashed flesh with spurs and raced on through the night.

He entered the Cross T by a back pasture gate. A hundred yards short of the barn he dismounted, making sure hoofbeats wouldn't be heard. He led his mount cautiously to the barn and unsaddled. The lathered flanks would dry before morning. Patterson hung the saddle on its proper rack. The blanket, being damp with sweat, worried him a little. He carried it through the dark to his cottage.

Among old papers he found the deed signed by John Riley. Patterson had kept it, because if he'd succeeded in cashing all of the loot the house would no longer incriminate him. Now he laid the deed on his hearth and set fire to it. The mantel clock told him that daylight was still more than an hour away. All the Cross T would swear he'd been here all night. A sense of triumph swept through Patterson. How many bullets had he pumped into Woodford? At least four, perhaps six. When the last crumb of the deed was ash, he pulled off his boots and went to bed.

CHAPTER
TWENTY

Faith stood forlornly in the Hospital corridor. It was the Arapahoe County Hospital located on Cram Street, between Evans and Fourteenth. This was the fourth day she'd been here and still they hadn't let her see Terry Woodford.

Not that she could do anything for him. The doctors had given up all hope of saving him. Shot five times, they said. Literally riddled with bullets. Only his vigorous youth and a superb physical condition, they said, could explain the miracle of even a temporary survival.

A week had gone by since they'd brought him here. Most of the time since then he'd been unconscious. Once, when asked by Sheriff Brewster, "Did you see the man?" he'd weakly shaken his head in a negative. He didn't know. And even now neither did the law.

What they did know was sensational, and the news sheets had been full of it. Police had crashed into the Larimer Street cabin for a search. Under a floor they'd found two quart fruit cans — one full of gold dust and the other with only an inch of its treasure left. More important even than that, in line with them were five circular prints made by five similar cans whose weight, in the moist soil under the floor, had made impressions of startling significance. The solution in simple arithmetic was there and the dullest wit in Denver could see it. Two and five made seven.

There, beyond reasonable doubt, had been cached the gold stolen from Frank Barber.

And Faith knew now she hadn't been entirely fair to Terry Woodford. Twice she'd quarreled with him, and once she'd rather rudely sent him away. Now it was clear that on one point at issue he'd been right.

The thieves, she'd maintained as had nearly everyone else in Denver, had been Lopez and Brockmeyer. She'd been sure no other guilt was involved. Terry had contended that the two stage-station hostlers were only outsiders trying to cut in.

And clearly he'd been right. Lopez and Brockmeyer were dead. So guilt other than theirs had come creeping to the cache, there to find Terry waiting and to shoot him down. It left Faith sick at heart. She wanted to see Terry if possible; at least she could smile and say she was sorry.

Certainly she'd be too generous to remind him that on their other disagreement he'd been wrong and she right. For although a major criminal existed somewhere, he definitely wasn't Milo Patterson. Milo, that night, had been twelve miles from Denver at the Cross T. The Tomlinsons and their Chinese servant vouched for it.

A nurse came out into the hall. "It's no use for you to wait any longer, Miss Harlan."

Faith looked at her hopefully. "You mean he's asleep?"

"Not asleep. His eyes are open but he wouldn't know you." The nurse smiled sadly. "And perhaps you'd hardly know *him*, either. His loss of blood was terrible." A man was coming down the hall. She stopped him. "You can't go in, sheriff."

Chet Brewster shrugged. "Okay. He already shook his head when I asked if he saw the guy. Just thought I'd ask him again."

Faith was moving away and the sheriff caught up with her at the front walk. His horse was tied at a rack there. "You're Frank Barber's niece, ain't you?"

"Yes."

He cocked an eye, smiling. "You can tell your aunt, miss, that it's gonna come to about sixteen thousand dollars."

"You mean Uncle Frank's estate?"

Brewster nodded. "It's up to the court, y'understand, and it'll take a long time. But we got one more reason, now, for thinking it's Frank Barber's dust we found under that floor."

"One more reason?" The question came absently from Faith. Her mind was on Terry Woodford.

"On a shelf of his Elk Valley cabin were some unopened fruit cans. Pendleton Pears, in quarts. Those two cans we found in West Denver still had the labels on 'em, *Pendleton Pears*."

"I'll tell my aunt," Faith said.

The sheriff stepped into his saddle. Faith stood on the walk and watched him ride away.

He came again to the hospital, as did Faith herself. With an amazing vitality Terry Woodford clung to life.

Many came to inquire about him, or to bring flowers, but it was mid-December before visitors were admitted to his bedside. It would take a long, long time, the doctors said. But the impossible had happened. The crisis was passed and some day this cowboy would ride again.

Five months, they estimated, or six. Probably by April or May Terry could leave his bed.

Those who came oftenest were Slim and Jase. Slim's grin spread from ear to ear when he learned Terry would eventually get well. They wouldn't let Terry talk. But Slim was permitted to stand by the bed and joke about last month's election, and about how long the icicles were that hung, Slim swore, from Judson's mustaches on the day they'd left Elk Valley.

"We brung down five hun'erd head, kid. Everything over two year old. Brung 'em down last week after they'd been knee-deep in that mountain vega since August. We was sure lucky. Ordinarily winter would've covered the feed a month sooner."

"It was that extra month," Jase put in, "that made beef outa them steers. Shovin' 'em down the bill was plumb easy. Shipped 'em to Omaha and what do yuh reckon they brung?" Jase took a telegram from his pocket and waved it.

Terry, his eyes dull and his bony face still pale, didn't seem to grasp what it meant.

"Means you an' me are outa debt." Slim grinned. "We don't owe Jase a dime. And they's still five hun'erd yearlin's up there in the hills. Every head that pulls through'll be velvet." He turned to the nurse. "Anybody told him how the 'lection came out?"

The nurse smiled and shook her head.

"They done us Democrats dirt, kid. We rounded up more votes than they did. Our man Tilden won it, hands down. But they worked a shenanigan. Tossed it into Congress for some kind of a post mortem showdown. By the time they got through makin' passes, they figgered Hayes was elected by one vote."

The nurse intervened. "That will be enough for today." She shooed the callers from the room.

Just as they reached the Cram Street sidewalk a ranch rig drew up. It was a Cross T rig with Arch Tomlinson driving. Arch helped his sister Victoria as she stepped down on the carriage block. Both of them knew Jase Judson and Jase presented Slim.

Victoria raised her veil. She looked with interest at Slim. "I've been wanting to talk to you, young man. Your partner Terry Woodford once quoted you on the subject of alfalfa."

"It's right good feed, ma'am. Down in New Mex they mow it three times a season."

"If pests get the first two crops," Victoria remembered, "you still have the third one left." She seemed to consider it tremendously important.

"That's the way it works," Slim affirmed.

Archie broke in. "And we'd like to have you tell us about the cattle you're wintering in the high country." He had a florist's box under his arm. "Tell you what. Soon as Vic and I pay our respects to the patient, why don't you meet us at Charpiot's for lunch?"

At Charpiot's the head waiter led them to a table for four. It was by a window looking out on Larimer Street where buckboards and buggies, carts and freight wagons, passed in an endless stream. The driver of a street car team clanged his bell at a huckster who was blocking the track.

Arch Tomlinson, the perfect host, ordered of Charpiot's best.

His sister gave most of her attention to Slim. "This alfalfa?" she questioned. "Is it easy to get started?"

"No ma'am. It's *hard* to get started. You got to plow deep. Then you got to sow it with a nurse crop. Oats, we used down in New Mex."

"A nurse crop?"

"Yes'm. If you plant the alfalfa seed by itself it'll sprout up so thin and tender the sun'll kill it. So you plant oats with it. They come up together and the oats grows tallest, for the first month or two, and shades the skinny little alfalfa stalks. That way the sun don't hurt it none. You irrigate it plenty and when the oats gets stirrup-high you mow it. By that time the alfalfa's strong enough so the sun won't hurt it any more. And it keeps comin' up year after year. Heck, I know alfalfa meadows down along the Rio Grande that was planted long before the Civil War and not a seed dropped on 'em since. And they still make three pea-green cuttin's a year."

Jase told them about the cattle in Elk Valley. And Slim, looking out, saw a buckboard drive up. In it were Milo Patterson and Faith Harlan. Patterson helped the girl down, tying his team at Charpiot's rack.

226

Sight of the man made bristles rise on Slim's neck. "Me an' that guy's gonna have a showdown some day," he muttered.

"Why?" asked Arch Tomlinson.

"'Cause nobody'll ever make me believe he didn't gun Terry Woodford. And look at him now! Sparkin' that nice young gal after robbin' her dead uncle!"

Archie stiffened a little. "You're rather mistaken, aren't you?" he corrected. "He was at the ranch that night. I myself was with him. The chap happens to be my partner, you know."

Patterson was bringing Faith inside. They appeared in the dining room and a waiter seated them at the rear. Victoria met their eyes and nodded a greeting. Her brother waved a hand.

"Archie's right," Victoria said to Slim. Her British sense of fair play was working. "Mr. Patterson was at home that night on the Cross T."

Slim grimaced. "Sorry I popped off," he said. He looked out at Patterson's rig and saw what seemed to be a sack of groceries in the back of it. "Patterson batches in your bunkhouse — I mean your guest cottage? Lives all alone there?"

"Right," Archie said. He steered the talk back to crops and cattle.

Slim fixed his mind on Patterson. Usually the man rode horseback to Denver. His use of a buckboard today meant that he needed to haul back groceries for his bachelor quarters at the ranch. The sack suggested that the marketing had already been done.

An idea came to Slim. His mind closed on it. Even Jase didn't know what it was when, a few minutes later, the group parted company on the walk outside.

The Tomlinsons went to their rig and drove away. Jase sauntered up Larimer toward the Grand Central. Patterson and Faith were still in Charpiot's dining room.

People on the walks paid no attention to Slim Baker as he went to a one-seater whose team was tied at a rack. Calmly Slim took a sack of groceries from it and walked half a block to a parked farm wagon. He dumped the groceries in its bed. If any passerby noticed him at all, he'd suppose Slim to be the wagon's master.

With the empty sack Slim proceeded to the nearest grocery store. "Gimme seven quart cans," he said, "of Pendleton Pears."

The grocer brought them from a shelf. Slim paid for them, put them in the sack and walked out.

A minute later he placed the sack exactly where it belonged, in the back of Patterson's rig.

Patterson whistled cheerfully as he drove home. An aura of contentment hung over him. Faith was getting friendlier all the time. He had a feeling he was making progress with her. He wouldn't rush her. There was plenty of time. When the stakes were big Milo Patterson had the gift of patience.

He opened the Cross T gate and drove through.

Yes, everything was rosy. Dividends from the Columbine Club had doubled his expectations. Mort Jardine was already paid off in full. True, Patterson had failed to cash in the last fifth of the Frank Barber stake.

But it made no great difference. A year from now he'd be a millionaire and take his bride to the finest house on Colfax Hill. A year after that he'd be lieutenant governor and two years later they'd send him to Washington. With a future like that how could Faith Harlan, or any other girl, say no?

At the Cross T barn he unhitched, hung up the harness and turned the team to pasture. Twice he'd offered to employ a roustabout at his own expense, but the Tomlinsons' stiff pride forbade it. When grass grew again and the place was on a paying basis, they'd go in with him to re-stock and re-man the ranch. Until then the austerity operation must continue.

Still blithely whistling, Milo Patterson carried his sack of groceries to the cottage. He dumped them on the table — then froze at what he saw there. Not the sugar, salt, coffee and beans he'd bought, but seven quart cans. Pears! Pendleton Pears!

It meant someone knew! Not Terry Woodford, for that snooping cowboy was bedridden. Yet someone knew his guilt and was taunting him with it. Serena! Who else could it be? Serena with her veiled threats, her hints of holding a whip-hand over him!

It had to be Serena. Opportunity? After buying the groceries he'd hitched briefly in front of the American House. She could have tipped a bellboy or porter to do it; or she might even have made the exchange herself.

Why? She'd do it to make him realize her power. To remind him that she knew; that she could control him at will; could command him, if she liked, to stop seeing Faith Harlan. For a long time he'd been aware of her

229

fiercely smouldering jealousy. He'd ignored it. And more and more, these late weeks, he'd ignored the woman herself. Except as a gambling partner he'd pushed her out of his life.

Now she was fighting back. Black blood climbed Patterson's cheekbones as he stared at her challenge. She must be dealt with at once.

CHAPTER
TWENTY-ONE

Serena stood at her hotel room window looking out on Sixteenth. Gray dusk was descending on Denver. A man with a short ladder moved briskly up the opposite walk. He set his ladder against a lamp post, ascended three rungs and from there reached up to light a gas jet at the top. Off he went to the next lamp post; then on to another. Serena watched in abstraction as, one by one, the night lights began glimmering along the street.

Frustration left her restless and indecisive, with a growing feeling of checkmate in her campaign to control Milo Patterson. True she knew things which could destroy him. By smileveiled hints she'd let him suspect she knew them. It hadn't helped her any. He was still running around with Faith Harlan. This very day he'd taken her to lunch. Hints had failed. Nothing was left except to threaten boldly.

Fear of him kept her from it. He'd killed Tony Raegan and had emptied his gun ruthlessly into Terry Woodford. So why would he hesitate to kill Serena? Fear of it drew her fangs, nullified her power.

That was her dilemma. At first it had seemed easy. Until the Raegan killing she'd known him only as a bold adventurer, a sky-limit gambler and a princely spender. She'd supposed their common knowledge of his guilt would draw him to her.

Now she knew better. He'd have no scruples against killing her.

Dining alone tonight had no appeal for Serena. She summoned a hotel boy and told him to bring coffee to her room. Then she began dressing for her duties at the Columbine. The green gown she brought out put salt in her bitterness. She'd paid for it herself. Patterson had stopped her charge account at Joslin's.

When the knock came she supposed it was the boy with the coffee. Serena covered herself with a negligee to let him in.

The smile, as she saw who was there, froze on her face. "Oh, it's you! I thought you were out to the ranch, Milo."

He came in, the black-blooded flush still riding his cheekbones. It made her back away from him. He kicked the door shut. Then step by step he advanced toward her and what she saw in his eyes flooded her with terror.

"Thought you were smart, didn't you?" His voice lashed. "Real cute, weren't you?" She had no idea what he meant.

She tried to laugh but panic choked her. She was still backing away from him when the bed stopped her. His challenge chopped at her again. "What are you trying to do, anyway? Shake me down?"

She managed to gasp, "I don't know what you mean, Milo!"

232

"Oh! So you don't know a thing about it?" As he reached out for her she screamed. It was only a half scream because by then his hands had her throat. Fury made him livid as his fingers cut into her flesh. "Listen, you sweet little witch! Don't lie to me. I know what you did. If you ever do it again I'll kill you. You hear me?" His fingers pressed harder, stopping her breath, bulging her eyes. "This is only a sample. I'll kill you, next time."

He flung her from him. She fell across the bed with her head bumping a brass bedpost. Only half conscious, she lay on her back staring up at him. "Remember this," he lashed at her, "next time you feel like getting smart."

He turned and walked out, slamming the door with a force that rattled the windowpanes.

For minutes Serena lay fighting for breath. When the knock came she didn't at first hear it. Then the hotel boy's voice called to her. "Your coffee, Miss Chalmers."

She got weakly to her feet, pulling the negligee around her. The boy mustn't see her. "Take it away," she said hoarsely.

It would need something stronger than coffee now. She found it on her closet shelf. Brandy. Her hand shook as she filled a glass. The liquor burned its way down her bruised throat.

Patterson! What did he think she'd done? The mirror showed her bloodless face and her shoulders shrugged convulsively. If he'd come *that* close to killing her on a mere suspicion, what would he do if she really gave him cause?

After a second drink an hysterical vindictiveness began supplanting fear. Presently it drove her to a decision. She'd fight back at Milo Patterson. He'd think she wouldn't dare, that he'd cowed her into cringing submission. But there was a way to fight back and she'd do it.

Her wits were too shattered to make any detailed plans now. She summoned a boy and sent word to the club that she wouldn't go on duty tonight.

Then she bolted her door. Suppose she told tales on Patterson! Just what tales would she tell and to whom?

If she told the police they'd arrest her for suppressing evidence till now. To cut off Patterson's nose she'd be spiting her own face. Her revenge would be dearly bought. There must be a safer way; a way to control him and still hold him at bay.

In all, what did she know about Patterson?

First, he'd stolen a girl's photograph at the time seven quarts of gold had also disappeared from the same cabin. She'd seen the photograph in his wallet. However, he'd deny it and she could offer no proof except her own word.

Second, he'd been contacted by Manuel Lopez just before Lopez had acquired a hundred ounces of the stolen gold. There again was a point she knew but couldn't prove.

Third, he was the real owner of the Columbine Club. That fact she could expose by inviting an inspection of the corporation books. The exposure would prejudice Patterson with Faith Harlan but wouldn't particularly interest the police.

Fourth, she could prove he owned the log house in West Denver. That would incriminate' him because the loot had been cached there, Terry Woodford had been shot there, and Tony Raegan had been murdered near there.

Serena's wits fastened on item four. She could establish it anonymously without any jeopardy to herself. Once Milo had told her about a poker game at Fairplay. He'd mentioned the players: himself, John Riley, Swede Olsen, Chuck Ferris and Hank Delaney. The unique thing about the game had been Patterson's winning of a house and lot from John Riley.

He'd told her about it in a letter while she was still at Santa Fe, at a time when ownership of the house had been in no way incriminating. Serena still had the letter. That was why she could name the players with certainty and spell their names correctly. "Ask Swede Olsen, Chuck Ferris and Hank Delaney," she could anonymously tip the police, "who won John Riley's house in a card game at Fairplay."

Police would follow it up. The result would tie Patterson to the house and to its guilty secret.

But Serena was still disturbed. What she needed most was complete protection against Patterson. Also she wanted a sword over his head. She must load a gun, cock it, point it at Patterson, then be able to say to him: "It will go off, Milo, if I'm found dead or if I mysteriously disappear."

Putting her evidence in a safety bank box didn't occur to Serena. Private bank boxes were an innovation and she didn't have one of her own. Valuables, such as jewels, she usually kept in the safe of her hotel. She couldn't quite see how to safeguard her secret in a hotel safe in a way to insure its exposure after, and only after, another assault on her by Patterson.

She lay restlessly all night, back of her bolted door, trying to conjure up some solid, safe way to defy Patterson.

At breakfast in the morning she read the latest papers. In vain she looked for some item about Patterson. Something which would suggest a reason for his fury. But the papers didn't mention him.

An item said that Jase Judson and Slim Baker were in town to see Terry Woodford. Today Judson and Slim were going out to the O Bar ranch south of Littleton. Occasionally during the winter they'd ride up to Elk Valley to check on their cattle there.

The same item said that Terry Woodford was expected to pull through but would be hospitalized till April or May. The doctors wouldn't permit his removal to the O Bar ranch, his condition requiring expert nursing.

The vague idea first came to Serena when she went out into the hotel lobby and saw a ranchman in the act of registering. "I left a bag in storage here," he reminded the clerk.

Range folk, Serena knew, were always doing that. Since only a slicker roll could be carried back of a saddle cantle, a rangeman would otherwise have no change of clothes for his weekend in Denver.

Terry Woodford, probably, would be no exception. According to the papers he'd stayed at the Grand

Central on Larimer. Being now bedridden at a hospital, he'd have no use for his bag there. Almost surely the hotel was holding it for him.

Serena brooded over it all morning. At noon she walked three blocks to the Grand Central Hotel. She took lunch there.

After lunch she whiled away an hour in the lobby. A bellboy brought her a magazine. "Isn't this where that cowboy lived?" she asked him. "The one who got shot over in West Denver?"

"It sure is, ma'am."

"His things are still here, I suppose."

"They sure are, ma'am. We're holdin' 'em in the baggage room."

Presently Serena wandered to the rear of the lobby and on to an alcove where guests could write letters. For a short while she seemed to be writing a letter. Actually she wrote nothing at all. But when some diversion in the street attracted the clerk and the boy and a few guests to the front windows, Serena made a quick reconnaissance.

She darted down a corridor. The corridor led to an open alley door. Just short of it another door gave into a sample room. There was one quite like it at the American House, and Serena went in for a quick look.

A drummer had a trunk open and was putting drygoods samples on a table for display. Humming as he worked he paid only casual attention to Serena. She passed him and went to a tiered rack where cubbyholes held checked baggage. Each nook had a tag with a name on it. Serena looked from name to name. The drummer perhaps assumed she was a hotel guest who needed something from, a bag she'd checked here.

Serena touched nothing. Soon she spotted the name Woodford. The cowboy had left a battered black Gladstone here. By it lay a slicker roll. Serena murmured: "Oh, bother! It isn't here after all." That was for the drummer's benefit as she swished by him and out.

Later, in her room at the American, she printed information on a sheet of white paper. Neither her own name nor Patterson's appeared.

ASK SWEDE OLSEN, CHUCK FERRIS AND HANK DELANEY WHO WON JOHN RILEY'S HOUSE IN A CARD GAME AT FAIRPLAY, LAST APRIL. THEN YOU'LL KNOW WHO SHOT WOODFORD AND RAEGAN.

She sealed it in an envelope which she addressed, in square printing, to Terry Woodford. It was in her muff as she went to a late supper at the Grand Central.

The place to put the envelope, she'd decided, was not in the bag but in the slicker roll. During convalescence a hospital patient conceivably might send for his bag but not for his slicker roll. That he would need only when ahorse on the range.

After supper Serena pretended to write letters. When the coast was clear she darted down the rear corridor. At this late hour the sample room was empty. She took Terry's slicker roll from its rack. Only one blanket was rolled in it. Serena put her envelope in the folds of the blanket, re-rolled and re-roped everything, put it back in the proper nook.

This time, covered by the darkness, she left via the alley. The alley emerged on Seventeenth and presently she was safely home at the American. From there, by cab, she went on to her evening duties at the Columbine Club.

"Feeling better?" the manager asked her.

"Rotten." And she looked anything but gay. "By the way, if Milo Patterson drops in tonight, tell him I want to see him."

Around midnight Patterson did drop in. He came to her and looked sullenly apologetic. "Okay, Serena. So I made a mistake. I just found out you didn't do it."

"Didn't do what?"

"You were at a hairdresser's between ten and noon. That was the only time you could do it. Never mind what. Sorry."

"You'd better be. Because I've just taken out some insurance, Milo."

"Insurance?" He gaped at her. "What kind?"

"Life insurance." Serena smiled bitterly and put a hand to her throat. Fifty customers saw but couldn't hear them. "Now get this straight, Milo, and be warned."

She told him everything about her hidden message except its place of concealment. "It's where it's certain to be found, Milo, unless I take it away myself. Which is something I can't do if I'm dead."

She turned her back on him and walked away. Joining a group at the roulette table she balked every attempt Patterson could make for further words with her. He kept trying, tagging her from game to game. Always she managed to keep a third person present. At three in the morning Patterson was still there, seething under the surface, and the look on his face panicked her again. "Alfred," she said to the club's immaculate bouncer, "I'm a little dizzy tonight. Will you see me home in a cab?"

Alfred was devoted to her. He saw her home in a cab. Patterson, impotently fuming, stood on the Holladay Street walk and watched them drive, away.

For many nights after that Serena slept behind a bolted door. Her gun was loaded and cocked and pointed at Milo Patterson. He knew that any violence of his own would unleash its trigger.

Twice he waylaid her in a restaurant. Each time she smiled sweetly, invited him to sit down, then beckoned a waiter. Before a waiter he was mute. Many times he knocked on the door of her room. Never would she unbolt it when she knew he was there. Then: "I'm dressing, Milo. See you at the club."

A dozen dealers, plus Alfred, were her armor at the club. The Christmas season came and went. Two light snows fell in late December and another just after the new year began. Each day Serena read the *News*, alert for all mentions of a cowboy invalid. His improvement was slow, she learned. He'd be confined in the hospital at least till May.

240

Other items told about a grazing experiment of epic import for the Colorado range. Five hundred head of young cattle had been left in the high country, and would either survive or perish there. Stockmen from all over the west were writing inquiries about it. The *News* published them. One old lady wrote in to insist, indignantly, that the owners should be prosecuted for cruelty to animals, letting those poor yearlings stay out all winter without anything to eat. A letter from Slim Baker answered her.

Lady, we'd like to keep them critturs alive same as you would. You tell us where some feed is and we'll sure fork it to 'em. We could ship 'em to the packin' house, but that'd be kinda cruel too, wouldn't it? All we're doin', lady, is givin' 'em a chance to live a couple of years longer. Some of 'em will and some of 'em won't.

Good luck struck Slim and Jason and was duly reported. A warm chinook blew down South Park and made the Platte Canyon, for a week in mid-January, almost balmy. In the high country around Shawn's Crossing only the drifts were left to cheat the elk and five hundred head of O Bar cattle from life-giving forage. Slim came down to sit by Terry Woodford's bed. "We ain't lost but three-four so far," Slim exulted. "Which could happen in any man's pasture, high or low."

Terry, flat on his back, gave a pale smile. "How bad are they scattered, Slim?"

"All the way from Crow Hill to Turkey Crik," Slim said. "Over on Buffalo Crik they's about two mile of open fiats where the wind swept the grass bare. Hundred head or so of our stuff are doin' right good there. Funny how they can find them places, first blizzard comes along."

Two weeks later he came again and was less cheerful. "That Buffalo Crik patch is a foot deep, cowboy. It driv our stuff downhill some. They're gantin' up and if we don't get another chinook we'll lose plenty."

Deep snow blocked Kenosha Pass, he said, and the stage road to Leadville was closed. "But all our stuff's this side of Shawn's Crossin'. What I could find of it had its backs humped and you can count ribs again. Every pine limb in the woods has got icicles."

That was the first week in February. Terry didn't see Slim again all month. But Faith called twice, once with her aunt and once alone.

Terry felt pampered and useless — and guilty, for instead of thinking of poor old Slim, out battling to keep their stock alive, here he lay like a stupid drone watching the door for Faith, waiting to hear her footsteps come down the hall.

When she did come her cheeks were whipped to a cherry red by the raw winter wind; soft tendrils of her hair escaped from the parka of her cape and Terry just sank back on his pillow, surrendering to an adoration which grew with each new sight of her.

She pushed back the parka and held out an icy little hand. "I've been sleighing, Terry. Everything is so white and beautiful."

242

Terry wanted to ask, "Who with?" But he could easily guess and some of the brightness left his eyes. "Sleigh waitin' for you?" he asked instead. She nodded and their moment was gone. Patterson was outside.

"So I can't stay but a minute," Faith said. "Just long enough to tell what Slim and Jase Judson are cooking up. A big celebration for May first out at the O Bar ranch. I mean if everything turns out all right."

The few details she gave absorbed Terry. For a minute he forgot Patterson and the sleigh.

But Serena Chalmers couldn't, not for a single breath. Restlessness grew within Serena. Her scheme for holding Patterson at bay had no future, no permanence. Before May she must substitute another. Otherwise her cocked trigger would fall and expose the man. Maybe he'd be convicted and maybe not. If not he'd be free to kill her. And if they convicted him she'd lose her soft and highly remunerative berth at the Columbine. Right now, with dividends and salary, it was reaping her a fortune.

It could go on indefinitely except for the deadline of a cowboy's release from a hospital. Serena tried to think of some other container, for her evidence, something permanent which would serve the same purpose.

An idea came when she realized the complete devotion of the giant bouncer, Alfred. Whenever there'd been any danger of running into Patterson, she'd make Alfred take her home in a cab. The man had the strength of Goliath combined with loyalty and a calm discretion.

Early in March she decided to take the envelope from Terry Woodford's slicker roll and give it to Alfred. She could say to him: "Keep this in your room till I ask you to give it back to me."

No bank would be safer than Alfred.

On a balmy noon Serena took lunch at the Grand Central. Later she slipped back to the sample room. Again a drummer was putting wares on display and again she drew no especial attention.

Until a gasp of alarm escaped her. She stood staring at an empty cubbyhole. The bag and the slicker roll weren't there.

After a shocked moment Serena hurried forward to the lobby. She found a bellboy and asked him, "Isn't Terry Woodford still at the hospital?"

"Yes'm," the boy said. "Be laid up a month or two yet, they say. But his side-kick came by the other day and picked up his baggage. Took it out to the O Bar ranch. Whatsematter? You feelin' sick, lady?"

CHAPTER
TWENTY-TWO

The cocked gun had been fired. Or rather an arrow was in flight and couldn't be called back. The fact in turn terrified Serena and in turn gave her a savage elation. The evidence would destroy Patterson. With equal passions she loved him, hated him, feared him. Now she'd unleashed a force which would destroy him. And why not? That question she asked herself over and over. He'd walked out on her, hadn't he, for another woman? He'd throttled her to within an inch of her life. So why regret sealing his fate? Or fear him, since her own name didn't appear in the evidence?

How long would it take? The cowboy's release from a hospital was no longer the deadline. The thing would come to light, now, only when he rode out on the range and got caught in a shower. Or when he needed to take the camp blanket from his slicker roll. He might be back on the O Bar a month or more before either of those things happened.

Serena waited, holding her breath, half minded to run, electing finally to brazen it out. On duty she hovered close to Alfred. Off duty she barred her door against Patterson.

★   ★   ★

On the last day of March callers at the hospital found Terry sitting up in a wheelchair. His face was beginning to fill out and his eyes, which had been dark caves, had recaptured some of their old sparkle.

"Howdy, folks," he greeted. "Awful nice of you to send me that candy, Faith."

"You deserve it," she smiled, "after the bird seed they feed you here."

"I could eat a steer," he boasted. "It's sure nice to see you, Miss Tomlinson. And you, Arch."

The Tomlinsons, who'd brought Faith with them, drew up chairs. The nurse brought one for Faith and then left the room. "Patched you up, have they old fellow?" Arch asked.

Terry nodded, grinning. Rolling a cigaret, he looked guiltily at the closed door. "If that nurse smells this twirly we'll claim you smoked it, Arch."

Faith pretended to look stern. "You have to obey rules," she said.

"Mr. Jase Judson," Victoria announced, "came by and invited us to his celebration. It's set for May first, you know."

"And they're taking me along," Faith put in. "Slim says you'll be home by that time, Terry."

"Half the valley'll be there," Arch predicted.

"Including the Denver Board of Trade," Faith added. Then she laughed. "Slim sent a special invitation to a certain banker. The one who turned you down on a loan last fall."

246

"No one believed it was possible," Victoria said. "So now they must see it with their own eyes."

Terry knew the general plan of it. About four hundred of the winter-bound cattle had survived. Which was a loss of only twenty percent. No further loss was likely, since the herd had drifted down to the six thousand foot level where the first green of spring grass was beginning to show. Should April storms come, they could be safely weathered. Slim planned to time his drive into an O Bar pasture for the morning of May first.

And there Jase Judson would have a barbecue prepared for perhaps a hundred guests. Terry looked at Faith and grinned. "It'll sure be somethin' to show 'em. Cattle wintered in the high country, just like the deer and the elk."

Out on the O Bar, in rich bottomland along Plum Creek, Jase Judson was plowing. Except when the ground was frozen he'd been doing it every day since February. He'd made a stout four-horse evener out of a black locust sapling and he'd hitched four Percherons to it. They'd had to grain the team generously, to get the power needed for deep plowing.

Slim Baker, with another team hitched to a harrow, came along behind. The smell of the black earth was good. Circling the bottomland ran a ditch, ready to flood this meadow at will. Jase came to the end of his furrow. He unlooped the reins from around his neck, bit off a chew and waited there for Slim.

"We'll be done by nightfall, fellah. A hun'erd acres. Hope it sprouts by May first, Slim. I want them folks to see it."

"It won't be more'n an inch high by then. Just enough to make the ground green."

"Tomorrow I'll let you broadcast the alfalfy, Slim. I'll come along behind with the oats."

Planting the meadow took three days. A planting of alfalfa seed with oats added for a nurse crop. When the last seed was dropped, Slim towed a log drag over the field. The drag made it smooth as glass. The sky was overcast and fluffy flakes began falling just as he finished.

All that night and the next day the flakes came down. It was a wet, heavy snow which melted almost at once. Jase was elated. "Just what the doctor ordered, Slim."

"Heap better'n an irrigation," Slim agreed. "Didn't wash any seed away."

Across the South Platte, along Bear Creek, Jase had two Mexican boys keeping an eye on the cattle. He rode over for a check on them. And Slim, hitching up an O Bar rig, drove into Denver.

Terry was waiting impatiently. This was the day set for his release. He looked at the rig and complained: "What? Still babyin' me? Why didn't you bring me a saddle horse, Slim?"

"Don't get funny, kid. You couldn't ride a burro, the shape you're in."

"I already picked up your duffel," Slim said as they drove through town, "and took it out to the ranch. So we don't need to stop at the hotel."

248

The road followed the Rio Grande track to the settlement of Littleton. Plum Creek came in from the south and Slim took a rutted ranch trail there. A few miles up the creek they passed through the O Bar gate.

Spring was on the ground and in the air, winging to them from the blossoms of wild plum and wild cherry. The cottonwoods were still gaunt, leafless. A great crane flew from one of them and flapped awkwardly upcreek. Terry saw a fenced meadow, plowed and harrowed and dragged, black with moisture. Something jumped in him and he wanted to sing. A crop would come there which grasshoppers would never completely despoil. Like Slim said, they wouldn't need to insult this range any more by calling it Grasshopper Valley.

The buildings above the meadow were crude, adobe-walled and flat-roofed. Nothing fancy like the Cross T on Clear Creek. "We're home, kid," Slim announced. Jase Judson came out banging on a tin pan. "Come an' git it, cowboys. Jackrabbit pie and frijoles."

Inside Terry found a battered hotel bag on his bunk. "Where's my slicker roll, Slim?"

"Out at the barn," Slim told him. "I tied it back of your saddle."

Terry saw it there when he made a tour of inspection. Jase noted a yearning look in his eye. With the result that the next time Terry walked down to the barn he failed to find the saddle at all. "I hid it," Jase admitted with a wink toward Slim. "Only way I can keep you from gettin' bucked off."

"We promised Faith," Slim said solemnly, "we wouldn't let you bust any broncs for a while yet. You gotta ride a bunk fer another coupla weeks."

Terry beat that estimate a little. By mid-April he'd found his saddle and was in it. All he did was circle the meadow to look at tiny green shoots sprouting there. "Oats," Slim said. "The alfalfy won't show for a few days yet." He cocked an eye upward at clouds. "I see we're gonna get another free irrigation."

The wet snow in late April was the best of all. After sunshine had sopped it up the oats grew like magic. Jase picked out a grove along the creek and dug his barbecue pit there. For two months he'd been graining a young steer.

When the big day came, Terry and Jase were waiting at the lower gate. They were asaddle, Jase in his Sunday best and with his mustaches neatly combed. Neither man wore a gun belt. Today they were hosts armed only with smiles and open hands.

The morning sun shone brightly. "But it's been cloudin' up a bit every afternoon, lately," Jase worried. Each of them had a slicker roll tied back of his saddle.

"There they come!" Terry announced.

A cavalcade was in sight, heading this way from Littleton. In the interest of pageantry the Denver Board of Trade had arranged for all guests to arrive in a single impressive column.

On it came, ranchers from the lower Platte, from Bear and Clear creeks, and some from as far away as Greeley. Bankers and shippers were there, hotel men and merchants, anyone interested in the agrarian future of this range. Buckboards, buggies, surreys and saddle horses. As each rig passed through the gate Terry yelled a greeting and waved his hat. All the Denver papers were represented. The *Rocky Mountain News* man pulled up by Terry. "Hi, cowboy. Don't get the idea we've quit on you. The *News*'ll never quit — till it finds out who shot you up. You and Tony Raegan."

The last rig was from the Cross T with Arch Tomlinson driving. Victoria and Faith sat on the back seat, the Englishwoman holding an open parasol.

"Sure glad to see you folks." Terry greeted them all but with eyes only for Faith. Faith in a blue dress with a tight little basque and a white frill at her throat, her eyes sparkling.

"Follow me!" Judson yelled. He rode toward a cottonwood grove, guiding the caravan to a barbecue pit there. Two of his neighbors had loaned him their cooks. These stood by with huge forks, ready to serve. "Come and grab it!" one of them shouted.

There were camp seats and trays for the ladies. Ranchwomen from distant valleys mingled, gossiping energetically. Some of them scarcely ever saw other women except at rangewide picnics like this. Those who'd arrived first made room for Faith and Victoria.

"This *is* a treat!" A Morrison girl laughed gayly. "Men waiting on us women!"

Terry was passing out trays to them loaded with juicy beef and sourdough bread. "Everybody's been waitin' on me." He grinned. "My turn now."

251

Men stood in line and served themselves. A farmer from the lower Platte gazed off across the meadow. "Looks like a purty good stand of baby oats you got out there."

"Oats ain't all," Jase said proudly. "Tell 'em what's under it, Terry."

"The oats," Terry told them, "is just a nurse crop for alfalfa."

Some weren't familiar with alfalfa. Denver had been settled originally by colonists from Georgia and later by immigrants from the midwest.

"Slim Baker gave us the dope on it," Jase said. "Tell 'em Terry."

"You plant alfalfa only once," Terry said. "Then all you've got to do is mow it and stack it three times a year. Last cutting comes in October after all the hoppers, if you had 'em that season, have come and gone."

A feed merchant put in: "I've seen it along the Arkansas below Pueblo. Plenty of it down along the Picketwire. Every cowshed on the Rio Grande's got a falfy stack on it. Wherever you find Mexicans you'll find alfalfa."

"Anybody know," inquired the *News* man, "when they first started growing it?"

Terry didn't know. Neither did Jase. Surprisingly the answer came from Faith Harlan. "When Terry told me about it at the hospital," she said, "I went to the library and looked it up. The Spaniards brought it to South America in the sixteenth century. In 1854 some gold seekers brought alfalfa seed from Chile to California.

About that same time it came up from Mexico to the Rio Grande Valley. Since then it's been the base of the entire agrarian culture of the Southwest. In California they still call it 'Chilian Clover.'"

Terry grinned and gave a low whistle. "Those are awful big words, Faith. But I reckon you're right. And if we do the same thing up here along the Platte, maybe we won't have any more feed famines like the last two years."

A lowing of cattle came from downcreek and drew attention that way. A long line of red and white was moving toward them with Slim Baker riding point. Behind, whirling ropes and shouting, were two Mexican boys.

"That's the O Bar outfit," Jase announced proudly. "Everybody take a look."

"And if I'm not mistaken," a Board of Trade man added, "it's just made Colorado history."

Food was deserted as all guests moved forward to the open meadow. The herd was nearly opposite them now. "It's long yearlings and short two-year-olds, mostly," Jase told them. "They wintered in the high country, right along with the deer and the elk."

The *Rocky Mountain News* man had the figures. "You put a thousand head up there last August, didn't you, Jase? Skin-and-bones stuff ready for the glue factories. By early December they had enough flesh to make beef and you shipped five hundred to market. The rest stayed in the mountains and you saved four out of five."

Jase nodded. "There they are. Count 'em."

The stock was thin but not dangerously weak. From now on they'd gain daily. Every stockman present was impressed.

But a Denver banker missed the point. "I can't see you've proved anything, Judson, except that Elk Valley had a little less snow than usual."

"What we proved," Terry Woodford cut in, "is that mountain grass is a sight stronger than we thought it was. Once it's cured, with a head on it, it's got the strength of grain — a strength prairie grass doesn't have. High country grass goes farther, stays longer on a cow's ribs. If it didn't, every one of those cattle'd be dead."

The herd was stringing by, a big O Bar showing on each flank. One cow seemed a year older than the others. "That's Bessie," Jase boasted. "She wins the ribbon. 'Cause Bessie wintered up there *two* years 'stead of only one."

"What counts," Terry persisted, "is that it can set a pattern for Colorado stock raising. You put your stuff in the mountain forests all summer and fall. You let that strong feed up there work its magic. Meantime you're down here on the flats stackin' alfalfa. Three crops of it. If grasshoppers get two, you still got one left. So you feed it to those mountain-fat cattle when snow drives 'em home to you."

A low rumble was heard overhead. Terry became aware the sun wasn't shining. "Speakin' of snowtime," a farmer said, "it'll be raintime in a few minutes."

However no one minded. Most of them trooped back into the grove to re-fill coffee cups. Most of the

254

stockmen looked thoughtful. One of them asked Terry, "Where could I get some of that falfy seed, son?"

Another stood pulling at his lip. "Reckon we'll ever get to ranchin' that way, young man? Like you said, high country grass for summer and low country hay for winter?"

"I'd bet on it," Terry said. "And I'll bet on something else. High country grass and low country hay, in the long run, will put more money in Denver banks than all the gold in Gregory Gulch and all the silver in Leadville."

"Hi, folks!" Slim Baker came loping into their midst. "Did you save some for me?"

Faith filled a plate for him. As she was getting his coffee a drop of rain spanked her cheek. Again came a rumble from the sky.

Some of the crowd moved uneasily toward the rigs. "It's a long way to our place," a Golden man said as he began hitching up. A light sprinkle was falling and Arch Tomlinson found a raincoat in his buckboard. He offered it to Faith; but the girl made him give it to his sister.

"Guess you'll have to wear mine, Faith," Terry said. He took a slicker roll from his saddle and unroped it. An odor of horseflesh made him hesitate. Then the shower quickened and he saw drops hitting Faith's bonnet. He unrolled the saddle pack and took the slicker to her. "It'll be better'n nothing, I guess."

She thanked him and put it over her head like a parka. "You dropped something, Terry," she said.

255

A sealed envelope, addressed to Terry, lay where he'd unrolled the saddle pack. It must have been enfolded in the blanket. "Wonder how it got there!" Puzzling, he opened the envelope and inside found four printed lines.

ASK SWEDE OLSEN, CHUCK FERRIS AND HANK DELANEY WHO WON JOHN RILEY'S HOUSE IN A CARD GAME AT FAIRPLAY, LAST APRIL. THEN YOU'LL KNOW WHO SHOT WOODFORD AND RAEGAN.

Terry blinked. With a blank look he showed it to Faith. "How strange!" she exclaimed. One of the names stirred her memory. "John Riley! It must mean that log house on West Larimer!"

Newsmen crowded around. The cryptic message was passed from hand to hand. A man yelled, "Anybody know a Swede named Olsen?"

"Never heard of him," another answered. "Nor Chuck Ferris. But I know a miner named Hank Delaney. He's tendin' bar now, down at Pueblo."

Terry put the paper in his pocket. "I better show it to the sheriff," he decided. "If you don't mind, Faith, I'll ride along with you to town."

CHAPTER
TWENTY-THREE

No one could dissuade Terry. Jase and Slim took a look at the stubborn set of his jaw and gave up. When the Cross T buckboard rolled out through the pasture gate, Terry was riding at its wheel.

At Littleton it bumped across the narrow gauge track and took the trail for Denver. "Might be someone's spoofing us," Arch offered cheerily.

"Could be," Terry admitted; but he didn't believe it.

Faith, on the back seat with Victoria, looked more and more disturbed. The import of the message had had time to jell in her mind. Only the cabin's owner would use it for a loot cache. The message named three men who could identify the owner. "Where," Faith wanted to know, "has your saddle roll been all winter?"

"In storage at a hotel."

An occasional drop of rain fell but no one gave it a thought. Arch whipped his team to a trot. A sense of crisis gripped all of them. Terry's mind was on Milo Patterson. But wild horses couldn't have dragged the name from him. Faith believed in the man. So did the Tomlinsons. Today Patterson was out at the Cross T irrigating a meadow.

They rolled in on Wazee Street, turning up Fifteenth to Lawrence. Terry stopped at the courthouse there. "Here's where I leave you." He waved his hat as they drove on.

Chet Brewster was in his office. Newsmen were already there. They'd preceded Terry from the O Bar and had told Brewster about the mysterious message.

"Let's see it." The sheriff snatched it from Terry's hand, read it twice. "Humph! A Swede named Olsen had a placer claim up in South Park. It played out on him and I heard he went to live with in-laws in Cheyenne."

He reached for a pad of blanks and wrote a telegram.

DID YOU SEE JOHN RILEY BET DEED TO WEST DENVER HOUSE IN CARD GAME AT FAIRPLAY LAST APRIL stop IF SO WHO WON POT

The sheriff called his clerk. "Send one copy to Nels Olsen care the sheriff at Cheyenne. Send another copy to Henry Delaney care the sheriff at Pueblo. Get 'em off right away."

The newsmen scattered to file their stories. "If you want me," Terry said, "I'll be at the Grand Central."

He rode there and registered.

When his horse had been stabled, Terry took a walk down to Sixteenth and Blake. At the desk of the American House he inquired, "Milo Patterson in?"

"No sir. He's out at his ranch. The Cross T near Golden."

258

"Is Miss Chalmers in?"

"Yes sir. Room 218."

Terry went upstairs and knocked at 218. A woman's voice asked cautiously, "Who is it?"

"Woodford of the O Bar. Could I talk with you a minute?"

After a delay the door opened. Serena stood there alert and tense. "Yes?" She seemed braced for a shock.

"Any idea who put a message in my slicker roll?"

"No. Why should *I* know about it?" The denial came too promptly and in an almost hysterical pitch.

"I didn't think you'd admit it," Terry said. "Better keep an eye out for Patterson. When he reads the morning papers he won't like what he sees there."

Her face went a shade paler and her voice cracked. "What do you mean?"

"I mean if you've done anything to make Patterson sore, you'd better keep out of his way." Abruptly Terry left her and went back to the Grand Central.

It had been a big day and weariness swooped over him. By the time the gas lamps were lighted along Larimer he was in bed and asleep.

When the sun was less than an hour high a rattling of his door aroused him. Chet Brewster's voice hailed him. "Wake up, cowboy. I got big medicine."

Terry pulled on his pants and let the man in. Chet waved two slips of yellow: "Read 'em and weep, cowboy."

Here were answers from a Pueblo bartender and from a retired miner at Cheyenne. Collusion between

259

them would have been impossible. Yet the responses were identical: MILO PATTERSON.

Terry had never doubted it. His face scarcely changed expression as he finished dressing. All he said was, "You convinced now?"

Brewster gave a grim nod. "How can I help it? Patterson was alone with Frank Barber when he died. Patterson took a pack-mule up there a few days later. He gave a reason he couldn't prove. Now we know he owns the house where the gold was cached."

"So what are you gonna do, sheriff?"

"This." Brewster brought out a warrant. It was for Patterson's arrest on suspicion of grand theft and murder. "I stopped by the American House. They tell me he's out at the Cross T. That's in Rankin's county. So I'll ride to Golden. Rankin and I'll go to the ranch together and pick him up."

A fierce desire to be in on it gripped Terry. "Swear me in as a deputy, Chet," he pleaded. "Then let me look for him in Denver. I mean in case they're wrong about him bein' at the ranch."

"You're in no shape for it, cowboy."

"Never mind what shape I'm in. Just give me a badge and a warrant. Look, Chet, it's not fair to leave me out of it. Tony Raegan was my friend. And I soaked up a few slugs myself. I was right all along about Patterson."

Brewster shook his head. "You shot it out with him one time, remember? And he downed you. So this time it's a job for sheriffs. Two of us. Me and Rankin. But I ain't had breakfast yet. We can talk while we feed."

260

Terry kept pleading all through breakfast. He made no mention of Serena. Or of a hunch that Patterson had come in during the night to deal with her. Arriving at the Cross T late yesterday, the Tomlinsons would tell Patterson about the mystery tip. No reason they shouldn't, since it didn't mention his name. Nor could Terry doubt Patterson's reaction. He'd strongly suspect Serena Chalmers. Who else would know the names of players in a long-ago card game? In which case the man would saddle up for Denver.

"Have a heart!" Terry coaxed. "Don't freeze me out of this. Gimme a warrant and let me keep an open eye for him, right here in town."

"You saw the Tomlinsons yesterday?" Brewster queried. "Did they say where he was?"

"Yes, they said he was at the ranch irrigating a meadow."

"Then he's still there," the sheriff concluded. Being entirely convinced of it he finally gave in. "Okay, cowboy. If you promise me you won't leave town till I get back, I'll make you a pro tern deputy."

"I'll stick right in Denver." Terry grinned and held up his right hand. "Swear me in."

Brewster swore him in as an emergency deputy. "I made the warrant in duplicate," he said, and gave Terry a copy of it.

"What about a badge?" Terry wheedled.

"You'll find one in the top drawer of my desk." Brewster stood up and took a hitch at his belt. "Now stop pesterin' me. And stay out of trouble. It's time I got started for Golden."

Terry followed him to the hitchrack. There Chet Brewster swung aboard a piebald sorrel. He went loping down Sixteenth toward the river bridge.

Terry hurried to a livery stable for his horse. While there he looked in all the other stalls. Patterson's iron-gray wasn't in any of them. The stable hostler said he hadn't seen the man.

A second livery barn gave Terry the same information. But at a third, on Fifteenth just off Holladay, he found the iron-gray in a stall. A stable boy was feeding it. "How long's this bronc been here?" Terry inquired.

"You'd have to ask the night man, mister. Came in during the night."

So Patterson was in town! Arriving during the night he hadn't gone to his room at the American. Where else would he go?

Pushing it around in his mind, Terry rode to the courthouse and went into Brewster's office. At this early hour it was empty. He opened drawers, found a deputy badge and pinned it on his vest. In a gun closet he found a cartridge belt with a holstered forty-five.

It was hooked around his waist as he rode down Lawrence and turned north along Sixteenth. The day's traffic had hardly started yet. The new Daniels and Fisher store hadn't opened its doors. A block beyond it Terry crossed the Larimer Street tram track. A porter was sweeping the walk under the arcade of the Broadwell House.

Terry cantered on two more blocks and tied his mount in front of the American. "Miss Chalmers up yet?" he asked there.

The desk clerk looked at the badge on his vest. "I hope there's no trouble, sir." His tone seemed a bit nervous.

"Why should there be?"

"A chambermaid just reported that Miss Chalmers' bed hasn't been slept in. And the night clerk saw her leave just after dark with a small bag."

"Anyone else called to see her?"

"No sir. That is, no one except Alfred. Alfred keeps order at the Columbine Club, where she's hostess."

"What did Alfred want?"

"He just stopped in on his way home, about three this morning, to ask why Miss Chalmers hadn't reported for duty."

"Milo Patterson been in?"

"No, we haven't seen Mr. Patterson for several days."

Terry went out on Sixteenth. A two-horse hack was waiting for customers. "Do you know Serena Chalmers?"

The cabman grinned. "Who doesn't? I haul her to work and back nearly every night."

"But not last night?"

"Nope. Alfred asked me the same thing, a bit ago. He looked worried."

"Where does Alfred live?"

"Potter's Hotel, 370 Blake. It's right around the corner."

Terry went to the Potter's and found Alfred at breakfast. "Where's Serena?" he asked abruptly.

"I don't know." The giant's face had no guile in it and his tone was respectful. "I wish I did, sir."

"Why?"

"Because lately," Alfred said, "she's acted like she might be afraid of someone. Sometimes she made me take her home from work. Last night she didn't show up at all."

The man seemed dull-witted but entirely loyal and honest. Terry felt sure his concern was sincere.

The easiest way Serena could avoid Patterson, Terry reasoned, would be to hide in another hotel till the man was safely in jail. He decided to make the rounds of hotels. The nearest was the Interocean, diagonally across the intersection from the American.

Terry led his horse there and went in. "Did Serena Chalmers take a room here last night?"

"Nope," the clerk said. "Milo Patterson asked me the same thing, 'bout an hour ago."

Tension, and a sense of climax, possessed Terry. So Patterson too was making the rounds of hotels! Logically he'd try this one first, because for Serena it would be more convenient than any other. Only a few steps from the American.

Terry dropped a nickel on the desk and picked up a morning paper. The front page had a story about yesterday's celebration at the O Bar. A parallel column told about a mystery message which had tumbled out of a slicker roll. The message was printed verbatim. So were the telegrams of inquiry sent by Sheriff Brewster to two men.

But the paper having gone to press before answering wires had arrived, Patterson's name didn't appear. Brewster wouldn't want Patterson warned. So in all likelihood he'd withhold further information until the arrest could be made.

Nevertheless Patterson *had* been warned. And no less Serena Chalmers. No doubt they'd both read this paper. And to them the story would mean more than to anyone else. They, and they alone, would know in advance what the answering wires were bound to say. They'd know the identity of the fifth of five men in a Fairplay poker game last April. Milo Patterson!

Panicked by Terry's call at her room, Serena had packed a bag and disappeared. And now Patterson was hunting her down, from hotel to hotel, an hour ahead of Terry himself.

CHAPTER
TWENTY-FOUR

There were four hotels on Larimer Street and Terry made them from west to east. Serena wasn't at Charpiot's, directly across from the *Rocky Mountain News*. Registering under a false name would do her no good, because the hostess of Denver's most glittering palace of chance was too well known.

Moving half a block east Terry tried the Broadwell; then, at the Seventeenth Street corner, his own hotel the Grand Central. From there he went to Taylor's Rooms, across from the Occidental Pool Hall. Serena had appeared at none of these places; nor at any of them had Patterson inquired for her.

Then Terry remembered a sedate and quiet hotel on Curtis Street. The Wentworth House. Serena could find more privacy there than at most places. Terry rode up Seventeenth at a canter, skipping a frame boarding house at the Arapahoe corner. A block short of the Wolfe Seminary he turned right, past small shops and cottages.

The Wentworth House lobby had potted palms and chintz curtains. A spinsterlike lady looked up from her knitting. She proved to be the day clerk and Terry asked her, "You know Serena Chalmers?"

"No, but you're the second man who's inquired for her this morning."

"You mean Milo Patterson's been here?"

"I don't know Mr. Patterson. He was a tall dark man in a rancher's hat. It was about thirty minutes ago, I believe."

Terry went out with a growing uneasiness. Patterson might get to her first. What would he do? Twice the man had proved himself a ruthless killer. Why would he so persistently hunt Serena unless he was afraid of what she knew?

Likely she knew a good deal more than his ownership of a house in West Denver. Finding her was vital, not only to save her life but to save her testimony. Maybe she'd caught a train out of town. Terry didn't think so because she'd only taken one small bag. She'd hardly quit Denver abandoning the expensive wardrobe in her room at the American.

However he had to check it. Back down Seventeenth he went at a lope, drawing stares from the walks. Hard-riding, gun-slung cowboys were common enough in Denver. But this one wore a brass badge and had some grim purpose on his face.

He whirled into Wazee and made a streak of dust to Twentieth, pulling up at the Denver Pacific depot. A board there told him the only train Serena could have caught out of town had left two hours ago. Terry questioned the ticket seller and the station master. Both knew the Columbine hostess by sight. They were sure she'd boarded no train here.

The only other station from which she could have skipped town was the D & R G, at Nineteenth and Wynkoop. Terry went there and got the same answers. But here again he found that Milo Patterson had preceded him — this time by a full two hours. Patterson had evidently put trains before hotels.

There were several shabby hotels near the depots. Terry tried the Rock Island on Twentieth, then the Planters on lower Sixteenth. Serena hadn't been seen at either. Neither had Patterson. A thought startled Terry. By now Patterson would know that Terry was on his trail. Because they weren't making the hotels in the same order.

At some Patterson would inquire *after*, instead of before, Terry Woodford. "Serena Chalmers? No, she's not registered, Mr. Patterson. But a cowboy was just here asking for her. A cowboy with a badge on his vest. He asked for you too, Mr. Patterson."

Which would alert and fully warn Patterson. No chance for a surprise now. Terry moved on to the Commercial House at Thirteenth and Holladay, then remembered he'd overlooked the Overland just opposite the depot. He doubled back there. "Patterson?" The clerk fixed a squinty eye on Terry's badge. "Yeh, he was by here about ten minutes ago. Why? What the heck's going on?"

"Was he wearing a gun?"

"He sure was. Looked kinda on the prod too. You're Terry Woodford, ain'tcha? How come they made you a deputy?"

Terry worked his way up Eighteenth, generally walking along the trash-strewn gutter and leading his horse. On this street about every third address was a rooming house. Terry made them all without success. Impatience dogged him. The morning was waning and time was running out. Because when Brewster discovered Patterson wasn't at the Cross T he'd come agallop to Denver and take command.

Turning west on Larimer, Terry again made the routine inquiries at his own hotel, the Grand Central. Neither Serena nor Patterson had been there. "But a Miss Harlan asked for you a little while ago," the clerk said.

Faith! "What did she want?"

"She didn't say."

Puzzled, Terry went out to his horse and rode another half block west along Larimer. An idea brought him to a stop. Dismounting he tied his bay in midblock and walked on to the next corner. It was Denver's busiest intersection, Sixteenth and Larimer.

He'd been using his legs too much, instead of using his head. For the surest way to catch up with Patterson was to wait for him. The man was systematically making all the hotels. In time he was sure to make the Broadwell House on this corner. Terry went into the Broadwell and again asked the clerk if he'd seen Patterson. "Not today," the clerk said.

"Thanks." Terry crossed Sixteenth to Joslin's Department Store. He stood with his back to a plate-glass show window, watching the Broadwell. The hotel had two entrances, one from Sixteenth and the other from Larimer, and from here Terry could watch both of them. A sidewalk throng screened him; many were women shoppers darting in and out of Joslin's.

Half the town's population seemed to be concentrated at this intersection. On its northeast corner stood the First National Bank, on its southeast corner the Broadwell, with Joslin's on the southwest corner and Brooks-Giddings on the northwest. Horse car tracks made a T here, one rail line running east and west along Larimer, another turning south from it along Sixteenth. Bells clanged as the trams stopped and started. Newsboys dodged in and out of the traffic. But no extra was being shouted, so Terry knew the press hadn't yet learned about the sensation implied in answers to two telegrams.

Yet many who passed by looked at Terry with an almost prescient speculation. They could see the badge on his vest. Nor could they have failed to read the mystery message story in this morning's papers. They'd know two wires had been sent and they'd wonder about the outcome. More than that, gossip could spread like a fire in Denver. There'd been time for a dozen hotel clerks to talk and give people ideas. Woodford asking everywhere for Patterson! With a badge and gun on! Why? Did it connect with yesterday's slicker-rolled message?

Denver wasn't dumb. Its eyes were open and its wits were nimble. Why was Terry Woodford playing hare-and-hound with Patterson?

A tram bell clanged. Terry kept his eye on the Broadwell's main entrance. A carriage drew up over there. A derby-hatted man helped a lady to alight. She wore a shovel bonnet and a ruffled skirt which she had to hold out of the dust. The Broadwell porter opened the door for them as they passed inside.

Terry, from this vantage, could see both ways along Sixteenth but only one way along Larimer. Half a block up Larimer he saw his own tethered horse. A girl stood on the sidewalk, at the bay's head, in a pose of waiting. With a shock Terry saw that she was Faith Harlan.

Almost at once he solved why she was there. She'd been with him at the exposure of the cryptic message. All night she'd be in suspense about it. Morning papers would tell her two telegrams had been sent. Had they been answered? Any normally curious young woman would want to know. Faith more than anyone else because the whole thing had begun with the murder of her uncle. So why shouldn't she ask Terry?

Terry's conclusion was that she'd gone to his hotel to ask him if answering telegrams had arrived, and if so whom had they named. Then she'd noticed his bay horse tied half a block west of the hotel. She knew the horse well. He'd ridden into her life on it, playing croquet from a saddle. So now she was simply waiting by his horse till he came back from whatever errand engaged him.

Terry was glad she hadn't seen him. Nor was she likely to see him with all this traffic streaming by.

He looked across at the Broadwell. His eyes shifted left, right. A tall man in a wide-brimmed cattleman's hat was coming down the sidewalk. A tall, swarthy man with black, brass-studded leather at his waist. Milo Patterson!

A freight wagon rumbled by and for a moment obscured him. One of its four mules shied at some windblown scrap of trash; the driver shouted, cracked his whip. When the line of view cleared Patterson had reached the hotel's canopied entrance. He was about to turn in when Terry stepped off the opposite walk and called to him.

"Patterson! Got something for you, Patterson."

The man heard him and turned. Only his eyes made response. They jerked with alarm and then fixed with a glassy stare on Terry. The man's holster had a gun and his hand slid a little nearer to it. Terry was crossing the street toward him.

At that moment all of Denver, it seemed, stood still. Half a thousand people were at or near that traffic-packed intersection; a thousand eyes flicked from Patterson to Woodford and back to Patterson.

At the car track, in midstreet, Terry stopped. His left hand produced a paper. "I've got a warrant for you, Patterson."

He wanted that much clearly fixed. Best for a hundred witnesses to hear him say it. Then there'd be no talk of a grudge fight, no angle of personal vengeance. This was the law speaking. And there, under the Broadwell's sidewalk arcade, stood a wanted felon.

Those who saw and heard held tautly still, waiting.

Then Patterson called back, "What kind of a warrant?"

"A murder warrant." Terry moved on toward him. Even then he didn't think the man would shoot. Not on a crowded street like this. Any missed shot could kill a bystander.

But an uncontrollable swell of passion ruled Patterson. The huge irony of it swept over him. Here was he, Milo Patterson, on the road to fame and power and riches, run to earth by a common cowboy! By Terry Woodford who, from the very first, had been like a cactus spine in his flesh!

In a blast of fury Patterson drew and began tripping his trigger. Bullets burned by Terry's head. Back of him, plate glass from Joslin's show window shattered and showered on the walk. Terry's own gun was out. He was standing still, only three paces from Patterson. Fear that he'd miss all but unnerved him. If he missed, his slug would fly straight into the Broadwell lobby.

Again Patterson fired and Terry's hat bounced. He stepped a pace sidewise, stooping as Patterson let go his fifth bullet. More glass crashed from a Joslin show window. A buggy horse snorted and reared. A woman screamed.

Then Terry squeezed his own trigger. Once, twice, three times. He felt three kicks at his wrist and a great weariness. He thought he'd missed Patterson. The man turned as though to run. He took three steps, then reeled a little. Terry closed in on him. Policemen, too, were closing in from two directions.

Before anyone could reach Patterson the man fell. He sprawled on the board walk, his gun clattering.

From the street a raucous voice yelled: "You got him, kid; you sure got him!"

Then everyone was shouting and when Terry reached the policeman bending over Patterson he could hardly make himself heard. One of the officers looked up and saw a warrant in his hand.

The other one said: "He's dead. Where'd you get that badge, cowboy?"

Terry said wearily: "Ask Sheriff Brewster. He's got a warrant just like this one."

A swarm of reporters emerged from the crowd to bombard Terry. He gave short, impatient answers. Mainly he said, "The answer to those telegrams was Patterson."

A wall of people stood around him. Beyond it Terry saw one small, pale face and he pushed that way. "Faith!"

Getting to her wasn't easy. She was on the flagstone sidewalk in front of the bank. Terry literally had to drag a reporter who clung to his coat. Another had his arm. He shook them off and came at last to Faith.

Her stunned look hurt him and what he said to her wasn't coherent. "They found out about him." Humility was in his voice but no regret. "They gave me a warrant for him." His only thought was to forestall her rebuke. "Listen, Faith. It was he who . . ."

She cut him off. "Don't say anything, please. You don't have to. I saw what happened." She put her hands on his shoulders and her eyes had tears in them. "Are you hurt, Terry?" Then everything he wanted to see was in her eyes and his arms went around her. He heard a babble of talk but none of it came from Faith.

Most of it erupted from the newsmen who again closed in. Some of it came from store clerks and shoppers. A Broadwell bellhop shrilled: "She's all yourn, cowboy!"

A volley from the newsmen: "Where's Brewster?" . . . "What'd you dig up on that guy, fella?" . . . "You say he owned the old Riley house?" Terry barely heard them. A pale, frightened face at a window, at the Broadwell's second floor level, briefly captured his attention. Less than an instant it was there, peering between the curtains, and then was gone. Serena! *If she wore a veil and registered under a false name, a night clerk might not recognize her.* "Look, Woodford." A reporter tugged at Terry's sleeve. "The Tribune wants your story. Under your own picture and by-line. We'll pay . . ."

Terry pushed him away. He turned savagely on the others. "Get outa here, will you?"

He looked both ways for a hack. Anything that would get Faith away from them. Then he saw a street car. It turned off Larimer on to Sixteenth and stopped for a passenger.

"Come on, Faith." Terry took a grip on her arm and headed for the tram. His free hand brushed people right and left. He heard the driver clang his bell and call out, "Giddap."

A voice shouted from the walk, "Hang on to her, cowboy!" Terry did just that, half dragging Faith to the car steps. He got her aboard and followed himself. Newsmen came in hot pursuit. He gave the leader a shove which toppled him back on the others. The car moved on, creaking sluggishly south along Sixteenth.

Terry paid the tram man two nickels. A dozen passengers were gawking. He found an empty seat and slid into it beside Faith. Neither of them said anything. The car had a flat wheel, thumping the rail at every turn.

It stopped at the next cross street, Lawrence, where an Indian woman got off. From then on the driver called each stop. "Arapahoe!" "Curtis!" "Champa!" "Stout!" "California!" At each of these one or more passengers got off. The retail district petered out and, after Graham Street, Terry and Faith were the only passengers left.

The driver looked back at them. "How far you folks goin'?"

"To the end of the line." Terry's quick answer had a buoyant lilt, and a prophecy.

The tram man grinned. "That's kinda what I thought. Giddap."

By now they'd veered on to Broadway, with a cow pasture on the left and a bean patch on the right. Terry dropped an arm around Faith and drew her close. Ahead of them a jack-rabbit went zigzagging in high leaps down the track. The tram team plodded on.